OPEN GRAVE

Also by Kjell Eriksson

OPEN GRAVE

Kjell Eriksson

Translated from the Swedish by Paul Norlen

MINOTAUR BOOKS

A THOMAS DUNNE BOOK ☒ NEW YORK

A THOMAS DUNNE BOOK FOR MINOTAUR BOOKS.
An imprint of St. Martin's Publishing Group.

OPEN GRAVE. Copyright © 2009 by Kjell Eriksson. Translation copyright © 2015 by Paul Norlen. All rights reserved. Printed in the United States of America. For information, address St. Martin's Press, 175 Fifth Avenue, New York, N.Y. 10010.

www.thomasdunnebooks.com
www.minotaurbooks.com

The Library of Congress Cataloging-in-Publication Data is available upon request.

ISBN 978-1-250-02549-4 (hardcover)
ISBN 978-1-250-02548-7 (e-book)

First published in Sweden in 2009 as *Öppen grav* by Ordfront Förlag

Minotaur books may be purchased for educational, business, or promotional use. For information on bulk purchases, please contact the Macmillan Corporate and Premium Sales Department at 1-800-221-7945, extension 5442, or write to specialmarkets@macmillan.com.

First U.S. Edition: July 2015

10 9 8 7 6 5 4 3 2 1

OPEN GRAVE

The notification came unexpectedly. Bertram von Ohler was eighty-four years old after all, somewhat frail, his legs did not always hold, the numbness in his hands created difficulties, especially at the dinner table. The dizziness in the evenings was getting more troublesome and meant that he socialized much less often. Bridge nights were sacred, however. There were some who thought he did not have much time left; the whispering about his ill health had increased.

Some were old colleagues who took pleasure in backbiting the old professor and competitor, or else they were simply acquaintances who for lack of other diversion spread unfounded rumors. One day it was some neurological disease that would soon break him down, the next the problem was advanced prostate cancer. There were also friends around him who listened eagerly, perhaps contributing a detail or episode and in that way kept the fire going.

Everyone took part in the rumor spreading with the same poorly masked enthusiasm. It was as if the sight of the old man, or the news that always

flowed in during the autumn's customary speculations, automatically elic-
ited comments about his imminent demise.

His real remaining friends were few. Some had left earthly life, others
were senile and put in homes. A professor in a related discipline, obviously
demented, was shunted aside to a family estate in Skåne. But the few with
whom Ohler socialized were upset.

"I'm used to it, many have tried over the years to take honor and glory
from me and now it's my life they're after," was his calm comment when
his friends complained. But deep down he was distressed, disappointed at
the pettiness and ill will, sometimes even genuinely angry.

He had reconciled himself with many things. Old grudges were buried,
injustices that had been harbored for decades receded in a forgiving forgetfulness. Even Associate Professor Johansson, who lived only a stone's throw
away, could now exchange a few words with his former rival. Most recently,
the other day they discussed Obama and "the other guy," neither of them
wanting to admit that for the moment they had forgotten his name. The
professor stood on the sidewalk, the associate professor with a rake in his
hand on the other side of the privet hedge.

Even the memory of his wife, deceased for many years now, had something conciliatory about it. Bertram von Ohler had developed a theory that
in reality he had her to thank for his successes, indirectly and without her
conscious assistance, but even so. She who the last thirty years of their life
together constituted an unimaginable torment for him.

How could a phenomenon as lovely as Dagmar had once been turn into
such a monstrous creature? He had consulted colleagues to get some explanation for her behavior with the help of academic expertise. No diagnosis
could ever be made. "Some people are mean, it's that simple," a professor
in psychology once stated when Ohler let slip what a virago he was living
with.

Every breakfast in the Ohler home was a minefield; a single false step
and the morning's peace was shattered. Every dinner was trench warfare,
with ambushes and snipers, and on really bad days it escalated to veritable
carpet bombing of reproaches and suspicions.

He did not desert his marriage, something which even his children advised him to do, but he fled to the department as often as he was able, and stayed until late in the evening. Sometimes he slept there in a little storage room.

Perhaps it was this fact, this absence from home and wife, that was the basis for his success in the medical field. He had Dagmar's quarrelsome and her suspicious nature to thank for his research results and his professorship, and for this belated crowning of his career.

The word came late in the morning. Bertram von Ohler had just come home from a short walk and was preparing to have a pasta salad, which Agnes had prepared the day before, when the telephone rang. It was Professor Skarp at the Karolinska Institute.

Ohler had only met him in passing at a few gatherings. For that reason it was somewhat surprising that after the introduction he started with the word "brother," as if they were members of an order, which Ohler doubted.

"Brother, I have the great honor and happiness to report that Professor Emeritus Bertram von Ohler has been awarded this year's Nobel Prize in Medicine."

"Good for him," was the only thing Ohler got out, incapable of putting these simple facts together into a coherent sentence.

"What did you say?" asked Skarp.

Bertram von Ohler, that's me of course, the thought passing like a projectile through his head.

"What did you say?" he let out like an echo.

Professor Skarp left out "brother," but otherwise repeated the sentence word for word. When he got no response this time either, other than labored breathing, he added something to the effect that he understood that this was overwhelming news, not unexpected in any way, but still no doubt difficult to take in immediately.

"Professor von Ohler, dear colleague . . . are you all right?"

"Fine, thanks. And I was just about to eat pasta."

"Now it will have to be something more festive," said Skarp, laughing with relief.

"I must call my children immediately. I'll have to get back to you."

"Of course. You can certainly expect an onslaught of phone calls and visits, brother, so perhaps it's wise to notify those closest to you first."

As if someone had died, thought Ohler.

"You don't want to hear the motivation?"

"No, thanks, I think I understand. If you'll excuse me now."

They ended the call and he hurried to the toilet.

"Now I'm pissing as a Nobel Prize winner," he said out loud, managing to squeeze a few drops from his wrinkled sex.

Instead of calling his two sons, both professors, one in Lund, the other in Los Angeles, and his daughter, who was research director at a pharmaceutical company in town, he pulled out the phone jack, quickly shoveled down a little of the pasta, took a few gulps of water, and left the house.

It was a radiant day, so he found, as he expected, Associate Professor Johansson in his yard. Marching in through the gate and ringing the doorbell would seem too forward, they were not on such good terms with each other.

The associate professor looked almost happy as he stood with the rake in his hand, surrounded by parallel rows of leaves. The associate professor had explained to Ohler that leaf raking must be done in a systematic way, and he understood now that his neighbor was about to combine the rows into neat small piles.

"It's a good thing it's not windy," the professor began, but realized at once that this was not a particularly apt remark.

"I would never rake on a day like that," said the associate professor.

"No, of course not."

The associate professor took a few swipes with the rake. Ohler realized that he could not linger too long, and decided to get right to the point.

"A few minutes ago I got some happy news and I decided to share it with you first of all."

The associate professor looked up.

"Yes?"

"We are colleagues, after all, we shared a laboratory for many years, we took part in joint projects, shared successes and disappointments, I don't need to remind you of all that, but I'm doing it anyway, on a day like this."

The associate professor stopped his work, leaned the rake against the trunk of a copper beech and took a few steps closer to the gate.

"That is an amazing tree," said the professor, pointing toward the beech tree. "Surely the most magnificent we have in the area."

The associate professor looked even more surprised. It was uncertain whether it was due to the unexpected praise or that the professor used the word "we," as if he included the whole neighborhood as owner of the tree.

"I'm guessing that it's the same age as the house," the professor continued.

Now the associate professor was standing right inside the gate. His long, thin face expressed a touch of impatience, perhaps irritation, but he was trying to smile anyway, uncertain of what occasioned this unexpected charm offensive. But the smile mostly remained a twitch in his face.

"I've won the Nobel Prize."

The cheeks rosy from sun and wind, the watery eyes, the narrow mustache, a barely visible streak over an open mouth, where a few fangs were visible, the narrow, sloping shoulders and the delicately built chest, all that was visible of the associate professor above the wooden gate, expressed an astonished distrust.

"The Nobel Prize," he repeated awkwardly.

The professor nodded.

"In medicine?"

"Yes, what else?"

"For IDD?"

"I assume so," said the professor.

IDD was the abbreviation they had used in the research group for the discovery that had been presented about twenty years ago and for which the professor had now been granted the honor.

"Assume?"

"I didn't ask, I had to take a piss when Skarp called."

Associate Professor Johansson shook his head and the professor saw doubt change to conviction, and he understood why: Never in public life had he used swear words or other strong expressions, never before had he uttered the words "take a piss," not even in his youth or in family circles. At the most, "have to pee."

He thinks I've lost my mind, thought Ohler, and at that moment it struck him that perhaps he had been the butt of a cruel joke. He was barely acquainted with Skarp, they had not had so much contact that the professor could say he would recognize the voice with certainty, in other words it could be anyone at all pretending to be the chairman of the Academy of Sciences. Someone sufficiently familiar with his background, his research, in the procedure around how the prize winner in medicine is named. Someone who wanted to play a trick on him, have a good laugh at his expense. That the person who called had addressed him as "brother" was a hint that something was amiss.

This sudden insight, that the whole thing perhaps was a deception, made the ground sway. He took hold of the gate, tried to suppress the dizziness by closing his eyes, lower himself somewhat with bent knees and arched back, the technique he always used. The fireflies behind his eyelids glistened in rapid bright streaks, there was singing in his head, and he had a slight taste of iron in his mouth.

When the attack was over and he opened his eyes, he discovered that the associate professor was glaring hatefully at his hand, as if it was a violation of his private life and property. But the professor did not dare release his hold on the gate.

"Excuse me," he said, "I haven't eaten properly today."

The associate professor did not say anything.

"Could it be a joke? I mean the phone call."

"Maybe so," said the associate professor, and now the hint of a smile could be seen at the corner of his mouth.

"Do you think I'm mentally deranged?"

"Of course not, what makes you say that?"

"You think I'm bluffing, don't you. But Skarp called!"

He was staring at the associate professor, whose Adam's apple bobbed. *I see, you're swallowing your words*, thought the professor bitterly. He stared at the wrinkled neck, which concealed esophagus, trachea, and the artery where the blood was pumped up to the brain. *You don't dare talk, afraid of saying too little, or too much. You haven't changed.*

He had decided to seek out the associate professor to show his willingness to share the honor. I go to an associate professor to spread luster over the entire research group, as if to say, "The credit is not all mine, we were a whole team. And then I am met with scorn."

He shook the gate. Nothing remained of the associate professor's smile other than a grimace.

He had done it without an ulterior motive, wasn't that so? The thought had come quite spontaneously, what else would be possible, besides the presumptuousness of rehearsing his comments and actions in advance, to have them ready when the Nobel Prize committee called. Or was there, on an unconscious level, a degree of calculation? Because immediately in his mind he had formulated his first statement to the media: "I am overwhelmed and obviously very grateful"—something like that as introduction. And then the hook itself on which to hang his own excellence: "The first thing I did was go over to a neighbor, a dear friend and research colleague, Associate Professor Johansson, to share the joy with him, because the prize is not mine alone, it is shared with a whole staff of untiring, dedicated associates. Without them I would be nothing. Then I returned home and called my children."

That was how the humility would be formulated. Not a dry eye. Perhaps he should mention the pasta salad?

The associate professor interrupted his train of thought.

"If it was even him."

"I know him."

No one was going to take the prize away from him now!

"Ferguson then?"

Allen Ferguson was an American researcher, active in Germany during the eighties, who had arrived at similar research results as the colleagues at Uppsala University Hospital. There were those who thought that his efforts were more pioneering and just a hair ahead in time besides.

"Ferguson based his results on our research, you know that very well."

The associate professor was smiling again.

"I'm going to mention Ferguson," the professor snapped.

"You'll have to list a lot of names."

"I thought you would be happy," said the professor. "But clearly I was mistaken there. Of course I'm going to list a lot of names. Your name included."

"Mine?"

"Why such surprise?"

The associate professor laughed, a laugh that resembled the hacking sound of an Angola hen. He made a grimace and twisted his mouth in a sneering smile.

Is this how it's going to be? thought Ohler, but decided to make a new attempt. He was the one who could, and must, be generous.

"Your efforts were decisive, we both know that. So why put on a show? We are both old, I'll turn eighty-five in December and you'll soon be eighty, we can disappear from earthly life sooner than we know, so why this pretense, this playacting? We know how it works. There is never any absolute justice, above all not in our world. It could have been a Ferguson, it could have been a Johansson, now it turned out to be a von Ohler."

"A von Oben."

"What do you mean?"

At that moment a taxi turned onto the street. The old men saw it slowly approach, to finally stop outside Ohler's driveway. In the backseat of the car a figure could be seen reaching out an arm, presumably to pay. The driver laughed, took the payment, and during the seconds that followed the duo by the gate breathlessly observed the scene. In order to see better the associate professor had leaned forward and supported himself against the gate, so that his hand almost touched the professor's. Unaware of this nearness, almost intimacy, which perhaps was reminiscent of something twenty, thirty years ago, when they stood leaning over a flickering screen, a diagram, or a report, they watched the driver get out of the car, still laughing, and open the back door.

Bertram von Ohler's cloudy eyes did not perceive what was happening, other than that a figure released itself from the inside of the taxi. But he heard how the associate professor took a deep breath, and realized that this identified the passenger.

"I think I have to piss," said the associate professor, and this unexpected comment, which the professor immediately understood as an outstretched hand, a conciliatory gesture, made him sob.

"Splendid, Gregor," he said. "Splendid."

The driver hurried up.

"Mr. Olon?"

The professor nodded in confusion. The driver took his free hand, raised it and shook it frenetically, while with the other hand he patted the Nobel Prize winner on the shoulder. His broad smile and his entire appearance testified to great excitement and unfeigned delight.

"A good day," he said.

The passenger, who had fallen behind, had now joined them.

"On behalf of the entire university I want to congratulate you."

The taxi driver reminded him about the flowers.

"So true!"

When Bertram von Ohler later summarized the day, the congratulatory call on the street would stand out as the most successful tableau. First the people's tribute, in the form of taxi driver Andrew Kimongo, followed by academic bloodred roses and the university rector's torrent of words, at the head of the long line of callers who then followed in quick succession.

It was a restless night, he was constantly wakened from the unsettled slumber that characterizes persons born under the sign of Sagittarius, in Ohler's case on the fifteenth of December. It was a theory that was championed by his daughter, Birgitta: Sagittarius dozes through the night,

Taurus sleeps heavily, Libra gets up early. She herself was Aquarius, whose most distinctive feature was dreaming intensely.

Bertram von Ohler was somewhat concerned. His daughter was actually scientifically educated, a medical doctor, but still firm in the intellectually lightweight, stupid theory of astrology. It didn't fit together.

She was a lesbian besides—a pure defense measure, she asserted, in this era of male violence—and for the past ten years living together with a nurse with Finnish background. A woman of whom Bertram disapproved. Maybe it was the Finnish accent. Liisa Lehtonen had been a successful competitive shooter and won medals at a number of international competitions.

If anything could be associated with violence it must be firearms, the professor asserted, but according to his daughter this was solely about mental balance and psychic energy. Liisa was a Virgo.

But despite the astrology, her sometimes meddlesome lifestyle advice, which might concern diet, exercise, wine drinking, open window at night, or basically anything at all, and as the cherry on the cake Liisa with accent and gun cabinet, and thereby self-imposed childlessness—despite all this Bertram von Ohler loved his daughter.

She was the youngest of the siblings and therefore also the one who fared the worst due to their mother's capricious moods and increasing misanthropy. The two sons, ten and thirteen years older, had moved away from home as soon as possible and thereby avoided the worst tumult.

The oldest was christened Abraham, as a concession to his mother. He had studied in Lund and remained there, even adopted a Scandian accent.

Carl, named after his grandfather, moved into a student apartment belonging to the Kalmar student association. By tradition the family was registered there. Bertram's great-great-grandfather originated from a family of pharmacists in Kalmar.

Like his brother Carl studied medicine and after several turns at various Swedish hospitals ended up in California, where he was now a moderately successful researcher in diabetes. According to his father a completely worthless field, an opinion he never uttered to anyone however.

He was proud of his children, happily bragged about them, as fathers do, remembered their birthdays, likewise the wives' and grandchildren's. Abraham had three children and Carl two. When Liisa's birthday was, however, he had no idea.

He had actually never needed to send money to his children after they left home, except for the costs for university studies. They never talked about money at all. It was there, had always been there. Since the seventeenth century.

The progenitor of the Swedish part of the Ohler family, originally from Hannover, had been recruited by Axel Oxenstierna to build up the administration of the Royal Mint. Apparently a lucrative occupation, because already after a decade Heinrich Ohler had built up a considerable fortune. That Queen Kristina contributed a few estates on Öland and right outside Västervik did not make circumstances worse.

From that soil the Ohler family tree sprouted, where one branch became the "pharmacists/doctors." There was also a minister branch, an officer branch, and an agricultural branch.

Just as happily as Bertram talked about his children and grandchildren, he could also, not without pride, tell the story of poor Heinrich, who came to Stockholm with an empty hand. In the other hand he had a knapsack.

In his bed, whose headboard was war booty from Bratislava, the professor argued with selected representatives on the extensive tree and came to the conclusion that the Nobel Prize outshone all else that had been presented to the family: being raised to nobility, loads of medals and distinctions, and through the centuries membership in a number of learned societies.

A conclusion even his father Carl would have endorsed—that was the professor's final, triumphant thought before he fell asleep at four o'clock in the morning.

✦

Two

The voice was not reminiscent of anything he had heard before, sharp and aggressive but at the same time anxious.

It was Swedish, with no obvious dialect or accent—he was always attentive to that sort of thing—but still a voice foreign to the extent that when he told his daughter about the episode a few hours later, he hesitated when she asked if it was a foreigner.

"In a way," he said. "Maybe it was an immigrant, someone who has lived here a long time."

"Maybe someone who was disguising their voice," his daughter suggested, "someone you know."

"Who would that be?"

"Have you called the police?"

Bertram von Ohler laughed, even though he'd had that thought himself, because half-awake in the early morning hours he had experienced the call as an actual threat, just as real as if someone stood in front of him with a weapon raised to strike.

"It's the sort of thing you have to expect."

"But what did he say exactly, is there something you've missed?"

Misunderstood, he realized that his daughter meant.

"No, he said he would see to it that I 'would never receive the prize,' and then he muttered some vulgarities."

"What were they?"

"You don't want to hear that."

"Of course I do!"

"Abusive language never deserves to be repeated. Besides, it didn't mean anything."

The fact was that what he called abusive language was what perplexed him the most, but there was no reason to drag his daughter into that.

He regretted mentioning the episode to her at all, and tried to guide the conversation to something else, said that Agnes showed up, even though she was supposed to be off. She had obviously congratulated him, but in that reserved way that only a person from a Roslag island can do, as if a Nobel Prize did not mean all that much, whether in Söderboda or in Norrboda.

No, she had viewed the matter purely professionally. The house must be, if not decontaminated, then gone through anyway and more thoroughly than what Ohler had allowed until now. She had threatened to bring in her sister Greta to help out.

"Then I gave her free rein, just so she doesn't involve that ghost under any circumstances."

Birgitta laughed heartily and the professor understood that for the moment he had diverted the danger, but to be really certain he continued.

"Agnes will order new curtains in the drawing room and the library and 'polish' all the floors, as she says. Then it will be the silver's turn."

"You're lucky to have her."

"Of course," said the professor.

"That was lovely of you, those statements you made on TV. But you must be sure to use a comb, your hair was standing straight up."

"It was windy."

"But why didn't you go inside the house?"

"Agnes phoned and forbade me from letting anyone in. If she hadn't been on Gräsö visiting her sister she would have come here and organized the world press."

He was rewarded with another laugh. He felt a need to keep his daughter in a good mood, perhaps as apology for not telling the whole truth about the telephone call at dawn.

"But it was beautifully expressed, that part that you weren't alone."

I was *alone,* he thought.

"Do you wonder what Mother would have said?"

That was a question that the professor found no reason to speculate about.

"Do you ever miss her?"

"No."

Perhaps he ought to have said something beautiful here too, even if it wasn't true? He knew that his daughter was of two minds about her mother.

"Do you suppose they're excited here at work?" she continued, apparently unperturbed by her father's abrupt responses. "Angerman called from Milan to congratulate, but I think he was mostly thinking about the company, because he said something to the effect that it was good I kept my maiden name, that it could benefit us in contact with customers, especially in the U.S. He invited me to go along to Boston next week."

"Pill-rollers," said the professor.

"If they were even that," said Birgitta with a sigh.

Under normal circumstances he would have asked what she meant, but he was bothered by his daughter's unnecessary talk about Dagmar.

He had not thought about Dagmar at all, not even on a day like this one. During the night's review of the family tree she did not even show up in his thoughts. She was as if erased; never before had he experienced that so clearly.

"I'm not going to invite any of her relatives," he said unexpectedly vehemently.

"But Daddy! Not even Dorothy?"

He knew that his daughter kept in contact with Dorothy Wilkins, widow of Dagmar's brother Henrik, whom he despised but never commented on. He was convinced that Dorothy maintained contact with his daughter solely to keep herself informed about the Ohler clan, primarily the patriarch himself. Now as before he chose to pass over her with silence.

Birgitta sighed.

"She's old," she said.

"She stays alive just to get to see me die," he mumbled. "There is something vulture-like about her."

"That's not true!" his daughter countered. "You can be generous now."

I'll never invite her, he thought, increasingly embittered, and he realized that he had to end the conversation before it got out of hand completely.

Dorothy was otherwise the one who had followed him the longest of all, from his student days in the 1940s. She was the daughter of one of his father's friends from youth, who'd come from England to Uppsala in May of 1945, right after the war ended. Perhaps her father had the idea of marrying off his daughter to the young and promising Bertram. The project had failed because no interest ever arose—from him in any event.

Dorothy went back to England but returned later and was introduced to Dagmar's brother. They took a liking to each other and she and Henrik got married after only a few months.

Early a widow and childless she had visited all the family gatherings in the Ohler house as long as Dagmar was alive but after that more and more seldom. Now it must have been ten years since she last visited the house.

Should he let her return now? Never! Not even a Nobel Prize and a large portion of generosity could get him to change his attitude.

"No, now I have to rest a little," he said, an argument his daughter could not oppose, as she often insisted that he ought to take it easier. "I'm going to meet some journalists this afternoon. I have arranged it so there is only one meeting with the press today."

"Do you want me to come over?"

"That's not at all necessary. I have Agnes. She's as good as three people. Besides, the meetings will take place at the hospital. I wanted it that way."

When they ended the conversation he thought about whether he had been too brusque toward his daughter. She meant so well and was actually the only one, besides Agnes, who seriously cared about how he was doing. His sons showed a formal interest, called now and then and questioned him about the "situation," perhaps told some piece of news from work or family life, that was all. They never discussed any scientific questions or asked for advice. They probably considered his knowhow antiquated. No filial affection was ever expressed by either Abraham or Carl, not even indirectly. Bertram was not surprised, and not particularly distressed. It had always been that way in the Ohler family.

He himself had never been molly-coddled by his parents, even though he was their only child. On the contrary. His father, Carl, prescribed corporal punishment, and his mother, Lydia, carried it out, when it was considered necessary to shape Bertram into a respectable son and citizen. "Respectable" was one of his father's favorite words; "proper" another.

Bertram was not bitter about this after the fact. Those were the times. They didn't know better. When he became a father himself other upbringing methods had replaced corporal punishment. For that reason he had never hit his children.

The sun was shining in through the windows that faced southeast and revealed that the study belonged to an old man. The piles of books and folders, the old kind in a depressing dirty shade of brown that cluttered up a few side tables, had something tragically forgotten about them. The glass of the bookcases was not smeared even by the handles, no one had consulted any medical works for a long time. Only the flies marched back and forth across the frosted glass leaving their tracks.

A stuffed, shabby kite hawk—a gift from his colleagues at the clinic on his sixtieth birthday—hung its head tiredly and its eyes had lost their former luster. Only after many years did he understand the slightly malicious gibe in giving him that particular kind of bird, but he let it sit there on its perch above the liquor cabinet, which these days contained only a lonely bottle of port wine and an almost empty bottle of cognac.

Should he have his old friend Hjalmar take a look at the kite? Then he remembered that he had seen the obituary. The taxidermist was gone. There was a time when they used to meet and discuss specimens.

He decided to draw the curtains but instead went around the desk, sat down on a neglected visitor's chair—God knows by whom, or when, it was last used—and observed the room from a different perspective. He studied the bird, which did not look any more spry from that direction.

A Nobel Prize winner's study, where during an entire professional career he had honed his theories, despaired and suddenly become optimistic, wandered around, slapped his palm on the desk in a moment of brilliant clear-sightedness, or touched his head when he realized a chain of thought had broken.

He could imagine it that way. He visualized the study, the whole house, as a future museum. He would always be there, if not physically then at least through the objects, in the way they were arranged. The ingenuity, originality, and industry would shine, but in gentle colors. An Ohler did not need to shout. It was enough to point to all the branches on the framed, glass-covered family tree that his father Carl had made in the forties: thought, governing, the Word, in the form of members of Parliament, officials, and ministers; natural science, the systemization the pharmacists and doctors were responsible for—a Julius von Ohler was helpful to Linnaeus; the prosperity and improvement of agriculture were the noblemen's contribution—a Gustaf von Ohler was particularly active in the development of Swedish plant cultivation. And to defend this construction there were the warrior Ohlers who fought at Narva as well as in Copenhagen and in the Finnish archipelago.

They were all hanging like lightly curled leaves in an extensive crown. He himself was there in the upper right-hand corner of the chart. When the chart was made he was a blank page; now he was a prize winner.

The family tree spoke for itself. Agnes would only need to clean the glass and dust off the frame. But wasn't it hanging a little crooked?

She would have to clean up in general too, he continued his reflections, but not too meticulously, it could be a little messy, right here in the study he could meet the horde of journalists that would stream in. He could have a tray brought in with a tea cup, a teapot, and a plate of crackers, set it on the serving table, a neat little piece of furniture that some relative had dragged home from China, feign activity, to show that there isn't time enough to leave the study, for even in the autumn of his old age, when his workmates were either buried or subjected to nursing care, Bertram von Ohler is still active.

He smiled to himself at his childish vanity. Wasn't the Nobel Prize good enough in itself, so why this mental theater?

✦

Three

Associate Professor Johansson's house was equipped with a four-meter-high glassed-in tower, where he cultivated his sun-loving plants. In the winter the thermostat made sure that the temperature was favorable for Mediterranean flora, around twelve degrees Celsius. He was particularly proud of a magnificent olive tree.

From his tower he had a good overview of the neighbors. Partly hidden behind foliage he could observe the peaceful life on the block.

He often had his morning coffee up there, read the newspaper, and puttered. So too this morning. The front page of *Upsala Nya Tidning* was naturally taken up by the news about the prize.

The associate professor lived at number seven and Professor von Ohler at number three. Sandwiched between these two scientists was a true humanist, Torben Bunde, literary scholar and writer, who from time to time entertained Uppsala residents with newspaper articles. It might be mental bric-a-brac about all sorts of questions—why the bells in Vaksala Church were tuned in minor, while those in Holy Trinity were tuned in major—or else flattering pieces appeared about some representative from the local rural gentry who happened to own a painting whose signature Torben Bunde found intriguing, or was simply of interest because Bunde played bridge in the house.

But principally his contribution consisted of very seriously intended reviews of books, preferably works that few had heard of and even fewer read.

It was a mystery to the readers that the editors let these screeds be published year after year. There were those who maintained that it was a conscious tactic. Through publication the image of the literary scholar as a fool, a charlatan, was reinforced, and the intent was thus that people should be amused at his expense. The section was called "Culture and Entertainment" after all; the literary scholar could very well be put in the latter category.

The price was high, however; those who were not initiated in the intricate academic game in the city, such as souls incorporated into the city from Östervåla or Lycksele, observed it all with wonder.

Associate Professor Johansson was convinced that Bunde in number five was now wrestling with considerable problems. He had seen him retrieve the newspaper from the mailbox by the street and immediately unfold it, and then remain standing as if paralyzed. Obviously it was there and then the news reached him that his neighbor had been presented with the world's most prestigious scientific prize.

How would Bunde react? Send flowers, like so many had done thus far—too expensive; visit his neighbor—an absurd idea, because it had never happened before; call—improbable, as Bunde was hard of hearing; write an article in homage—less probable, as despite unlimited self-confidence he surely had the feeling that he was not conversant in the subject; write a scathing article where he went on the attack against the selection of prize winners—more likely, even though he was no more conversant in that subject.

Or perhaps pass over all of it with silence? And when some acquaintance brought it up he could smile, tip his head, and mutter something indulgent that could be interpreted any number of ways.

By not showing so much as an ounce of desire to bask in the radiance that now fell on the whole street he could reject the selection of prize winners in an elegant way, while he high-mindedly did not utter anything obviously unfavorable. Perhaps he could simply let slip something about the professor's failing health.

There were several possibilities and from his lookout point the associate professor sensed that internally Bunde was in uproar. After the initial shock the neighbor had raised his eyes toward Ohler's house, and his look had expressed unfeigned astonishment, as if he had never noticed the building before.

The associate professor lingered in his tower. This morning the otherwise rather sleepy street would surely be somewhat livelier than usual. Already a number of couriers had delivered flower arrangements, curiosity seekers had cruised past in their cars. The professor's housekeeper, who had been there as long as the associate professor could recall, was no doubt hard at work arranging vases. The associate professor had seen glimpses of her in the windows on several occasions.

She would stop on the sidewalk outside his house, praise his plantings, perhaps comment on the weather or some everyday incident. Once, perhaps ten years ago, he had received a compliment. That was after he had given her a few violet tulips, which she had admired during the spring.

"You are a good person, associate professor," she had said when, embarrassed but very pleased, she received the package of bulbs.

He understood that it was an uncommonly generous statement coming from Agnes Andersson. Perhaps also a veiled criticism of the professor; hadn't she emphasized "associate" a little? He would like to believe that.

Now he glimpsed her in the professor's study on the second floor, as she drew back the dark-brown curtains, opened the windows, and fastened them wide open. The associate professor tried to smile sarcastically at the futility of trying to air out all that was old in the Ohler house, but it was not a convincing smile, more a grimace that illustrated the distress he felt.

He ought to be proud; as someone involved in the breakthrough in the IDD project he could claim a share of the credit for the prize. But the proper delight would not appear. Twenty-two years ago—he remembered it was a Thursday in May, as usual pea soup was served for lunch—he read the thirty-page summary in *The Lancet*, an article that landed as a sensation, and he saw that his own name was missing.

Decades of toil and his name was omitted. An inconceivable ignominy. As if there was room for only one. The one who got to shine, receive congratulatory telegrams and telephone calls from near and far, and now the Nobel Prize.

Associate Professor Johansson's entire worldview took a serious blow that spring day. In principle he had long been aware of the academic machinations, backbiting to maneuver colleagues out, fighting for funding, where no means were shunned. But now it struck him personally and with such force that he questioned his own research achievements, his entire career. The insult of being ignored he also read as a sign of a kind of general societal rottenness.

After that day he started to distrust everything and everyone. He never ate pea soup again. That, and the associated Swedish pancakes, came to symbolize the mendacity in the world.

The years up to retirement were marked by great indifference. The excitement and enthusiasm had disappeared. He was running on idle.

A lecture trip to Göttingen, Hamburg, and Berlin was the only occasion when he got to experience some of the sweetness of victory. It was intended for Ohler to travel to Germany, but his wife's death came very conveniently for the associate professor. He was sent as a replacement and got to receive much personal evidence of his German colleagues' appreciation. One of them he still kept in contact with. To him he could be completely frank. The conversations and correspondence with Horst Bubb were the valve where the excess steam, when the pressure got too high, could be let out.

Horst had also called early in the morning, something which nowadays otherwise happened only on the associate professor's birthday, and tried to cheer him up. The German, who had worked with Ferguson for fifteen years at the Max Planck Institute, understood the associate professor's feelings very well.

They happened to talk about Ferguson in particular, now retired and living in Vermont, according to Horst very aggrieved. The associate professor got the idea that his friend, by apportioning the bitterness to several researchers involved and in that way diluting it, wanted to alleviate the associate professor's disappointment.

His colleague had also mentioned something about an article that might possibly appear in an influential newspaper with a quiet but very clear criticism of the selection of prize winners. According to Horst this was being initiated by a certain Wolfgang Schimmel, an influential doctor from Munich, who intended to gather a number of significant names behind him.

The associate professor, despite his own frustration, strangely enough remained unresponsive to all this talk about the injustice that was now being committed. He was already tired of it all and wished that the festivities on the tenth of December would be over, the articles cease, and Ohler become a name, not for the day, but instead one in the line of prize winners, who after a few years only the chief mourners would remember.

Ohler was no Einstein, Bohr, or Curie, who would write themselves into scientific history, so let all this go away, he thought in his tower.

"Let it go away, let us die," he mumbled.

The lemon tree in front of him responded at that very moment by dropping a leaf.

✦

Four

Right before twelve the associate professor's doorbell rang, an event if not sensational, then still very unusual. Most recently it concerned a security alarm salesman.

The associate professor was in the kitchen making his usual lunch: a couple of fried eggs, a few slices of pickle, and an open-faced cheese sandwich. The menu had looked like this ever since retirement.

The first ring was followed by another, more drawn out and sharper in tone.

The associate professor was in a quandary: should he finish frying the eggs or move the pan to the side to go and answer the door? In his confusion he did neither. He remained standing with the spatula in his hand, while the eggs were transformed into inedible, dry flakes in the pan.

He thought later, as he disposed of the scraps, that it was like an illustration of municipal politics in Uppsala: While those in charge in other municipalities held discussions, made decisions and then implemented them, Uppsala's politicians remained standing with spatula in hand, year after year.

When the frying pan started to smoke he came to his senses, turned off the burner, took off his apron, and hurried out to the hall.

The associate professor peeked out through the peephole: Torben Bunde. He looked impatient, staring intensely at the door. The associate professor felt as if he was the one being looked at, not the other way around. His neighbor raised his hand and another ring resounded through the house. Now that he knew who the visitor was, he experienced it as even more insistent.

He knows I'm home, the associate professor thought, it's just as well to take the bull by the horns. He unhooked the security chain and opened the door.

"Is this how it's going to be now?"

Torben Bunde, Ph.D. was dressed in something that the associate professor thought was called a smoking jacket, at least back in the day when smoking was done in a fashionable manner.

His face bright red, he pointed with a diffuse motion in the direction of his own house and stamped one foot on the stone paving.

"What do you mean?"

Bunde waved his arm.

"A man," he panted, "a man sneaking around with an ax in his hand."

"On your lot?"

It was a strange feeling, talking to Bunde like this. Not because the associate professor had problems setting aside formalities with people, but it felt wrong somehow.

"I didn't see that well, if it was on mine or yours, or"—Bunde clearly experienced this unexpected neighborly contact and extended conversation as equally strange, because he hesitated suddenly—"or if it was on Lundström's, or whatever his name is, the new person."

Alexander Lundquist had moved in five years ago and was therefore observed with a certain skepticism. No one knew exactly what he did for a living, but there was talk about some kind of publishing activity. Bunde, whose property bordered the newcomer's, had cautiously let the surroundings know that it probably concerned pornography.

"I see," said the associate professor, uncertain how he should tackle the situation.

"Is this how it's going to be now," Bunde repeated, "with a lot of running around in the bushes, photographers and other riffraff, those kinds of paparazzi?"

"Photographers don't usually carry axes. Perhaps it was someone working on Lundquist's yard?"

"That! His yard mostly looks like a communal garbage dump."

Everything that had to do with municipal operations, including recycling stations, Bunde called "communal."

"All the more reason to hire someone," the associate professor replied.

He was finding an unexpected enjoyment in the conversation.

"I definitely think he mentioned something about that."

"Have the two of you talked?"

"Just in passing," said the associate professor.

"Yes?"

"Perhaps it was Lundquist himself you saw?"

"Very unlikely," Bunde said with a sneer. "He's never appeared in the yard before."

The associate professor had to agree.

"This man, you didn't go up and ask what he was doing?"

Bunde shook his head.

"I don't believe there will be 'running around' as you say. Have you gone over to congratulate?"

"No, I want to wait," said Bunde doggedly.

"Perhaps we should take up a collection for a little flower arrangement? I mean, those of us here on the street."

Bunde stared at the associate professor.

"I think I smell something burning," he said.

"I'll never be a cook," the associate professor said, smiling.

Bunde turned on his heels and almost ran toward the gate, which he had left open. It was such an unusual sight for the associate professor that he did not catch the neighbor's parting words.

"Close the gate behind you!" he shouted.

He observed the neighbor striding away. Bunde's hair was sticking out like a scraggly white broom from the back of his head. The sight reminded the associate professor of the only children's book he owned. In it a magician was depicted who at the end of the tale was put to flight by angry people. He wanted to recall that the magician had conjured away something valuable to a poor man in the village. Could it be a cow?

It must have been a cow. Otherwise he probably would not have gotten the book as a Christmas present. His father had been called the "Indian" at home in Rasbo.

The associate professor walked along the stone-paved walk, and to push away the memories flaring up from childhood and youth he let his eyes sweep over the yard, observed that the Öland stone ought to be reset, noted that the moss in the lawn had conquered even more ground, especially in the shadow of the privet hedge, and that the autumn crocus had never been so abundant and beautiful.

While he slowly shut the gate he thought again about the conversation with Ohler. Had the professor been sincere in his intentions when he came over? Perhaps he truly wanted to share the honor? Could it be the case that he had let his many years of disappointment cloud his judgment, that he had not understood that the professor had gradually changed character?

In yesterday evening's news broadcasts, which the associate professor followed on a couple of channels, the professor had repeated his preaching that the honor was not his alone. He had even mentioned Ferguson, which before, during his active period, would have been completely inconceivable.

It was during the last years before retirement that the associate professor's bitterness had grown; it was when forty years of work suddenly was perceived as worthless. To now come up with flattering remarks changed nothing.

He went up the stairs to the tower. The last bit, very steep, was becoming increasingly troublesome.

A pale October sun bathed the plants in a conciliatory glow. He let his hand run across the two-meter-long leaves of the multistemmed dracaena in a careful caress. Against all the green in the tower it shone bloodred. He dampened a rag and wiped off all the old dust so that the contrast stood out even stronger.

In the corner of his eye he thought he perceived a movement between the apple trees on Lundquist's lot. A branch swayed. The Katja tree's fruits shone like little lanterns.

The associate professor removed his glasses and wiped off the lenses with the rag, put the glasses on again and scanned the neighbor's lot. But now everything was quiet.

Must have been a blackbird, he thought. Lundquist never bothered to harvest fruit and berries, so the birds would feast far into autumn. At Christmas the waxwings came and pecked their way into Ribstons.

After pottering with the plants for a while it occurred to him that he hadn't had lunch. The Nobel Prize had certainly made a mess of life on the street, and he set aside the rag and started the descent to the kitchen.

"This stairway will be the death of me," he mumbled.

✦

Five

"Agnes, would you please get the medicine."

He had called several times before she heard his voice. Before they had a functioning bell system from the library too. That was when the male guests gathered there to have a cognac after dinner. Then sometimes the housekeeper's attention might be called for.

She was standing a couple of steps inside the room, looking at him with that inscrutable expression he had such a hard time with. It might entail willingness just as well as total repudiation and contempt.

Needing to involve Agnes in this was not something he was happy about, but now he was feeling so dizzy that he did not dare try to get up from the chaise longue.

Agnes organized most everything in the house but he wanted to take care of the heart medicine himself. He knew that she kept track of how many pills he took, because several times she had pointed out that he had to renew the prescription.

"Shall I call Birgitta?"

Agnes twisted her head slightly, her lips pressed together, the eyes somewhat clouded by cataracts, expressionlessly observing an oil painting that was hanging above the fireplace, a portrait of a woman attributed to Arvid Lagerstedt.

The professor had the feeling of being a very obstinate patient, who for the hundredth time was trying his caregiver's patience, and where conventional surface politeness alone kept the caregiver from slapping the patient across the mouth and then leaving him to his fate.

He chose not to answer the question, the customary tactic. It was theater, their single combat tested over decades. A theater where he always got the last line.

"Thanks, that's fine, Agnes, the medicine."

She disappeared without a word but returned immediately. While he rinsed down the pill he observed how Agnes circled the library, while she waited for him to set down the glass. He got the impression that there was something she wanted to say, but knew there was no point in asking.

"Do you remember, Agnes—"

She turned around.

"How long have you worked here, Agnes?"

"Fifty-five years."

"That's a long time," the professor observed.

She nodded. He wanted so much to hear her say something, make some kind of judgment, or at least make a comment, about the fifty-five years she had served three generations of Ohlers.

Agnes Andersson had never, as far as he could recall, let slip any appraisal of either the family or her position. She had always been there, like the so-called Stockholm bureau in the hall, the table service from France, the framed sketch of a bladdernut, signed Linnaeus, the oil painting by Roslin, the swords from the time of Charles XII that hung crossed over the fireplace in the library, the spear from the parts around Lake Tanganyika, and everything else that filled the house.

It was as if the news about the Nobel Prize, a kind of receipt for his achievement but also an endpoint, made him want to sum up, and Agnes was the only one he could talk with. It was the two of them, no one else, who could confirm each other's stories.

He was still holding the glass. She was waiting by the window, fussing with something on the windowsill. He got the impression that she experienced the tension in the room the same way he did. Wasn't there something unusually tense about her shoulders and the somewhat crooked back, perhaps an expression of a suppressed desire to speak?

While his story was public property hers was mute, and trying to coax it out of her was pointless, he knew that. That after a whole life of distance they could come together and write a common story was a vain hope.

I'm looking for affirmation from a domestic servant, he thought indignantly, *a woman who can barely read a newspaper, who never in her entire life lifted a finger to improve herself and considered learning as something sickly. I, a von Ohler who has received the Nobel Prize, am fawning on an illiterate fisherman's daughter from an inbred island. As if I needed her approval!*

He set aside the glass. Agnes turned immediately and gave him a quick glance. Once again he thought he glimpsed that desire in her to say something, before she hurried over, picked up the glass, left the room, and closed the door behind her.

He stared at the closed door.

"Ungrateful hag," he muttered, got up slowly, smiled contentedly when the fit of dizziness did not appear, and went into the bedroom. It was time to get dressed, to meet the first foreign journalists, who were surely already on the scene at University Hospital, where he laid the foundations for his Nobel Prize.

Agnes had chosen and set out clothes, newly pressed trousers, white shirt, bow tie, and a somewhat worn blazer. A slightly surprising choice— he had expected something more formal, if anything a suit with vest—but realized immediately how well the choice of clothing agreed with the image he wanted to create, and which Agnes immediately and intuitively seized upon.

In the hall were a pair of newly brushed dark shoes. Agnes helped him tie the laces.

"I've called for a taxi," she said. "Professor, you can go out and wait. It will be here soon."

He lingered at the door, hesitated, heard a car drive up, nodded, and opened the door wide.

"Thank you, Agnes," he said, "that's excellent."

"Professor Ahl will meet you at the clinic," said Agnes, closing the door behind him.

He felt driven out of his own home, but attempted a smile. In the near future he would be forced to smile a lot.

He didn't like smiling. In general he didn't like it when old people smiled, it looked like a death grin.

"Mr. Olen!"

The taxi driver's enthusiasm was if possible even greater this time. He opened the gate as the professor approached.

"You again?"

"Yes, Professor Olen, I asked for it. Stephania calls for me."

"So every time there is a fare from this address you'll be coming?"

"If I'm working."

This pleased the professor, it was like having your very own chauffeur. He got into the backseat, only hired hands insisted on sitting next to the driver, his father had maintained, and it was an understanding that Bertram von Ohler shared.

"Everything fine?"

"Thanks," said the professor.

The taxi took off. It was warm and pleasant in the car. The professor leaned back, closed his eyes, and for a few moments he was back in his youth, in the family's old Packard, with Olsson at the wheel. That was his name, Gerhard Olsson, strange that I even remember his first name, because no one called him anything other than Olsson. Then he disappeared during the military call-up, somewhere in Norrbotten, drowned in a river. The new one, what was his name, Wiik it definitely was, but no first name showed up. He was not many years older than Bertram himself, with one leg shorter than the other, which was probably why he was rejected by the military, smelled of tobacco. He stayed with the family until . . .

The professor opened his eyes. *Wonder if Agnes knows? She ought to.*

Then there was no more chauffeur. The caretaker had to manage the little driving there was, and then mainly in the summer to the house on Rådmansö that his father Carl bought during the war. It was a real find, a classic Victorian mansion, owned by an alcoholic factory owner who became insolvent and quickly needed cash.

It was Consul Wendt who had tipped him off about the house, because even though he backed Hitler while the Ohlers, despite their German background, had always been Anglophiles, they socialized. After the war all quarrels were forgotten and the Wendt son later was elected to parliament as a conservative.

But he did not want to think about former caretakers and Nazis. That led too far, there was simply not room for all the history. Or it was not allowed to take up room. Like the story with Wiik, his behavior when Anna quit, threatened unbelievably enough to report Carl. That invalid who could not even become a private, and whom Carl took on out of pure charity, threatening with the police!

Or else with Dagmar, why should he think about her? That they fell in love and got married, what did that mean today? Nothing! Three new leaves on the family tree were the result, good enough, but brooding about Dagmar and all the other dung in the story was of no use.

"My father always took taxis," he said.

The driver laughed. A happy fellow, the professor observed, yet not insistent. He drove nice and easy too, no sudden careening, an ideal chauffeur.

"Was he a professor too?"

"That's right. How did you guess?"

The chauffeur shrugged his shoulders.

"You see that sort of thing," he said.

"He was one of the country's foremost gynecologists."

"I see," said the driver, braking in front of the entry to number seventy. "That was quick."

The driver turned around.

"Here is my telephone number," he said, handing over a card. "Call if you need a taxi."

The professor pulled out his wallet with some effort.

"Keep the change," he said, extending a hundred-kronor bill.

"It's too much."

"I'm not exactly destitute," said the professor, "and it will soon be December. Then there will be replenishment."

✦

Six

Associate Professor Gregor Johansson was taking a nap. It was a lifelong habit. When he was a student and in the early years of his professional career it was sometimes hard to get away, find a place to stretch out for a while. No more than ten or fifteen minutes was needed, even if since retirement it had become considerably longer than that.

He used his father's method, and also his parlance. If he were to be encouraged to remember any special expression from his childhood it was just these words, "I'm going to lean back awhile," that would come to him unbidden.

There was also a childhood odor track: the smell of barn and a hint of sour milk, "pungent" as his father put it, born in Rasbo, a not completely unpleasant aroma, but "different" as his mother, originally from Karungi in Norrbotten, would have expressed it.

And then naturally the kitchen sofa bench, inherited goods that stood under the south window in the otherwise quite modern kitchen.

A completely misplaced piece of furniture, most of all because the associate professor had done nothing to improve its worn appearance. On the contrary, it was with great tenderness that he observed the worn, dirty brown original paint that could be glimpsed under the equally worn-down green outer layer that was his childhood shade.

It was the work of a village carpenter, with a few curves and flourishes on the back, a couple of carved, stylized flowers on the front of the drawer. Otherwise nothing exaggerated, instead a worthy and typical representative of the furniture used most by poor people, indispensable day and night. He had spent his first thirteen years in it.

He was lying on his back on the bench staring up at the ceiling. The usual calm would not appear. He understood what the cause of it was. They were arguing. His father in his languid Uppland way, his mother in her bare Norrbotten dialect. It was as if their respective provinces shaped their speech and gestures.

They carried on, wreaked havoc, pulsed in his circulation, his cheeks burned, made him remember and sense the sweet-and-sour in his childhood and life.

With the years the din had become louder and increasingly frequent. Perhaps natural, he thought, the older you get, the more strongly the odors and veins of memories appear, it's an old truth.

He had no major problems with these memories, there were seldom any really gloomy recollections that floated up, but sometimes they came traipsing, like the shabbily clothed men on the road outside the family's little cottage, those his mother insisted on offering coffee, sometimes a little food. Despite his mother's assurances that they were harmless, just hungry, he was afraid of their mournful appearance; perhaps he had been frightened sometime when he was very small. Perhaps it was his mother's words that it could just as well be themselves who were tramping along the roads.

It was called the "big road" but was no more than a narrow and crooked, poorly maintained gravel road that connected the station in Bärby with the highway toward the coast. There, a few kilometers north, his grandfather lived in a cottage on the farm in Ströja. These points—the cottage, his

grandfather's place, and then Frötuna, the estate where his father worked—
formed a triangle whose few square kilometers basically constituted Gregor
Johansson's whole life during his early years.

Sometimes they went to see Aunt Rut and her husband Karl in Selknä,
less than ten kilometers north. "Kalle" had been a road worker, and in
northern Sweden met his future wife. Later he got work on the Roslag line,
brought Rut with him, and moved to Selknä. Then, when his mother rode
the twelve hundred kilometers to visit her sister, she met the cattleman
Harry Johansson at a barn dance in Gråmunkehöga. So she too moved to
the province.

The outings to Selknä, and a few times by train into Uppsala, were ad-
ventures. The station hand in Bärby, also named Kalle, was already exciting enough.

Then came the black years, as his mother called the war. For Gregor
the period was a strange mixture of worry and a kind of expectation.
Worry that the strange men with hard voices from the radio would come to
Rasbo, but also a time when the adults seemed exhilarated. There had
probably never been so much talk between the farms and houses, gossip
and speculation, with constantly new rumors in circulation.

In 1943 came the deathblow. Just as the fortunes of war on the continent were turning, the luck of the family also turned. His father fell down
from the hayloft, broke his hip and an arm, opened an ugly wound in his
belly, with inflammation and blood poisoning as a result, an injury which
after five days in the hospital in Uppsala would prove to be fatal.

Gregor was then thirteen years old. His father had decided that his son
should be educated as a control assistant, he would work with livestock
but unlike his father he would not need to toil as a cowhand in the animal
stalls. Everything was prepared for him to start in the secondary school in
Uppsala, as a lodger with a cousin of his father, a childless widower who
was foreman at Nyman's bicycle factory.

There began the long migration that led to the university. A path he actually had not chosen himself, and which in retrospect he looked back on
with mixed emotions.

He had been helped along, with the combined exertions of a whole family and later with scholarships, and he realized already during the first month of secondary school, when it turned out that "things come easy to him," that he would never need to tramp along the roads and beg for a cup of coffee and a sandwich, perhaps an odd job.

At the same time, the absence of his father, of the odors of his childhood, sat like an aching wedge in his body. In times of worry it was as if someone struck a blow and drove the wedge a little further into his chest.

He woke from his slumber and sat up. Perhaps it was the overwhelming events of the past twenty-four hours, with the Nobel Prize and Bunde's unexpected appearance, that made the associate professor dream about strange things. In his dream his parents had appeared, but also the old people at the estate, Björks in Sandbacken, where he got to go to buy eggs, the smith who was called "Phew Pharaoh," his grandfather who outlived his son by twenty years, and many others, in a cavalcade where the dead appeared and talked about the sorts of things they had never been allowed, or even wanted, to talk about when they were alive.

He knew that it was time to get up, that lingering on the bench was not a good idea. Once the shabbily clothed started wandering it was time to get up and do something else.

He decided to have his afternoon coffee in the tower, ordinarily an effective cure for melancholy, so he brought a package of cookies from the kitchen and started the climb up the stairs.

The seesawing flight of a green woodpecker caught his attention. He had always liked woodpeckers and had left behind a stump from a pear tree as an intended food source and perhaps nesting tree and been rewarded. Every day the woodpecker came to visit.

From the pear tree the associate professor let his eyes wander over to Bunde's and then to Lundquist's. Immediately he caught sight of the figure crouching behind the overgrown honeysuckle. The man, because of course it must be a man, was standing completely still. The associate professor could only glimpse parts of his back and legs, and perhaps something that might be a dark cap.

"Strange," said the associate professor to himself, and looked quickly toward Bunde's.

He was right, thought the associate professor, there is someone sneaking around here. Should he go downstairs and call the police? No, that would seem almost silly. What would he say? That there is a man standing in his neighbor's yard? He would be laughed at.

The coffeemaker hissed and the associate professor left his lookout point to pour a cup and take out a cookie.

The whole maneuver did not take many seconds, and when he returned to the window the figure was gone. He quickly checked the surroundings but no stranger was seen anywhere.

He did not like that. He did not like obscurity and mysteries. There must be a reasonable explanation. Perhaps it was as he himself had said to Bunde, that this concerned hired gardening help. The honeysuckle really needed pruning, and not just that. All of Lundquist's yard needed a proper facelift. But the honeysuckle stood undisturbed, not a single branch was weeded out.

The man simply had to pee, was the associate professor's next thought, he had withdrawn, tried to conceal himself in the bushes at the back side of the house. A tradesman who did not have access to a toilet, perhaps the explanation was that simple. Perhaps some work was being done on the front side of the neighbor's house? Plastering the façade or window repair were two possibilities that occurred to the associate professor.

He decided to take a walk around the block to check the whole thing. He wanted certainty. Not least he wanted to have something to say to Bunde if they were to meet again.

Suddenly he saw the comic side of all this, this activity that had developed on the otherwise so calm little street. He stopped by the gate, laughed to himself, but quickly became hesitant.

He remained standing a good while, with his hand on the gate handle and his eyes fixed on the street, while his thoughts wandered back to the cottage in Rasbo and the "big road," in this strange interplay that had marked the whole afternoon.

No shabbily clothed people ever come here, it struck him, and the familiar irritation came over him. It was an irritation, not to say anger, at himself that he had felt so many times. Why in the world should he continue to go over the old days? Times are different now and the smells are different, so why?

I became a doctor, I became an associate professor, if not a Nobel Prize winner, nonetheless respected and appreciated by my colleagues, but still so afraid of the shabbily clothed. No, not afraid, more like ashamed that I was so afraid then. But I was a child. I was alone, with no siblings to defend me, explain to me. Mother's words that they were not dangerous did not take, because I knew intuitively that Father didn't like it that the shabbily clothed were entertained by the gate.

He went out onto the sidewalk and began his walk around the block. It was just starting to get dark. The associate professor quickened his pace. He walked with long strides, staring straight ahead, anxious not to appear curious.

At Tibell's he turned left. Linda Tibell shared his interest in Japanese maples and had a magnificent Ozakazuki, whose leaves were now orange-red, at one end of the house.

Then the associate professor turned left again. Lundquist's house was number three in line. In the other house, belonging to the Winblad family, with whom he shared the privet hedge on the back side, small lamps were shining invitingly in all the windows on the ground floor. On the steps Winblad's Irish setter was sitting, following the associate professor with his eyes.

He seemed to sense how the neighbors were also peering behind their curtains. What would he do if no one was seen in the yard? Could he go up to the house and ring the doorbell?

He stopped outside Lundquist's gate, pretended to retie his scarf. The morning newspaper was sticking up out of the mailbox. That convinced him that it was not Lundquist himself he had glimpsed in the bushes and that there was no point in ringing the doorbell. He continued his walk. A stranger, in other words; the question was whether he had a valid reason to be in the yard.

Suddenly the entry light above the front door came on and a figure emerged from the darkness between a pair of extensive spindle trees.

The associate professor stopped abruptly.

"Sorry, I think I frightened you."

The same man whom the associate professor had glimpsed earlier—he recognized the knit cap—came up to the fence.

"Yes, I was a little startled, I'll admit."

Just then the outside light turned off.

"It must have a loose connection," said the associate professor.

"No, the light is motion controlled, it senses a limited area," the man explained, and took a couple of steps back. The light came on again.

The man on the other side of the fence was in his sixties, perhaps a hundred ninety centimeters tall, and gave a forceful impression. His face was chiseled as if it had been worn down by wind or long-term hardship. He was dressed in a pair of dark slacks and a half-length green jacket of somewhat sturdier material.

"Perhaps you're wondering what business I have here?"

"No, not at all," the associate professor assured him. "I'm just out on a late walk."

"It wasn't my intention to frighten you."

"Of course not."

They stood quietly a moment.

"Do you live in the area?"

"Yes," said the associate professor, pointing a little vaguely in the direction of his house.

"Are you the one who has the splendid climbing hydrangea?"

"That's right."

"It must be incomparable when it's blooming."

"Are you interested in plants?"

The man smiled and nodded.

"The spindle tree is not so bad now that it's fall, otherwise it can be a little uninteresting. But now I won't keep you any longer," he said.

"No problem," said the associate professor.

They went their separate ways. The associate professor was happy about the comment about the hydrangea, which really was enormous and covered a large part of the east wall, but at the same time he was very displeased. He had been able to determine that he'd indeed seen a stranger on Lundquist's lot, but had not gotten any answer to what he was doing there. Frustrating to say the least. He definitely did not look like a burglar or photographer, as Bunde had suggested. And why would anyone sneak around? Ohler was no camera-shy movie star or member of the royal court who had to be photographed surreptitiously. On the contrary, he certainly welcomed all the attention.

The stranger had sounded so certain when he talked about the hydrangea and the spindle tree on Lundquist's lot. Could he be a gardener? The associate professor decided that was the case. What other person wandered around that way talking so naturally about plants?

He had been polite too, and well-dressed in practical, durable clothing. The latter also argued for gardener.

The associate professor rounded two street corners before he was back on his street. He glanced in toward Ohler's, where the lights were on, as in the past when the house was full of people. He tried to imagine what was going on in there, and above all what would happen in the future. Festivities, children and grandchildren gathered, colleagues on visits, media people driving up in cars for live broadcasts, dinners—in brief: life and motion.

He himself would go into his turret. The professor would point up toward the illuminated tower and say something about "my assistant, Associate Professor Johansson." He would stand out as a mossy hobby gardener, who for lack of anything else devoted his solitary life to "begonias or whatever."

A skinny shadow figure in a silhouette play who now and then was lit up by the cold blue glow from the lights the associate professor had arranged for his rare plants, while the professor could shine of his own force, surrounded by living, warm people.

He had remained standing on the sidewalk, staring straight ahead without seeing, afflicted by heart palpitations. He waited until his pulse regained its normal rhythm and took a deep breath. His throat was burning from all the coffee that gave him sour belches during the walk.

"What do you say, Uncle Gregor!"

He turned around. Birgitta von Ohler was standing in front of him with a broad smile and outstretched arms. She persisted in calling him Uncle Gregor, which she had done since childhood. He didn't like it, but now it was too late to correct.

"Birgitta," he said tamely.

"Are you standing here? Come in for a cup of coffee!"

"Thanks, but I think I'm fine."

"Don't be silly, Daddy will be very happy."

"I'm going to throw together a little food in my cottage," said the associate professor. "It will be a lot—"

"Of course it's quite amazing! After so many years. You did hear that he mentioned you?"

"How's that?"

"On TV."

The associate professor shook his head.

"'My best colleague,' he called you on the news."

The associate professor stared incredulously at the radiant Birgitta and then let his gaze disappear into a darkness of rising anger. The street and the sidewalk disappeared, likewise the houses and Birgitta von Ohler.

"How are you feeling?"

She took a step closer, took hold of his arm. The associate professor opened his eyes.

"Excellent," he said, but the paleness and weak voice were obvious signs to the contrary.

"Gregor! You're not feeling well."

The associate professor freed himself from her grasp, turned around and staggered toward his house. *I can't run,* he thought, *I cannot die on the street.*

He shoved open the gate and took a couple of deep breaths. Home. From Bunde's house organ music was heard, a Bach cantata, always this pompous Bach! Otherwise it was silent.

His heart had never protested. *Perhaps this is God's punishment for my unjust thoughts and my foolish anger,* thought Gregor Johansson.

He was astonished at himself. *Suddenly I am turning to God! Both brain and heart have become dysfunctional due to this damned Nobel Prize!*

He went over to the beech tree and pressed one palm against its trunk. The coolness of the bark was transmitted through his arm and cooled down his agitation a little.

Should I speak freely? Should I too, like Schimmel in Germany, write an article and tell how it really happened, about Ferguson, about the teamwork, about how one man steals all the glory for himself, as if it were the solitary genius who creates? I could testify. Schimmel can raise up Ferguson, I can push Ohler down from his pedestal.

The thought gave him a certain consolation, but he realized that few, if any, would be influenced. He would stand out as a bitter and jealous loser, as if he was only speaking on his own behalf. The professor was right on one point: There was no justice.

All that remained was to keep his mouth shut. As soon as he had drawn that conclusion the associate professor went into his house.

✦

Seven

Agnes Andersson stared at her feet. How far had they taken her? Or on the contrary, where had she taken her feet? Assuming now that it was the head and not the feet that decided the direction.

To a footbath. In a house where basically she had spent her entire adult life.

Agnes was the third Andersson sister from Gräsö who worked for the Ohlers. Carl von Ohler rented a house on the island a few summers in the 1930s and then came into contact with the fisherman and smallholder Aron Andersson, who supplied fish and helped out with odd jobs.

Then, when Carl needed a new maid for their home in Uppsala, the oldest of the Andersson daughters, Anna, was talked into starting. When she left the household after a couple of years her place was taken over by the middle sister, Greta, who stayed a few years longer, and who in turn was replaced by their little sister, Agnes.

Bertram and his family had use of the wing rooms, as they were called.

When his father died in 1959 he became sole master of a fourteen-room house.

At the time, there was one maid besides Agnes on the serving staff, and a half-time caretaker, all of whom had to take care of Bertram, his wife Dagmar, and the two sons, and as of 1960 a nanny who took care of the afterthought, Birgitta.

Now only Agnes and Bertram were left.

She was sitting in what the family always called the "small parlor." Fifty years ago it would have been inconceivable that as a servant she would be allowed to occupy a room that was reserved for the "ladies," then equipped with a couple of small couches and a handful of armchairs. It was intended that the female guests could gather there after dinner, drink a glass of liqueur, and exchange a little gossip. All while the men sat in the library drinking cognac and talking about their business.

Now it must have been thirty years since any ladies drank and gossiped in the house. The parlor had been redone into a kind of living room for her. Next to it was her bedroom. To start with, she had thought it was quite unnecessary, but Birgitta, who had taken the initiative, insisted on it and Agnes moved from her old room to a new one in the wing. And thus got her own parlor in the bargain.

The time she spent with her sore feet submerged in the tub of lukewarm water and Epsom salts was a break for her head too. Every evening she sat like that, ten minutes, a quarter of an hour.

She heard the professor rummaging about. Quite suddenly it had become important, after years of Sleeping Beauty slumber. He had instructed her in how he wanted it to be and she could tell that if he was often confused he was exact and clear where the arrangements for the study were concerned. The stuffed bird would be removed—"Toss it" was the professor's curt order—and that made her happy. She had wanted to get rid of it long ago, the ugly and malevolent-looking thing.

He had talked long and well about the picture with the family tree and lost himself in stories and kinsfolk. Tales she had heard ad nauseam. But she let him talk on without listening, while she dusted off the bookcase and stowed away old magazines and loose papers.

Suddenly the monologue had ceased. Their eyes met for a moment and in his features she could glimpse what she thought resembled distress, before he laughed.

"The way I go on, as if these . . . diagrams, these branches"—he threw out his hand toward the picture—"might interest you. You have your own family out on the island."

She did not really know what she should say but nodded instead.

"You never married, did you, Agnes," he observed unexpectedly.

"No, I never did. And there were no branches on the Andersson tree. I, and my sisters too for that matter, have been fully occupied with Ohlers."

The professor stiffened, without saying a word, and shortly thereafter left the room.

Perhaps there had not been a line of suitors outside her door, though at one time there had been men. But Agnes never married. That was not something she dwelled on or considered particularly notable or tragic, it was simply the way it turned out, she had always reasoned with herself. A fragile defensive wall, she realized that, but her background, as daughter of the fisherman and lay preacher Aron Andersson, founder of the congregation God's Army, had given her a fatalistic attitude. A fragile wall, for certainly she had longed many times to be out of the Ohler house, and the only way that had existed at one time would have been marriage.

Her father had impressed on her, sometimes with the rod, that her task was to serve God and all other masters, including himself. In his faith there were no mountains. His Old Testament attitude, which aroused a mixture of wonder, respect, and ridicule on Gräsön, left no room for thoughts of freedom.

The congregation God's Army, which in its heyday had two dozen members at most, of which five were from the Andersson family, was long since

departed. Her sister Greta and herself, together with a couple of other re-
tirees, were the only survivors who could testify to the reserve and mute-
ness that marked the interior life of the sect. There was not much joy and
consolation, only fear and hard work.

Smallholder Aron Andersson's faith in God was as merciless as the stony
ten-acre parcel he had to work, the family's life as poor of pleasures as the
patch of forest, mostly consisting of alder marsh and rocks, that belonged to
the place, and their worldly fate as uncertain as the harvests of the often surly
sea, sometimes plentiful catches of herring but more often half-empty nets.

For Aron life and the sea were a struggle, a precipice, resistance that,
if not overcome, in any event must be endured. That was God's idea.
Everything was meager and harsh but above all unpredictable. Only the
Word stood firm and the thought of the Son's descent was the only refresh-
ment to be had.

The father's doings left no room for any form of spontaneity or surprises.
The only thing that deviated was that all the sisters were allowed to leave
the island and the congregation to serve the Ohler family.

This was an anomaly that for Agnes was unfathomable at first. Perhaps
it was her mother's influence that made it all possible. There was a streak
of rebellious delight in her. Aron Andersson also harbored an obsequious
respect for Carl von Ohler and his lily-white wife, so when the question
came up of whether Anna might go with them into town Aron chose to
grant his permission. For a couple of summers Anna had been helpful in
the Ohler household on the island, so it was perceived by everyone as a
natural extension.

Perhaps the father, in all his stern religious zeal, felt a pinch of doubt
after all. Perhaps he wanted to crack open a door for his three daughters,
away from the island and the meager life. Even he could see how times were
changing. Not even the strictest remained unaffected.

When Anna was going to start in Uppsala Aron sailed her over the sound
to Öregrund and the waiting bus. When Greta followed later she could take
the motorboat and Agnes in turn could take the ferry that had started working Öregrundsgrepen.

Sending the daughters to the professor and the house in Kåbo was a guarantee besides that they ended up among "educated and cultivated folk." The expression was her father's. That the Ohler family were not believers, other than on paper, was less important. The family was a suitable acclimatization to a respectable life on the mainland. The father's greatest apprehension was that they would end up "at the factory" or "in a store" and thereby be lured into sinful ways.

Agnes observed her toes in the footbath. God's ten commandments in accordance with the childhood rhyme, where the words had been drummed in: "Thou shalt have no other gods before me." So long ago, but she could still feel the pressure of her father's fingers around her toes as he made her mechanically repeat commandment after commandment.

Sixty-five years ago. She felt dizzy for a few moments at the insight that she would soon die, be united with her parents. She would never get to experience someone pressing their fingers against any part of her body, not even the crooked toes.

Perhaps I wasn't made for that, she thought. *I was destined to serve. I have never loved anyone, not even Birgitta, who took shelter in her arms when it was stormy in the house, when Dagmar and Bertram crossed swords. And no one has loved me. Well,* she corrected herself at once, *Father and Mother.*

She remembered when her father had died quickly in his seventies. He dropped dead in the cramped cowshed. Actually, he had nothing to do there, the little herd had been gone for several years, like most of the cows on the island, but he used to go out there and "idle," as her mother said.

The news came the same day that it was announced that the "old king" had died, so the to-do around Aron Andersson's death was curtailed somewhat.

She went out to the island. Ohler offered to have her driven out, but she took the bus, got off in Öregrund, crossed the little square, read the newspaper placards about the nation's grief, and came up to the ferry landing soaked with sweat, even though a stiff breeze was blowing from the north-east. It was Fredell who ran the ferry and he expressed his sympathy; rumors spread quickly on an island. They were the same age and school-mates, and she wanted him to hug her, a completely unimaginable action for both of them. But he stood next to her during the trip across, silently with his hands on the railing. They looked out over the water, northward toward the island, where they were both born. She was cold, the sweat coagulated on her body, but she remained standing, and he remained standing, even though he always walked around talking. She said, "Thanks, Gösta, that was nice of you." He went to make sure that the cars got off the ferry. She would never forget Gösta Fredell.

She walked from the ferry home. It was only a few kilometers, if you counted like when she was a child. *I'll catch pneumonia,* she thought, but trudged on. There was a comfort in the landscape, late yarrow and columbines swayed at the edge of the ditch and the apples shone in the gardens. At old Lidbäck's a mare was standing that whinnied as she walked past. She stopped and said a few friendly words.

Her childhood home, a poorly built wooden shack, looked even smaller, as if the house had adapted itself now that it needed to house only two persons instead of three. It was a gray, melancholy house and had been like that since Anna's return from service with the "old professor." Later on she left for Stockholm, where she got a position with a businessman with houses in both Saltsjöbaden and in France.

She was replaced by Greta, who in turn was replaced by Agnes, a relay team of sisters to keep the Ohler home in good shape.

Agnes could still remember the short walk from the road up toward the house. It was as if it was the last time, even though she realized that was not the case. But it was a painful way to go, a farewell. Thirty-five years ago, she thought, staring at her feet in the bath.

"He went first," said her mother as Agnes stepped into the kitchen.

She was sitting at the table, and immediately poured a cup of coffee from a thermal carafe, as if she had been sitting there a long time waiting for her daughter's arrival. They had their coffee in silence. If her father had become somewhat more easygoing with the years her mother had changed in the opposite direction.

Greta was at the funeral parlor to take care of the practicalities. Agnes helped pack clothes in boxes and bags, which would most likely end up in the attic. Agnes did not ask what her mother intended.

"The office," the box room under the stairs, which Aron had furnished as his own little den, was mostly cleaned out. Agnes suspected that her sister had been there. But in a drawer she found her childhood. In the warped drawer in a worm-eaten cupboard he had stored the loose tobacco, the only vice he allowed himself. He did not smoke, instead he cut up the long braids and drew the tobacco into his nose. He did it to "clear his nasal passages."

That aroma was her father, but also a kind of worldly perfume, an almost sensory reminder that there was an existence beyond the home and the congregation.

She had pulled the drawer out completely and brought it to her nose, breathed in deeply, and experienced her father's mute devotion. So certainly she had been loved, in his reserved way, but loved all the same.

Agnes knew that Greta had tried to get hold of Anna and before she returned to Uppsala she asked whether their big sister had been heard from. Her mother did not answer and Agnes took that as a no.

A few days later Agnes got pneumonia, was bedridden, and could not be at the funeral.

The water had long since cooled in the tub. Her feet were wrinkled and softened. Agnes filed them long and well, a task that brought her a kind of pleasure.

✦

Eight

"There are rats!"

"It's mice," Agnes Andersson corrected.

"Doesn't matter." Birgitta von Ohler looked around the library as if she would discover more. "They are rodents," she continued, "and they can eat up a household from inside."

Maybe it was the fatigue that made Agnes's eyes tear up.

"Don't be sad," Birgitta exclaimed, taking hold of her arm. "It's not your fault. I'm just so surprised that it's happening in this house."

"Mice make no distinctions," said Agnes, freeing herself from her grasp. "They make their way indoors this time of year. I usually set out a few traps every fall."

Birgitta observed her wide-eyed.

"I've been doing that all these years," Agnes added.

"Have you talked with Daddy?"

"About what?"

"The mice."

"I didn't know you were so afraid of—"

"I'm not afraid! Don't you understand? People are coming here now, journalists and others, from all over the world, and you're walking around with a rat trap. And tonight Daddy's colleagues are coming here. I'm sure they'll be sitting in here after dinner."

Agnes looked at Birgitta with an expression that did not express any of what she felt inside, but possibly Birgitta sensed Agnes's fatigue, a fatigue that perhaps unconsciously let the contempt be glimpsed from behind the mask she had polished for half a century.

"I know what you're thinking!"

Agnes turned away.

"You think I'm stuck-up and impertinent."

"Not at all," said Agnes with her back toward Birgitta.

"Look at me!"

"I have a few things to do," said Agnes, but then turned around slowly, as if the movement were associated with an awful pain.

"You believe—"

"Believing you can do in church," said Agnes, but fell silent out of pure astonishment at her own reply.

Birgitta was staring at her.

"I must say"—this was one of Bertram's stock phrases that his daughter had inherited—"this prize has certainly stirred things up properly."

"It's been stirred up a long time," Agnes mumbled.

"What do you mean?"

Agnes walked over to one of the windows that looked out from the back of the house.

"Palmér planted the apple tree outside here the same week I came to the house. It was a cold October, I remember the steam from his mouth."

Agnes's voice was raspy, as if it hadn't been used in a long time, and she cleared her throat before she continued.

"I was standing right here, it's like it was yesterday. He was out there and I was inside here where it was warm. I remember that I wanted to call him into the kitchen for coffee, but that sort of thing was not done. I didn't know my place and the cook was not gracious either. Your grandfather and grandmother were still alive then, your father had a position at Academic Hospital and I . . . I didn't know . . ."

"What didn't you know?"

Birgitta had joined her at the window and also observed the tree, heavy with fruit. All that was heard was the sound of the rain striking against the window.

"How life would turn out."

"Who knows that when you're young?"

Agnes did not reply. Her eyes rested intently on the shiny fruit that rocked in the wind and was rinsed by the rain.

"I think I'll make an apple cake," she said at last.

"Do you regret taking a position here?"

Agnes cast a quick glance at Birgitta.

"Regret or not, I was sent here as a replacement for my sister."

Agnes made an almost imperceptible movement with her head and left the window, taking quick steps toward the door. With her hand on the doorknob she turned around to say something, but remained standing without a word.

"Are you not feeling well?"

"I should see about the food for dinner," Agnes replied, leaving the room and carefully closing the door behind her.

Perhaps it was the rain that made Birgitta von Ohler linger a long while by the window, the way you stay standing by a fire or in front of a fireplace, staring into the flames. Now it was the steady lashing against the windowpane and the stubborn, almost aggressive sound of the drops against the windowsill that captivated her.

She had come to the house to help Agnes with the preparations for dinner. It was obviously at Bertram's initiative, because when she showed up Agnes acted completely uncomprehending and unusually brusque, refusing all assistance in the kitchen.

Agnes's reaction was perhaps understandable but nonetheless Birgitta became lost in a gloomy state that corresponded well with the weather. The usually pleasant feeling of being indoors and able to observe the storm from a warm, sheltered position would not appear. On the contrary, she had an impulse to leave the house, expose herself to the foul weather, and let the rain and wind take hold of her.

Her father was in his study; according to Agnes he was spending several hours there every day, and did not want to be disturbed. God knows what he was occupied with. She had asked but didn't get an actual answer, other than that he was tidying up old papers and notes.

At times she feared that he would not manage the onslaught of callers and journalists and then the ceremony itself in Stockholm on the tenth of December. She could see him wobbling up to receive the prize from the hands of the king, but stumble and fall headlong. Or, in the usual conversation on TV with the other prize winners, lose the thread and start rambling on about inconsequential things, something he was doing more and more often.

Birgitta had carefully hinted something about her apprehensions to Agnes, but she seemed completely oblivious, or perhaps she was pretending not to understand. She had just looked disinclined, with her slightly protruding eyes surrounded by a blackness that suggested a poor night's sleep.

The fatigue that afflicted Bertram von Ohler seemed increasingly to spill over onto the housekeeper. But she's no longer a youth, thought Birgitta. Last Christmas, when the whole family had gathered for once, she had discussed the issue with her brothers. Perhaps she should see about hiring a younger person? Agnes could obviously continue living there. Throwing her out after half a century would be heartless, on that they all agreed.

No decision was made, perhaps partly because it felt unreasonable to hire someone outside the circle of Anderssons from Gräsö, who had served the family for almost seventy years. But there were no more sisters and no younger generation.

She decided to bring up the question again, now when Abraham and Carl would be coming to Uppsala. Agnes would surely protest indignantly but perhaps think it would be nice anyway to only work a couple of hours a day and let someone take over the main responsibilities. She had recently expressed a kind of cynical indifference about the condition of things, an attitude that would have been unthinkable before. Birgitta had looked for signs of whether this new attitude had left its marks in the house, but could not discover any. Everything was sparkling clean as before, the food preparation seemed to work irreproachably, and her father had not expressed even a word of dissatisfaction.

If Agnes had changed, then this also applied to her father to a large degree. The initial euphoria, the almost boyish delight about the prize, had been replaced by irritability. He was holding something inside, she was convinced of that, something that worried him. She had tried in vain to narrow down what it might be but had also been rejected by him, grumpily to start with but later, when she brought up the issue again, angrily and with an emphasis that made her mute with astonishment.

Her father was not in the habit of raising his voice, even if he sometimes sputtered a little. Often he was content to evade her questions. Then when he unexpectedly used that old harsh voice she relived for a moment her childhood and youth and remembered the occasions when her parents clashed.

Afterward he had seemed regretful, said something to the effect that he was stressed, but nothing else, no hint about what worried him. She knew him well and realized that he was withholding something.

Now he was rooting through his old papers, whatever use that could be, and barely answered when spoken to. He had even canceled playing bridge, an almost inconceivable measure. But he could not avoid dinner. In a weak moment, he had told Agnes that he regretted it immediately, he had invited Professor Ahl and a few other colleagues for a "simple meal."

Perhaps it was simply the excitement and a general worry about standing in the limelight that created this irritation and desire for isolation? She wanted to believe that, but the nagging sensation that there was something else refused to go away.

She had forgotten to ask if Gregor was invited. He had seemed strange when they met on the street. The associate professor was perhaps not a cheerful fellow, but she had always gotten along well with him. Now he had stared at her as if she were a ghost, and then rushed off like a frightened animal.

She breathed on the window and in the mist that was formed she wrote her name. A scraping sound from the top floor brought her back to reality and she decided to call home and say that she would be staying a few more hours. Regardless of what Agnes maintained, two persons surely would be needed to wait on a number of professors.

Liisa would not be happy, she had always had difficulties with Bertram and between them there was a kind of childish competition for Birgitta's favor. It could take on quite silly expressions, primarily from her father's side.

"I meant to ask you, is Gregor, Associate Professor Johansson, invited to the dinner?"

"No," Agnes answered, standing by the kitchen door. In one hand she had a basket and in the other an umbrella.

"I see you've made coffee. I'll have a cup."

Agnes nodded toward the coffeemaker and opened the door. A gust of rain-soaked autumn wind came into the kitchen. Agnes opened the umbrella and went out into the garden. A stab of melancholy and fear made Birgitta immediately rush over to the window.

It's like forty years ago, it struck Birgitta, *I'm a child who is standing in the kitchen and sees Agnes go out to pick fruit or berries in the garden. I have become a middle-aged women while she is unchanging.*

She observed how Agnes carefully selected the apples. Sometimes she used the umbrella to knock down fruit. Birgitta made an attempt to leave her spectator's position, perhaps to help out, but it was too late: Agnes already had the basket full, and was immediately back in the kitchen.

She had a pleased look, an expression that Birgitta knew well. In her way of resolutely shaking off the umbrella, closing the door after her, and placing the basket of fruit on the little table under the window—surprisingly exact and nimble movements coming from an elderly woman—she demonstrated an efficiency and sovereignty that Birgitta had always admired. No one performed their tasks as energy-efficiently.

"The rain doesn't want to give up," Agnes noted.

Gone was the harshness in her voice.

"Shall I peel the apples?"

Agnes stopped for a moment, then filled a plastic tub with water which she placed on the table, took out a peeler, and pulled out the kitchen chair.

"Not too small pieces," she said.

"What kind is this?"

"Cox Pomona."

They worked in silence. Birgitta sat at the table and peeled and cut up the fruit while Agnes cut up onions and root vegetables at the counter.

"You know, Agnes, when I was little I thought you would disappear every time you left the house, even if you were just going to pick a few currants or go down to the store and buy a liter of milk."

Agnes gave her a quick look, but did not say anything.

"That was a horrible time, wasn't it? That I put up with all those quarrels"—Birgitta took another apple out of the basket—"but I had to, I was only a child."

"Your mother drank," said Agnes.

Birgitta's peeling knife stopped in mid-motion.

"Your mother was unhappy."

Birgitta stared at the housekeeper's hunched back. Only the sound of the knife against the cutting board was heard.

"What do you mean?"

Agnes turned around with the knife in her hand. The smell of onion struck Birgitta.

"Exactly what I'm saying—your mother was unhappy and drank."

"My mother was sick."

"She *got* sick, yes."

Birgitta stared at the older woman, tried to see something conciliatory in her facial features, some opening to a different conclusion, a different story. But in the housekeeper's face there was only the determined look that Birgitta recognized so well. No compromise was possible. It was a stern implacability that Birgitta guessed had been impressed on Agnes during prayer and self-denial since she was a child.

She held an apple up to her nose to drive away the smell of onion.

"But there's nothing to talk about now," Agnes decided, and resumed her work.

Birgitta took a bite of the apple.

"I'm going to make two apple cakes," Agnes stated with her back turned toward her. "If you want to eat the apples you can go out and pick for yourself."

She went over to the refrigerator, took out a package of bones with some meat on them, perhaps pieces of oxtail, and Birgitta understood that Agnes was preparing a stock and that most likely there would be roast fillet with mushroom gravy and fried potatoes with herbs for dinner, a classic in the house.

Birgitta got up and pulled on the old, cutoff boots that Agnes always had standing by the door and went out. She realized that Agnes was watching her and when she turned her face toward the sky there was a fine drizzle that settled on her face like a cool, refreshing film. She knew that it would irritate Agnes.

"You'll catch cold," was also her immediate comment when Birgitta returned to the kitchen.

"I wish I could be at the dinner," she said.

"I doubt if it will be much fun," said Agnes.

"I was mostly thinking about the food."

Agnes's neck twitched.

"Can't we eat in the kitchen, the two of us? Like before, when—"

"I'll be serving," said Agnes.

"You'll have time for that too."

Agnes did not answer but shook her head.

"I can help you," said Birgitta, but realized at once that it was the wrong thing to say.

"Think how that would look."

A sudden fury came over her and she caught herself cursing Agnes's lack of imagination. "Think how that would look," she silently imitated the ill-tempered comment, but the fury changed just as quickly into a kind of melancholy that affected her more and more often when she visited the house. It seemed as if the uncertainty of her childhood returned even stronger with increasing age, as if the smells in the house, the sight of the heavy furniture and the threadbare carpets brought her back to the unpredictable aspects of her early years, the feeling of constantly moving in a minefield, where a quarrel could detonate at any moment. Freedom had always been outside the house, in the garden or in the old playhouse that some distant relative had cobbled together in the early 1960s, places that neither Bertram nor Dagmar visited.

Liisa always joked with her, called the Ohler family "the headshrinkers" without ever explaining what she meant, but Birgitta herself had started to think of the family as a clan that wandered around with shrunken skulls, a ridiculous but also anxious image that sometimes came to her.

"Why did you think I would disappear every time I left the house?"

"What?"

The breadth of Agnes's question, and perhaps the fact that she asked it at all, produced a landslide of emotions inside Birgitta.

"I guess I was afraid of being alone," she answered with her eyes directed out the window. Between the branches of the trees and the black-soiled leaves some patches of blue sky were visible.

"No risk," said Agnes. "I stayed here. Always."

"Do you regret it?"

"Maybe I was scared too," said Agnes at last.

She fetched a pan—it was her firm conviction that stock should always be cooked in an iron pan—dumped in the bones, the oxtail meat and vegetables, salt, whole pepper, bay leaves, poured in a little water and half a bottle of red wine, Portuguese Birgitta noticed, set the pan on the stove, and turned on the heat.

"There now," she murmured.

Birgitta had peeled and cut up the last apple and let the segments disappear down into the tub of water. She wished there had been more fruit to peel.

"As luck would have it I brought black chanterelles with me," said Agnes.

"From the island?"

Agnes nodded.

"I should have made the stock yesterday, but I didn't find out until this morning that there would be a dinner this evening."

"I'm sure it will be really good as always," said Birgitta.

Agnes was standing by the stove and would do so until she could skim the stock a couple of times, and then leave it to simmer for several hours.

"Afraid of the life out there," she said unprovoked, making a movement with the ladle toward the window. "Here I had an income and a place to live anyway."

"But you've been happy, haven't you?"

Agnes snorted.

"You all thought I couldn't manage anything else," she said. "Anything other than scrubbing, dusting, and cooking, cleaning up. And maybe that's right."

"Now you're being unfair."

Birgitta got up and went over to the housekeeper. "Look at me!" she said.

Agnes slowly turned her head. Her eyes looked uncommonly fish-like, perhaps it was the heat in the kitchen, perhaps the talk about happiness and all the thoughts that brought with it that made her eyes stick out even more.

"We have always appreciated you, you know that! The whole family, even if Daddy is the way he is. Even Mama wanted to have you stay."

The ladle stopped in the pan.

"What do you mean 'have me stay'?"

"It was nothing," said Birgitta, her face turning bright red.

"Yes it was," said Agnes, as she resumed the skimming.

Birgitta thought she could perceive something triumphant in her voice.

"I know that the professor wanted to fire me, but that Dagmar intervened."

"That's not at all true!"

"As true as I'm standing here. And what is *really* true? Is there more than one truth?"

"Sometimes," said Birgitta, who was relieved that she got off so easy.

"I'll stick to mine."

Agnes turned down the heat on the stove.

"And one day perhaps you will find out why your father wanted to drive me out onto the street."

"He wanted to save on the household," said Birgitta.

"That's the silliest thing I've heard."

Agnes made a smacking sound with her tongue as if to underscore what she thought about Birgitta's understanding.

"Now you'll have to excuse me," she said, "but I have to prepare the roast."

"How should I find out the truth? Daddy's not likely to say anything."

"You'll have to wait until I die," said Agnes. "And that can be at any time."

"Don't say that!"

"What do I know?"

"Ridiculous!" Birgitta hissed.

"That may be, but you'll have to wait."

Birgitta left the kitchen without a word, pulled off her stockings on the stairs, and took a few easy, girlish barefoot steps out on the lawn, with a flightiness that in no way corresponded to what was going on inside her. She needed to get away from Agnes and her evasiveness. Bitterness was the worst thing she knew, when people dug down into old injustices, many times imagined, and dwelled on them over and over again.

What did Agnes really have to complain about? She had been free to leave the house at any moment whatsoever but had chosen to stay for over fifty years. She had reasonable pay and free food and lodging, had never needed to suffer want, after only six years of elementary school and a couple of courses at some kind of housekeeping school as her only asset.

She wanted to scream out this simple fact in the kitchen, but realized that it would not lead to anything good. Birgitta was aware that it was crucial to keep Agnes in a good mood, because after all she was the one who kept the household running. Her father, Nobel Prize winner or not, would be in a bad way without her, and Birgitta was the one who would have to step in. Bertram would never accept any kind of municipal home assistance, he would rather die of neglect.

Behind her restraint was also a lingering respect for Agnes from her childhood. It would never disappear, she realized that. Agnes was unapproachable, always had been, with a kind of lower-class sovereignty that, without putting it into words, Birgitta still felt if not fear then a certain discomfort about. Birgitta had always felt as if the servants saw through her, they could look into every corner where the family dirt accumulated, and their expressions never revealed what they were thinking, what conclusions they made.

Their relationship to the servants was based on a contract where the foundation was obedience and silence. Agnes, and others in her position, were assumed to be loyal, but no one could take that for granted. The threat of a Trojan horse by the pans in the kitchen, serving in the dining room or cleaning the bedroom with the most intimate garments and stenches, always awakened an apprehension of a conceivable fifth column, a worrying factor and a source of irritation that never left the upper class.

Liisa was the one who, in her efficient Finland-Swedish—it was as if the tone in the language underscored the thought—put Birgitta on track, draped the unspoken discomfort into words. It was only in recent years that Birgitta could fairly confidently look back on her childhood and adolescence.

With her calm and her coolness, certainly acquired during many long training sessions at the firing range, Liisa served as a factual corrective when Birgitta digressed in metaphysical explanatory models about how and why things developed as they did in the Ohler family.

To the general picture could be added the peculiarity that Agnes's background offered. Not because she preached—Birgitta had never heard her resort to religion in the form of an apt Bible quotation, never seen her pray. But God was present, or rather the sense that God was greater than everything, more significant than Ohler's combined prestige and worth, and that He thereby had priority when paltry earthly matters were to be organized or interpreted. Agnes had always viewed the family tree with a certain skepticism, always listened to the tales of the family's achievements with an absent expression.

The damp grass did Birgitta good. She looked around, studied the wobbly prints she produced and then let her eyes travel around the surroundings. From the neighbor's house organ music was heard. Hyllenius had hoisted the flag, perhaps it was someone's birthday in the house, but she then discovered that it was hanging soaked at half mast and realized that someone had died. In the tower Gregor was visible among his plants. Somewhere the sound of some kind of machine was heard, a power saw Birgitta thought, perhaps it was at the publisher, the most anonymous neighbor.

She sensed that Agnes was keeping an eye on her through the kitchen window, just like when she was a child, and that produced mixed emotions in her, like so much else that concerned the house. And not just the house, it struck her, the whole neighborhood called forth a claustrophobic feeling, as if the whole area was enclosed in a fog, an unhealthy haze, where the same shadow figures schematically moved year after year. Who was directing this mechanical dance of death? Perhaps Liisa's words about headshrinkers applied to all of Kåbo?

She raised her eyes and observed Gregor Johansson in his tower. Perhaps he was heading for confusion and dementia, their encounter on the sidewalk had suggested something along those lines. And then this Torben Bunde, who staggered around in an organ rumble, a comic Bach poisoning, which made him write such peculiar things. Farther away Hyllenius, now in mourning, who was trying to maintain a kind of respectability with his purchased titles and poorly imitated mannerisms. In mourning? Perhaps it was just the opposite? Perhaps they were celebrating an inheritance.

Better to have grown up in Salabackar or at Kvarngärdet in a family without ancestry and fortune, then I would not have anything to defend other than my right to live more or less respectably. That was a thought that constantly occurred to her, and more and more often, now as she approached the age for summation, fifty.

She felt a kind of loss of something, of what she didn't know, what it smelled or tasted like, but that obviously must be there.

This something, which the Ohler family and the entire neighborhood despised, spoke badly of, and lived in fear of, enticed with words in a language that she had never mastered.

It was a fear that sometimes took comical expressions. Birgitta had never seen it that way until her Liisa pointed out that the fear of others was completely unfounded and pathetic. The people from Kvarngärdet, whatever they smelled like, would never invade Kåbo. It was as if Agnes were to revolt, a completely absurd thought.

Birgitta peered toward the kitchen window. Agnes was toiling away in there. Birgitta was filled with compassion but also anxiety that a person had been locked in so long. She herself, like her brothers, had fled.

What she understood was that Agnes never had a man and was most likely a virgin. A married housekeeper was inconceivable, if she was not living together with a man employed by the family. Birgitta had seen that sort of thing during her childhood, apparently happily married servants, and been astonished, tried to imagine Agnes with a man. An impossible thought, not least considering what a contrast it would have made to her own parents' embittered, and later downright hate-filled, coexistence.

The organ music from Bunde was booming ever louder, clearly the piece was approaching its resolution, and Birgitta suddenly started laughing. It was as if the built-up tension was released in a violent paroxysm, which was only interrupted when an apple fell down with a dull thud in front of her. She leaned over, picked up the apple and stroked it against her face.

✦

Nine

Karsten Haller had drawn the conclusion that the woman was Bertram von Ohler's daughter. Who else would be stumbling around barefoot in his yard? There was something frightening about her, like when you observe a person unable to contain herself, control her movements or bodily fluids. She was a grown woman, not a child that could be excused, and it was a cold and damp October day. It all made him feel very ill at ease.

Then when she broke out in hysterical laughter he got the impulse to call to her to stop, pull herself together.

Then an apple dropped and she fell silent immediately. Despite the distance he could see with what a blissful look she rubbed the apple against her cheek. By no means did this make him calm; on the contrary, it underscored a kind of capriciousness in her that he sensed could lead anywhere.

He knew nothing about her. Maybe she was crazy?

For a few moments he toyed with the thought of calling her to him, exchanging a few words, perhaps coaxing a little information out of her. But her look made him give up on that idea.

Now she was standing under the tree, lightheartedly leaning against the trunk, chewing on the apple she had previously handled so lovingly. He got the impression that like a female spider she devoured her lovers.

It was a strange environment, so quiet, aside from the music from the neighboring house that he had noticed with surprise was playing almost all the time, and whose ominous organ rumble only underscored the desolation that rested over the neighborhood.

The only one who generated any kind of activity was the man in the glassed-in, illuminated, and circular greenhouse on the roof of his house. The same man he had run into the evening before and who had given a somewhat confused but nevertheless sympathetic impression. It was not just the greenhouse and the gigantic climbing hydrangea that testified that he was interested in plants. On the lot were several interesting bushes, even one he could not identify at a distance, and whose deep red leaves caught your eye.

He tried to imagine how it had looked here decades ago. Probably not much had changed, all the houses appeared to have been built eighty or ninety years ago, solid stone houses, on good-sized lots, which left room for fruit trees, lawns for croquet and sunbathing, and in a few cases pools.

A nature reserve, it struck him, with protected species that were treated with the greatest respect and care and which in contrast to Etosha, where he had worked as a guide for several years, was not subjected to caravans of insolent tourists with binoculars and expensive photographic equipment.

He was an intruder, carefully disguised and equipped with tools that gave him access to the domains of the elect, to the cream of Uppsala's population, to the "educated and cultivated," as his mother had called them.

Those who owned at least a couple of expensive cars parked outside the house, who sailed in the Caribbean and skied in the Alps, shopped in London and New York, while they complained about the tax burden under the dictatorship of the social democrats. All this as his father had talked about and which during his youth often sounded like envious complaining.

It was his experiences from Africa that first caused him to understand more of the context. It took a village in north Namibia to understand Uppsala.

The cold crept up his leg. The woman had left the garden long ago. He did not understand why he was still standing there, what he could achieve by this insolence. He had no plan. Not even a sensible idea, other than the thought of the deep injustice that Bertram von Ohler was being honored in every conceivable way.

Injustices exist to be fought against, his father had maintained, and he, if anyone, ought to have known. Yet in his attitude there was an indulgent aspect, in the midst of the rhetoric he might fall silent and laugh, at himself and his tirades, belittle what he had just asserted and with emphasis at that.

Perhaps the weight he carried when he came ashore at Trelleborg, with his son pressed against his skinny chest under a stinking coat, was so great that it made everything else seem small?

Shortcomings and everyday discord paled in light of the evil he had experienced during the war, turned into a temporary irritation like when a fly buzzes around your head. Was that how his father would have seen it? Was that how he himself should view Nobel Prize–winner Bertram von Ohler? Like a fly?

But you swat at flies by reflex, he thought. You don't always think you'll make a hit, it's more a movement to give vent to the fury at the persistent presence. And then the ridiculous pride at your quickness when surprisingly enough the little carcass tumbles around and down, struggles with its shitty feet and pale wings, dies a painless, bloodless insect death, an insect's kind of reasonableness. Blame yourself, you think a little carelessly, perhaps a trifle ashamed that you resorted to violence against such an insignificant and in most respects, strictly speaking, innocent creature.

No plan, no idea why he was still standing there. Only a growing anger.

He should forget it all, for who was really served by dragging old rubbish out into the light? Perhaps his parents would not have approved? What has been cannot be made undone, they would surely reason in their heaven.

But the anger was too great.

His father would have taken action! The insight came traveling like a black projectile that struck his body with such force that he was forced to support himself against the wall. That's the way it was! Ludwig Haller's love for his family was greater than anything else, unashamedly unconditional. A love that cleared its own paths, ground down all resistance, overcame every obstacle, even his own history. Against the painful memories of a whole continent Ludwig Haller, who had lost everything and almost everyone, a refugee who had seen everything a human eye should never have to see, against all this he placed love for his only son and his wife.

In that case revenge, when it concerned those near and dear, would also be just as obvious, categorical, and immediate as love. His father would not have hesitated a second.

Vacillation was betrayal. His grandfather, Ludwig's father, had vacillated and it had cost him and several in his family their lives.

Were there perhaps other reasons he spent so much time staring at a house with an old man personally unknown to him, a man he had never met, only heard and now read about? And who by an unfathomable chance now found himself so near to.

It felt as if he had pulled off a cistern cover and was now staring down into a deep, dark well, whose stone-lined sides were dripping with dampness and covered by spotted moss that resembled black, clotted blood.

Down there in the depths were his parents, they spoke to him. His father with his slight accent and his mother with her gentle voice, two things he instinctively despised when he was a child.

Down there Nouibiwi was also lurking, or Miss Elly as she preferred for him to call her before they got married, and which he continued to call her, despite her express disapproval. Otherwise she did not talk that much, neither then nor later, but what she said was often filled with wisdom.

She did not say anything from the depths of the well either, only looked at him with her big eyes, the whites shining in the darkness, and encouraged him to do something for once!

He looked over toward the Ohler house, which had now assumed quite different proportions, been reduced. The plaster façade, with its dark patches after the rain, no longer looked as imposing. If you looked at it closer the cracks could be seen, perhaps depending on the seepage from the heavy clay that everything in the city rested on. The birches were simply too close to the house, he said to himself, they ought to be removed, if only to let more sun onto the lot.

The windows, so inviting before with their neat candlesticks and potted plants, now in the dark of the afternoon resembled black eyes that malevolently stared out over the surroundings.

From the wheelbarrow he picked up a trenching shovel, for its form and usability his favorite tool, and weighed it in his hand. On the shaft, at seventy and ninety centimeters, notches had been carved, like bowl hollows, to make planting easier. They were not really necessary, he had the measurements ingrained in him, but it was a habit to carve in these markings.

He stared at the tools in the wheelbarrow: a sledgehammer, a string trimmer, a crowbar, and much more.

I ought to rough-hew a pillory, he thought, rough and scratchy, and erect it in the midst of this reserve of high culture. The organ music could rumble.

"I ought to," he mumbled, before he set aside the trenching shovel and instead reached for the concrete shovel and spade that were leaning against a tree.

He continued his strenuous labor. The ground was hard and invaded by all kinds of roots; once again he muttered something about the birches. He had decided to excavate to a depth of forty centimeters. If he encountered large stones he would let them be. The planting depth should be at least sixty centimeters, but when he discovered how hard it was to dig, he decided to raise the beds somewhat. He had proposed that to start with but the homeowner rejected it, thought it would look unnatural. Now it had to be like that anyway. He could explain it such that in time the planting would settle somewhat.

Normally he would have rented a small excavator and done the work in a jiffy, but on that issue too he was met with opposition. No machinery could be brought onto the property. So now he had to dig by hand, though actually he had nothing against that. It was hard work that tried your patience, but after a while the precisely weighed movements created a pleasant pace, an almost hypnotic rhythm, where the repetition gave him the time he needed for reflection, or rather a kind of meditative calm.

The rain did not bother him—on the contrary, it made the ground softer. He toiled on as always, occupied by the monotony. Every shovelful demanded a similar thought and muscular effort, but with a little variation in every stroke, invisible to an outside observer, a kind of automated and polished finesse that amused him, granted him satisfaction. A visitor at the edge of the excavation would think, Nice that I don't have to do this mechanical job.

He had experienced so many times how the uninformed felt sympathy for him, that he should have to toil in this old-fashioned way, that he did not let it bother him. He saw it differently: Others were missing out on something valuable and were to be pitied. They saw only the sweat that appeared on his forehead and in his armpits and how his muscles were forced to work. Nothing else.

It was not until twilight came that he straightened up, set aside the spade, and surveyed the situation. It was at moments like this that he wished he still smoked. The thought came to him every day, even though he quit more than ten years ago.

The planting was intended to cover about fifteen square meters and more than half of that was dug up. He kicked at a stone on the bottom of the excavation and it obligingly loosened from the grip of the clay. He took it as a good sign. Tomorrow he would finish the excavation and then refill it with his own mixture for acid soil plants, needles, cones, and branches from spruce, peat, leaves, compost, and a little gravel. The proportions varied from time to time, it was not that exact, he worked by feel, tossing in what might be suitable at the moment. If he came across a rotten log or stump he threw that in too. This time he would layer the mixture with twigs from the pruned spindle tree in the front.

It struck him that there must be an excess of beech leaves on the neighbor's property. He had glimpsed the stately beech above the roof. Should he perhaps ask whether he could gather some leaves in sacks and carry them over?

He peered up toward the tower. The "tower man," somewhat hidden behind plants but completely visible, stood observing him. He raised his hand, but the old man withdrew without responding to the greeting.

A lonely old fogey, he thought, while he gathered up his tools and turned the wheelbarrow over, but he can probably part with a few leaves.

Once again he observed the excavation and made the association that he was standing before an open grave. Most recently it was at the burial of his mother; that was also a rainy day, six months ago. Those who were assembled huddled under umbrellas, a woman whispered something inaudible, another nodded at him, before they all dropped off, apparently reluctant to prolong the ceremony and their own presence more than necessary. And he appreciated that, no gathering had been arranged, no uncertain, wary talk over clattering coffee cups and saucers. There were too few mourners, five besides the minister. His mother's lonely life would have stood out as more pitiable if they had exerted themselves to observe convention with a funeral reception.

But afterwards, when the grave was filled in and the few wreaths and flowers laid out, when everything was quiet in the little cemetery, he thought, What memories did the others have of his mother? And then he regretted that they hadn't gathered to talk for a little while. It did not

have to be strained, he could simply have been able to express his gratitude for their presence in a more emphatic way, perhaps coax out a few
remembrances. He had no idea, however, who two of the guests were.

And those who were not present, what did they have to tell? There were
many gaps in his mother's own story and now there was no one who could
fill them in. The war years she had talked very little about, perhaps out of
consideration for his father, and he understood that quite well. But her early
years? He knew so little.

Now it was too late, was his only thought, as he stood in the rain in the
cemetery. Was that perhaps only an expression of self-pity? His own solitude stood out as even more obvious now that his mother was gone. And
she had actually expressed a wish to "be able to end it," tormented as she
was the last years by rheumatism and migraine-like headaches.

Not only was it too late to fill in the gaps in mother's life, it was also too
late for himself, for as far as he knew no one was interested in his own story.
Even fewer would come to his funeral, he was sure of that—a thought that
made him stop on the gravel path. A few broken lines from a hymn his mother used to sing when he was a child came to him. He wanted to cry but
pulled himself together.

From where he was standing in the cemetery he could see how the caretakers were waiting in the background, they had observed him, quietly curious. One was sitting in a garden tractor, the other was standing alongside
with a shovel in his hand, perhaps they had things to take care of, he
thought, but did not want to get started until he was gone.

He started to leave, as controlled as he could, nodded to the caretakers,
stepped out through the gate and caught sight of his car. At the same moment the tractor started up. He suppressed the impulse to return to the
cemetery, go up to the caretakers, shake their hands, say something appre-
ciative and then some small talk about the weather or about the signs of
spring that were also to be seen in a cemetery.

Instead he jumped into the car and drove to his mother's small apartment on Norrtäljegatan to start clearing up and cleaning out. There, in a
drawer under the kitchen counter, strangely enough, he found the diaries,

eleven small notebooks with black, soft covers of a kind he had not seen in many years. The slightly wavy lines were filled with his mother's barely legible scribbling. He realized that what he thought had been his mother's handwriting during old age had already been established in her youth.

Considering where he found them, in direct proximity to the garbage can, he got the idea that she had intended to discard them, but death in the form of a massive heart attack had intervened.

It's strange, he thought then with rising irritation, collapsed on a kitchen chair, how everyone hides their lives. Not just strange, but also dreadful, as if no intimacy was possible.

"It was just the two of us," he sobbed.

He had become agitated, not because she kept a diary, but because she did not have the sense to get rid of them in time, her typical indecisiveness, many times stemming from a kind of fatalistic passivity that always annoyed him. If she had not wanted to share while she was still alive, shown him that confidence, then why deliver a few limp notebooks reeking of garbage in a kind of scornful afterbirth?

Since then, after the initial irritation in his mother's apartment, he had been reconciled with her. He had read the diaries, depressed and confounded, but also filled with a mournful gratitude when little by little he realized her greatness.

And now he could stand by an open grave, which would soon be filled with rhododendron and other lime-intolerant plants, without introverted anger or tears, instead filled with resolve to let her life shine, just light up the dark corners where the "educated and cultivated" tried to hide their dirty laundry.

Her words, obviously written down in a mixture of resolve and terror, would grant her an hour of remembrance, he would see to that. For he had understood that much later, the thin figures at her mother's funeral were of the same make as his mother. Then they had looked like pathetic and pitiable individuals who by chance had been blown into the cemetery. Now they stood out for him as the only allies he had.

He smiled to himself, spat toward the birches, leaned over, picked up a stone, big as a fist, moved into the shadow of a bush where four lots met, weighed the stone in his hand before with a powerful discus throw he sent it away in a wide arc toward and over Ohler's house. He followed its track, a granite comet toward the dark sky, just as elated as when as a child one early May Day morning he pushed an abandoned baby buggy, filled to the brim with empty bottles he had picked up after the students' Walpurgis festivities the night before, bottles that he intended to redeem at Uno Lantz's junkyard in Strandbodkilen. The buggy rolled a little hesitantly to start with down the hill, before it took heart, picked up speed and became a projectile. In line with the statue depicting a student singer the buggy swerved, listed severely, and spewed out liquor bottles in a magnificent slow-motion movement.

The effect this time was not as noisy, but when the stone fell down on the roof on the front side of the house it produced a crashing sound anyway and then rolled clattering down the roof tiles. Then silence took over the block again.

He disappeared from publisher Lundquist's garden after, in his opinion, a job well done.

✦

Ten

The attack on the Ohler house was followed the next morning by another. If a thrown stone, in human history perhaps the most original form of attack, hits its mark, it can fell a giant.

An article in a German newspaper can hardly produce anything so drastic, but well formulated and buttressed with factual arguments in a clever sequence it can shake things up properly. The fact was that it struck like a bomb, and that it exploded besides during the All-German Medical Association's annual meeting in Düsseldorf did not lessen the effect.

The association, which was formed as early as 1768, was considered one of the most influential within its field in Western Europe. Its membership directory included such significant names as Waller, Haagendorf, and Schütze.

Over three hundred medical doctors were gathered and Horst Bubb could tell his friend Gregor Johansson that Wolfgang Schimmel's devastating criticism, published in *Frankfurter Allgemeine*, had great impact. The news the day before had dominated the informal discussions during the convention and Horst thought that the majority supported the article's main thesis: The Royal Swedish Academy of Sciences was compromised, not to say corrupt. Now, through the selection of the prize winner, it had used up the last remnants of its credibility.

The associate professor noted without difficulty with what excited delight his German colleague accounted for the atmosphere at the hotel's conference facility. Bubb saw no complications in an "overwhelming majority" so quickly and resolutely managing to assess that the Nobel Prize would end up in the wrong hands and wallet.

"It is, however, slightly annoying that we are meeting in Düsseldorf in particular," was his only more worried comment, but he did not explain why. It was after all his home town, he ought to be proud of being the host, but Associate Professor Johansson sensed that the city presumably was not associated with the scientific brilliance and weight that the sometimes rather vain and arrogant Professor Bubb perhaps considered necessary for such a distinguished group of scientists.

For fifteen minutes they discussed the effect the article might conceivably have, or rather it was Bubb who babbled on, convinced that the Academy of Sciences would now be forced to realize its blunder, review its decision, and perhaps let Ohler share the prize with Ferguson. The associate professor considered such a retreat completely inconceivable but expressed it a bit more guardedly. Out of sheer friendliness he did not want to undercut the German's enthusiasm, and for that reason not prolong the discussion either. He had not even had time to have his morning coffee before the call came from Germany.

Bubb was also seeking support from Sweden and inquired whether the associate professor had possibly taken some initiative, which of course he had not. He had been fully occupied with leaf raking, he thought about adding jokingly, but refrained.

He felt yesterday's listlessness and now, having a bad conscience, he felt all the more anxious to end the conversation and digest the information. He felt he was being disloyal, most of all considering the activity that the colleagues in Germany were developing, that they were actually also fight-ing for his cause, albeit indirectly. It was a disruptive feeling, he did not want to feel like a traitor, he simply wanted peace and quiet, but was un-able to say anything about his irresolution to Horst Bubb.

Instead he inquired about his wife's health.

"Unchanged," Bubb said curtly.

"I think the doorbell rang," the associate professor said mendaciously. "It may be the media wanting a comment. Perhaps they've been contacted by—"

"Excellent," Bubb exclaimed. "Let him have it! Don't hesitate to stress your own contribution. Do that, Gregor, speak out."

"Thanks, I'll do that," said the associate professor.

After hanging up the phone he remained standing awhile by the kitchen table, unable to sort his thoughts. The only feeling he could register for cer-tain was discomfort. There was something in Horst Bubb's voice that he could not come to terms with, a kind of shrill fervor, not magnificent, righ-teous revenge, but instead a petty revanschism, an attitude he was mor-tally tired of.

He understood that the cure this time too was coffee and then work in the garden. Yesterday's rain had accelerated the falling of the leaves, and then there was the compost to tend to. And he should prepare the winter covering of the Gloire de Dijon, one of the most beautiful roses he knew of.

A sudden movement caused him to look out the window. A police car came slowly cruising up the street. It was a remarkable sight, one the as-sociate professor could not recall ever having seen in the vicinity of the house. It slowed down in front of Bunde's gate. Had he really called the po-lice? thought the associate professor. The man whom the neighbor had seen "sneaking around" was a gardener and nothing else, that was quite clear. The associate professor had been able to study him yesterday—the gardener was industrious, as it was an effort to dig in the Uppland clay. Gregor knew that from his own experience.

But the car cruised farther and finally stopped in front of Ohler's house.

Two uniformed policemen got out. He positioned himself as close to the window as possible to see what was happening. The policemen walked slowly up the path toward the house. They gave an impression of being hesitant, as if they were not sure they had come to the right place. Or else they were simply impressed by the grand entryway—the flight of steps and floor in Jämtland dark shale, four cream-white pillars, without exaggerated details, which held up a balcony with a pointed wrought-iron fence, and a wide, dark brown door in some type of foreign wood with a brass knocker.

The associate professor had to resist the desire to open the front door and peek out. Then he realized that he had a better view from the tower and hurried as best he could up the stairs.

Once there he could see the professor himself, standing on the lawn in front of the house. He was pointing toward the house and then down in the grass. The associate professor, who knew him well, saw immediately that he was worked up. His white hair was sticking up in all directions, his one hand once again was pointing toward the house while the other waved at the street with irritation.

One of the policemen leaned over and studied something in the grass that was impossible for the associate professor to make out.

The policeman returned to the car and came right back with what the associate professor perceived as a bag. The object of their interest was picked up and disappeared down into it.

The professor continued his expressive gestures and his energetic speech. One policeman took notes on a pad. The other, bag in hand, took the opportunity to look around. He disappeared around the side of the house and when he had made his rounds and come out at the opposite end his colleague put away his pad and then saluted.

The associate professor was astonished. Salute! The policemen lingered on the sidewalk a minute or two before they left the street. The visit had lasted about fifteen minutes.

But what was it about? The associate professor thought and speculated while he made his way down the stairs to the kitchen, to finally make himself a cup of coffee. What sort of thing was that on the grass? Had there perhaps been a break-in?

He realized that the only way to find out what it was all about was to ask Ohler, and that was unthinkable. Hope rested in Bunde, but asking him, and thereby openly showing his curiosity, was an almost equally unpleasant alternative.

Then it struck him that the housekeeper, Agnes, naturally knew what this was about. With a little luck perhaps he could nab her as she went past on the sidewalk.

He set out a cheese sandwich that he had made the night before and put in the refrigerator. He did not like doing too much in the morning. Perhaps it was an inheritance from his childhood, the thing with the sandwich.

Mostly his father had left for work by the time Gregor woke up. He went off on his bicycle already at five o'clock. If there was snow on the ground he skied through the forest.

His mother had gotten up earlier, heated coffee and made breakfast, and then also made a sandwich for Gregor. The mornings when he woke up early were the best, his parents quietly talking in the kitchen, careful not to waken him.

When he sat up on the kitchen bench his mother handed him the sandwich and a cup of milk, and they sat gathered around the kitchen table awhile. During the dark time of the year his father might turn up the wick on the kerosene lamp a little. If it was summer the birds chirped so invitingly, as they never would later in life.

The associate professor worshipped his father, but on one point he had never relied on his father's judgment, and that concerned politics. After growing up in a cottage in the shadow of an aristocratic estate, it seemed inconceivable to him, almost a parody, that there could be a society where everyone had equal value.

Take the old crone Hult, half crippled and completely crazy, or Hanna

Björk in Sandbacken, who used to watch him when his parents went off by themselves somewhere, or the always filthy woodworker Kumlin, or for that matter Uncle Kalle in Selknä and the other workers on the Roslag line. Could they step forward as equal to the count, or to the manager, or even the inspector?

It spoke for itself, thought the teenage Gregor Johansson, that it was an irrational thought, more a fairy tale, like one of the tall tales his father liked to tell.

It never came to a conflict between father and son. Gregor listened to his expounding but never made any objections.

Every month, always on a Sunday, collectors came from the various farms in the parish with the subscription, the membership fee, for the union. His father was treasurer in the division in Rasbo.

The board of the division also gathered regularly in the cottage, all of them young or middle-aged men, often serious, but just as often a little exhilarated. A certain optimism prevailed after the difficulties and setbacks of the pioneer years. A labor government was in power, there was talk that the old farm worker system would soon go to the grave, there was talk about statutory vacation and much else. Books started showing up, other than hymnals and collections of sermons, in rural workers' homes. Victories great and small that were commented on in the little cottage. It was harvest time.

As a young boy Gregor had in an unconscious way shared their joy and faith in the future, as a kind of extension of the warmth and goodness he felt in his childhood home. But equality and equal worth, Gregor Johansson had never believed in that, neither then nor later. He would have liked to, but distrust was set so deep in him that he never let himself be engaged to participate in a political discussion or even vote in an election.

On one point, however, he had a definite opinion: He was a republican and despised everything that had to do with the royal family. The newspapers' writings about the princesses, the queen's plastic surgeries, and the blunders that every now and then popped out of the king's mouth, or whatever it was that concerned the court, tired him out.

Once he had even written a letter to the editor with a republican angle.

It was not published, however. Since then he did not subscribe to the local newspaper.

On the other hand he listened to the radio, always P1, and so too this morning. It was a news broadcast and in the first segment the associate professor already got wind for his antiroyalist sails. The monarch let it be known, in one of his attacks of inarticulate outspokenness, that wolves were copulating and thereby there were more of them in the Swedish forests. The king thought this was a problem, that is, he really wanted to shoot some. Or, well, what did he really want to say?

That he was some kind of honorary member of the World Wide Fund for Nature, whose mission was to protect endangered species, did not seem to worry him.

Gregor Johansson sneered to himself at the breakfast table. Sometimes it was easy to be a republican. But the sneer froze on his lips when, through some kind of unconscious and highly undesired association, he happened to connect the king with Ohler. From whose hand would the professor receive the Nobel Prize, if not Carl XVI Gustaf's?

The associate professor moaned. He was reminded of Bubb's exhortations that he should act and he felt tempted for a moment to immediately get to work, but then sank back in a kind of lethargic indifference, the defensive wall he had so laboriously constructed for his own peace of mind. He would not fight for a cause lost in advance. He was an old man, a wise old man, he convinced himself.

The coffee cup clattered against the saucer as he got up to clear the table and right then the doorbell rang. "Bunde" was his first thought, and strangely enough he became a little energized. Maybe it was the prospect of hearing a little gossip about the visit by the police that made him leave the kitchen with light steps to answer the door.

To his great surprise it was the gardener who was standing on the front stoop. He was smiling broadly, and his cheeks were rosy, which contributed to his active look. He began with an apology for disturbing.

"Absolutely no problem," the associate professor assured him, becoming immediately favorably disposed toward the stranger.

"I couldn't help noticing the beech tree," said the man, making a vague gesture with one hand, "and now, you see, I'm laying an acid soil flower bed and—"

"So you need beech leaves," the associate professor continued.

The man laughed and nodded.

"Beech leaves are first-rate goods, you know," he said.

The associate professor smiled.

"One moment then, I'll put on my . . . if you don't . . . then we can . . ."

The associate professor suddenly became eager at the prospect of taking a turn in his garden with the enthusiastic and obviously experienced landscaper. The man seemed to read his mind and assured him that it would be interesting to look a little closer at the garden.

It took more than an hour to inspect the over fifteen hundred square meter lot. Every now and then they stopped, made comments, and exchanged experiences.

"Oh, a witch alder!" the visitor exclaimed, when they came to the back side of the house. "I saw it from a distance but didn't realize what it was. What a magnificent specimen, what divine autumn color!"

The associate professor felt almost intoxicated. He caressed the deeply bloodred leaves with a loving motion, incapable of adding anything. He was filled with a deep gratitude that the man had pulled him from the kitchen table and his gloomy thoughts about the Nobel Prize and the royal family. He felt as if they were two good friends who had known each other for decades.

The visitor was very tactful besides. He generously overlooked a few less successful arrangements. To start with, the associate professor was ashamed of the obvious deficiencies, grateful that his yellow perennial bed was not in bloom and showing its peculiar mixture of pale and bright, but as he realized that the man's opinions focused on the successful parts of the garden his discomfort subsided.

It was hard for the associate professor to handle this natural friendliness and rare feeling of affinity. How could he repay it? Could he invite him in for a cup of coffee? Or perhaps even better, dig up a plant as a present to the man?

"Perhaps you would be interested in a witch alder," the associate professor suggested. "I mean, for the bed you're working on. It thrives in a slightly acid soil."

"Maybe so. Definitely a few white azaleas. I have a weakness for white."

"Yes, you need something that brightens things up."

So it continued a good while, a garden fanatic's ping-pong, while they slowly wandered back to the entry side, where they remained standing.

"You didn't by chance see the police earlier?" the associate professor broke the silence.

"Yes, and I meant to ask what they were doing here."

"They were at Ohler's," said the associate professor. "They picked up something from the ground and left."

"What was it?"

"An object," the associate professor answered crossly, who despised imprecise information.

"A stone," said the man, and his whole face was smiling.

"Stone?"

"Perhaps from an excavation," said the man in a gentle tone. "So it's okay if I fill a few trash bags with leaves?"

"Yes, sure . . . of course," said the associate professor, surprised by the sudden shift in subject.

The man extended his hand.

"Very nice," he said in a hearty voice.

The associate professor took his hand, but the thought that he wanted to offer the visitor something meant that he could not get out even the most trivial phrase. It was only when the man was standing by the gate that he found his tongue.

"Excuse me, but what's your name?"

"Karsten Haller."

"Gregor Johansson," said the associate professor, smiling too.

When Haller left the associate professor decided to dig up part of the witch alder later in the day. It had spread well and it would not entail any exertion at all to separate a powerful side shoot.

Then he happened to think about the strangely certain statement that it was a stone that the policeman found, and that perhaps it came from an excavation, and how Karsten then quickly started talking about leaves.

He leaned over the gate and looked but could not discover anything in particular, other than a car that drove up and parked outside Ohler's.

The associate professor decided not to be curious, mostly out of pure instinct for self-preservation; he did not want to think about the professor anymore. Today he would be happy about his new acquaintance. He sensed that they would soon see each other again.

✦

Eleven

"A swine, a damned Prussian swine!" the professor shouted.

Agnes backed away a step from the table.

"He visited me at the lab, do you remember that? Then he was a young, promising talent. Now he's sticking the knife in me. I even invited him to lunch here at the house! Do you remember that? Now that infantile swine is sitting there sneering in his bunker. German bastards should never be trusted!"

How could I remember every lunch? Agnes thought quietly. It wasn't her fault that some jealous German wrote something in the newspaper.

All morning he had been bossing her around, yelled at her, and to top it off now he refused to concern himself with the lunch she had carried in.

"The food will get—" Agnes tried to interject, but the professor was not to be stopped.

"What!" he shouted. "How . . . Scrambled eggs, what kind of food is that? You know I can't stand eggs."

"Professor, you have eaten eggs without difficulty your whole life."

"Nonsense! Take that goo away!"

Agnes chose to leave the dining room. A hellish day, which started with a visit by the police—cretins and bunglers, he had called the two constables—and then that devastating phone call, God knows from whom, about that German Svimmel, or whatever his name was.

She stared at the golden-yellow scrambled eggs and the sausage from Tuscany. A salad of arugula, tomato, and cucumber in a bowl, with a few splashes of olive oil. A bottle of mineral water. Linen napkin. Knife and fork.

She sat down at the kitchen table and ate her own food. He can sit there and shout at himself in the dining room, she thought.

Soon he would get dizzy and need help getting up and making his way to the library. As a substitute for lunch she would fix tea, toast a few slices of bread, one with salami and one with soft cheese, which he would put away muttering, and then take a nap on the couch, even if he stubbornly insisted that he didn't sleep, only "closed his eyes to think better."

Although his fury unjustly affected her she felt a certain satisfaction. Or downright schadenfreude.

The last few days he had been wakened out of the increasingly gentle rut that had come to mark both him and the house in recent years. The gradual winding down of the pace had occured, without her actually reflecting on it that much. The time of big gestures was over. Then came the news about the prize and everything changed. The professor was altered beyond recognition or, rather, he resumed his old form, but without the potency and energy of middle age. He became a whining, sometimes shaky old bag of bones that stamped around the house. It seemed as if he was searching for something, rummaging about, moving things that had stood unmoved for decades, except during her own intermittent dusting. He picked up and inspected objects as if he had never seen them before. In the study he took out papers whose print had faded long ago. He had even gone down into the cellar on his own, God knows why.

Every now and then he shouted for her and wanted her to help him, most recently with some boxes that had been shoved in under a table in a room on the top floor, a room that no one had set foot in for years.

"Pull them out," he ordered.

He was sitting on a piano bench, breathing heavily through his nose. His skinny, veined hands rested on the edge of the table.

"Why is that?" she ventured to ask.

"There are papers," he said curtly. "Don't babble so much, just pull out the boxes."

When an hour or so later she went up to check that everything was fine he was sitting leaned over quantities of letters spread out all over the table. He had pulled up a floor lamp whose sharp glow lit up the scene: an old man who when she peeked into the room twisted his body and set his arms on the table, as if to conceal what he was occupied with.

He wanted afternoon tea, but after to be left in peace. "Not a lot of running around," he said. A few envelopes had fallen on the floor and when she bent down to pick them up he had shoved her and shouted, "Leave it be."

"Leave it be," she thought at the kitchen table, observing the congealed scrambled eggs. *If I were to "leave it be" now* . . . That was something Greta had returned to upon Agnes's latest visit to Gräsön—what would happen to the professor then? Who would take care of him? Hiring a successor was impossible, times were different now, no one would accept the conditions that prevailed in the house. Birgitta could step in but not full-time. If nothing else the Finnish woman would never accept that.

And what would happen to her? Could she return to that island and the house she left in the fall of 1953? How would she and Greta manage? Neither of them were young, even if Greta seemed spryer than she'd been in a very long time.

It was as if the shove both literally and figuratively put her off balance.

The more she thought about it, the more inconceivable and offensive the action appeared. In reality he had not touched her in thirty-five years, other than involuntarily when he needed help getting dressed or to stand up when the dizziness struck him, and on those occasions he dared to lay hands on her.

That time, on June 20, 1973, the touch had been draped in alcohol-soaked talk and tears, but now it was with a kind of bitter irritation that bordered on loathing. She had done nothing to deserve this reception, this unprovoked rancor, this humiliating shove.

She stared at the increasingly unappetizing film over the scrambled eggs. So unnecessary, it struck her, for a hen's work to now go to waste. It was a thought that made her smile. She pictured the hens of her childhood, how while strutting and clucking they eagerly followed her wherever she went in the hope that she would toss them a few crumbs.

The terrain of her childhood stood out increasingly often and ever clearer to her. She sensed that it was age. She had reached the crown and could only look back, and down, at the laborious uphill ascent that had been her life. In retrospect the early years, before the move to Uppsala, stood out as the happiest. Despite the scarcity and privation. Despite the isolation, the congregation was small and tightly knit and the island lacked a ferry connection to the mainland and the summer visitors were few—despite all that there was joy, a kind of faith in the future. Perhaps it was the landscape that created this will to live and confidence? Or was it simply because she was young?

Her father had said something to the effect that to behold God a person had to be able to see far. You could on the island, it was enough to go up on the cliff at Sigvard and Tall-Anna's. There the whole sea was open. Glistening in the sunshine, or dark and threatening, with cloud banks towering up over the Åland Sea, or more often toward the inland. Because that's how it was: the storm might lay its shadow over the island, but if you turned eastward the sea was bathed in sun, only weakly rippling from the breeze. Perhaps God was out there among the islets and skerries? In that case she had turned her back on Him.

In Kåbo there was no such perspective. Here villas were seen in every direction, all of which expressed the same thing: money and power. Power to command, power to shove. No God was there to see. The fact was that Agnes had gradually lost much of her faith. It was as if there was no room for Him with Ohler. Or rather, He became superfluous, all the glory she dreamed about as a child: heat—no more cold floors and shocking chill in the outhouse; richly set tables—no more scarcity and the melancholy of tastelessness; beautiful, soft clothes—no more of her sisters' discarded rags and the roughness of the flour-sack towel; beauty—no more clumsily cobbled-together furniture and the flaking vase on the sideboard.

Everything was here. Everything was perfect. God was not needed.

During the first months she had wandered around the house and run her hand over the crystal, the foreign types of wood, the linen cloths, the decorated and gilded frames, marveled at all that was fragile, light, excellent, well worked.

Now she knew better. She would give a lot for a time with the roughness against her skin or for the sensation of drinking coffee from a chipped cup with a mended handle. But all the old things were long since thrown away or put away in a box in the attic or in some half-demolished shed.

The cliff at Sigvard and Tall-Anna's remained, however, in unchanged condition. The last time she "went home" to the island she had made the now strenuous ascent and remained there until twilight. Afterwards she could not account, either for herself or for her sister, what made her stay so long or what was going on in her head.

To her great surprise Greta did not criticize, or even comment on her unexpected expedition. Perhaps she too tottered up on the rock sometimes?

Agnes stood up, cleared the kitchen table, tipped the professor's lunch in the garbage pail, and did the dishes.

She happened to think about the policemen. One of them had a shrewd smile, the other mostly looked shy, while the professor was carrying on almost scared. Perhaps he was taken by the seriousness of the moment, being confronted with a Nobel Prize winner.

When the professor turned away the shrewd one said something in a low voice that it was probably not the last stone, but when she asked what he meant he just smiled. Did the police know something that she and the professor were not aware of?

The familiar buzz from the bell made her jump. She could picture him leaning over the dining room table with his finger prepared to repeat the ringing at any moment, if she did not show up quickly enough.

She went up to the window. There was movement in the bushes in the neighbor's yard. She assumed it was the same man she had seen digging so industriously the day before.

The bell buzzed again. She twisted her head and observed the shaking metal box. Let it buzz, she thought, and at the same moment a trembling went through her too, as if the connection from the dining room was linked directly to her body. It was an alarm that went from her stomach and spread like a shooting pain up through her trunk and down into her legs. It reminded her of the inner agitation she experienced on the cliff at the island.

She could not identify what happened but sensed that it was the professor's shove and the thoughts it awakened that affected her so strongly that she remained motionless when the bell rang. She heard but did not react. Fifty years ago this would have entailed a sharp reprimand, perhaps dismissal, and only a week ago an improbable defiance.

Just as it buzzed a third time she heard him call. She left the kitchen, took the long way, and entered the dining room from an unexpected direction. He stood, as she suspected, leaning over the table and the bell.

"Yes?"

He twirled around as if he had been struck by a blow to the back. The veins in his face were swollen and the forceful lower lip quivered.

"Have you gone on strike perhaps, Agnes?"

Saliva was spraying out of his mouth.

"No, but I've retired," she said with forced composure.

She could not keep from staring at the archipelago of drops of saliva on the shiny tabletop.

"Retired?"

"Like you did, professor, many years ago."

The words made her worried in an undefined way, as if she was guilty of something indecent and she was forced to repeat the word "retired" silently to herself to try to understand its full import.

"What kind of talk is that!"

She did not answer, did not dare try her voice.

"Are you feeling unwell?"

"Thanks," she mumbled.

"What kind of answer is that?" he barked, but immediately changed his tone. "You're simply exhausted, Agnes. There's been a lot going on the past few days. Isn't that so?"

She was unable to say anything.

"Make a couple sandwiches, please, but no salami or liverwurst. Then you can take off the rest of the day, in any event until dinner. Forslund is coming over, but he's not much for food, you know that. Just throw something together. He likes home cooking. You'll solve that splendidly, Agnes."

Algot Forslund was the lawyer who had served the family almost as long as she had. If he was not much for food he made up for it in drink. "Home cooking" in Forslund's case meant a plate of herring, but primarily aquavit.

She looked intently at the professor, but was unable even to confirm that she had understood his words.

"There's been a lot for me too," said the professor.

She withstood the impulse to go up and wipe off the table.

"Maybe we're burnt out," the professor said with a grin.

She left the dining room, mute and with a sense of having been betrayed.

✦

Twelve

"You can never have too many leaves," said Karsten Heller.

He smiled more broadly than the associate professor could remember anyone in his company having done for years.

The gardener had packed half a dozen trash bags full of beech leaves. They resembled swollen black eggs, ready to burst at any moment.

"You're sure that—"

"Take as many as you want," the associate professor assured him. "I'm just happy to get rid of some of them."

He appreciated his new acquaintance, who became loquacious where plants were concerned, but otherwise apparently preferred to work in silence. The associate professor sensed that he worked a lot on his own.

When another four sacks were filled Haller looked up. He resembled a hunter proudly observing the day's catch.

"I was thinking about something," said the associate professor. "When we last met you said something about it being a stone that the police picked up in Ohler's yard. How could you be so sure of that?"

"Because I threw it," Haller said simply.

"What do you mean?"

"I was the one who threw the stone. The evening before. It landed on the roof and evidently rolled down on the front side."

"Why is that?" the associate professor said sheepishly.

Haller laughed.

"Yes, why?" he repeated. "It was an impulse. It pleased me enormously. I could throw another, yes, I could let fly a whole flat of cobblestones. Preferably with a catapult, you know, one of these medieval devices, so that it would rain stones over the house."

He was smiling, but the associate professor could hear a kind of conviction behind the bantering tone.

"It truly was a spectacle," said the associate professor after a moment's silence, and they both joined in a laugh.

"Would you like a cup of coffee?"

"That would be good," said Haller.

"I only have a few almond cookies," the associate professor said apologetically.

The associate professor considered a moment whether he should invite Haller up into the tower but that didn't feel quite right. When the coffee was ready and they were sitting down in the kitchen, after a while he ventured a question.

"Do you know Professor von Ohler from before?"

"No, not personally," Haller replied.

"You know that he's been awarded the Nobel Prize in Medicine?"

"That has probably not escaped anyone."

The associate professor suddenly became thoughtful. He had been distracted by the talk about a catapult, imagined a siege, a boyish image, where showers of stones shot down from the sky, and for that reason he had been lured into laughter. But now he became wary. What did he know about the gardener on the other side of the table? There was something about him that did not tally with the image he had gotten of him yesterday.

"Have a cookie," the associate professor offered.

Haller inspected the associate professor before he sank his teeth into the cookie.

"What I do is probably pretty clear, but what is your occupation?"

For a moment the associate professor considered fabricating something, denying his background, inventing something new, but realized that it was simplest to stick to the truth.

"I'm also a doctor, a virologist like Ohler. We actually worked together for almost thirty years at University Hospital."

Haller looked a little surprised but said nothing. He seemed to be waiting for a continuation. The associate professor felt as though he had to explain himself, excuse why he had been a colleague of the professor for such a long time. It was as if that created a kind of distance to the gardener.

"But we don't socialize," he added.

"And you're not getting any prize," Haller noted.

The associate professor stood up to get the coffee.

"Refill?"

"Thanks," said Haller, pushing the cup closer to the associate professor, "but then it's time to get going."

"How long will you be here?"

"Just a few more days. I'm going to dig a couple more flower beds and prune the maple on the front side, maybe cut down a birch tree."

"Sensible," said the associate professor. "I've dug up a witch alder, in case you're interested."

Haller smiled and nodded. He emptied his cup and push the chair back from the table.

"May I ask a personal question? Not because it concerns me, but you seem to harbor a certain animosity with respect to Professor von Ohler."

"That was nicely put," said Haller. "But it's true. I don't know him personally, as I said, but to me he represents the worst thing about this town."

"And that is?"

"The so-called educated classes' contempt and suppression."

"And how do you know that the professor stands for such values? I mean, if you don't know him personally."

"I know him anyway," said Haller with a sarcastic smile. "As I assume that you know your colleague very well. And then you yourself live in this educated area in a millionaire's house."

The associate professor felt how embarrassed he became, at the same time as he was provoked by the other man's slightly scornful tone.

"Excuse me," said Haller. "I didn't mean to be insolent."

"What's wrong with education?" the associate professor asked calmly, but then it was as if an immense force filled him. "Tell me that! Is education wrong? I am sitting on a farm worker's kitchen bench, the bench of my childhood. Any education I've acquired I've had to fight my way for, inch by inch."

Haller was astonished at the other man's sudden transformation. He never would have expected such fury from him.

"Inch by inch!" the associate professor repeated and underscored his anger by striking his index finger on the table. "Not an inch for free!"

"Excuse me," said Haller again, raising his hands in a conciliatory gesture, but the associate professor would not let himself be stopped.

"I'm sitting in this house, yes, it's true, worth several million kronor today, an inconceivable amount of money. My father grew up in a drafty farm laborer's shack in Rasbo, full of snotty children and wall lice. Two of his siblings died from the Spanish flu. I speak several languages, my mother knew a little Finnish, that was all. My father only went to school for three years. I became a medical doctor in a specialty that he could not even conceive of. He could not have pronounced the title of my dissertation. I have traveled all over the globe, the farthest my father got was to Skinnskatteberg to bury a brother. My parents would burst with pride if they could see me today. Tell me, master gardener, have I done wrong? Should I regret it?"

"Excuse me," Haller repeated for the third time. "Of course you didn't do wrong. I didn't know about your background, the fact is that I—"

"You talk about contempt," the associate professor interrupted, feeling the heat in his face. "But *you* are the one who is contemptuous."

Haller looked at him with a mixture of admiration and sorrow, as if he had stepped on something valuable.

"I'm just a bitter mole," he said, "someone who digs and digs in the earth."

"But you're not blind."

"Blinded," said Haller.

"By what?"

"Perhaps I'll tell you sometime."

Haller fell silent and looked down at the floor, leaning forward with his elbows on his knees. He had pushed his chair out so far from the table that he seemed to be sitting in the middle of the kitchen. The associate professor felt exhausted. He had seldom if ever let his emotions run away like this.

"If there's an occasion," Haller continued.

It was this addition, expelled like a sigh, that made the associate professor regret his vehemence. He had also seen the solitary man's misgivings in his sorrowful eyes and tormented expression, and he sensed that Karsten Haller was simply a lonely person, like himself unused to contact with others. He felt that he was guilty of a blunder that he now wished he could undo.

"I'm sure there will be an occasion," said the associate professor, trying to adopt a more conciliatory tone. "You have a *Fothergilla* waiting," said the associate professor. "A cultivated witch alder."

Haller looked up and nodded mutely.

"But you are right on one point," said the associate professor.

"And that is?"

"Perhaps I can tell you some time," said the associate professor, and was rewarded with a cautious smile and a nod.

They separated in mutual silence, both of them embarrassed at how the coffee break had developed. Haller loaded the sacks of leaves on his trailer, after having declined help with a deprecating gesture, and took off. A few minutes later the associate professor could see him carrying the sacks onto the neighbor's yard and emptying them out. Against the wall of the house several yellow sacks were also visible that he suspected contained peat moss.

He realized that it would be a long workday for the gardener. There, at work, perhaps he was happy in his solitude, mixing a cultivation substrate— wrestling with a bale of peat and kicking leaves and spruce needles around—and demanded no social competence, no education either in the classical sense.

The associate professor went up to the tower and watered, increasingly sparingly the further into autumn it was. What was it that made him so upset? He could not remember when that last happened. At work he had seldom if ever taken sides; there he let pure idiocy and bullying pass by. He usually backed off to avoid hearing more, with a look that expressed the point of view of the morally superior, a silent demonstration that did not seem to impress anyone.

Was it out of pure cowardice? Or perhaps simply an expression of the sense of inferiority that he recognized as the driving force in Haller's primitive condescension? Because of course he had despised, downright loathed, many of his fellow students for their ill-mannered behavior and monumental ignorance of life outside the dormitories and student societies. There was a certainty in their demeanor, a lack of humility, as if they could never be wrong. If they were caught in a lie or momentarily bothered by something, they immediately dismissed the discomfort, as if to say, "Of course, maybe that wasn't so successful, but what of it?" They were protected, and knew it.

He never enlightened them about the life and conditions in a farm laborer's home, but instead assumed a passive attitude. Only a few of his fellow students came from working-class homes, and probably none from the rural proletariat. He was basically alone in his experiences, alone in his language. He was proud of his background but never took sides, never got involved in controversy, did not even respond to the worst forms of class-conditioned contempt and ignorance, as he had now done with Haller.

The associate professor had become righteously angry at Haller's impolite manner but at the same time in some strange way embarrassed on the other man's behalf and therefore he wanted to tell him off, and perhaps by that means himself. Because he understood very well that Haller's open contempt for the professor, and above all his apparently pleasurable hurling of the stone, had wakened his own bad conscience, reminded him of Bubb's insistent encouragement to take part in the campaign against the Nobel Prize committee's selection, as well as his own extremely real feeling of having been discriminated against, both before and now.

The professor's words that there was no absolute justice in the world, above all not in academia, had been grinding in his head and now the meaning of the words was clearer to him than ever.

At Lundquist's the gardener worked away, the preparation work was as good as finished, it was soon ready for planting. Haller knew his business, that was clear. He had laid out two planks as walkways to avoid trampling down and compressing the soft, inviting beds.

The associate professor felt a stab of jealousy. Haller could lose himself in meaningful work, while what he busied himself with in his tower resembled therapy. But I've done my share, he thought further, I contributed to a scientific breakthrough that reduced suffering and saved human lives. I don't need to apologize for my actions or because now I cultivate exotic plants in a tower. I paid back with interest what it cost society to educate me and I think I have the right to enjoy . . .

"But am I enjoying myself?" he asked right out loud and turned toward Lundquist's lot, as if the answer could be found there.

Haller looked up at the same moment. The associate professor understood that he was well outlined against the dull foliage of the olive tree. He waved and Haller waved back.

Perhaps Haller can become a friend? The thought was mind-boggling, as if the mere idea of the existence of a friend was beyond reasonable. It struck him that he had not even used the word "friend" in many years.

When would that have been? Well, perhaps when he wrote the obligatory Christmas letter to Düsseldorf, which he always began with *"Lieber Freund."*

The associate professor laughed joylessly at these ridiculous thoughts. Should Horst Bubb be the one he called and told about his worries, the one he asked for advice and sought support from? Bubb, who was filled by a single thought: disqualifying Bertram von Ohler, a person he had never met or had any difficulty with. Whatever he would say to his "dear friend," the German would reply with a salvo about the Academy of Sciences and Wolfgang Schimmel's heroic struggle for the melancholy Alan Ferguson in Vermont.

But he would not quarrel, he would not choose sides, despite the sense that an injustice had been committed. Did that make him a lesser person, a coward? Was it struggle that could lift the discomfort from his shoulders?

After a final glance toward Haller the associate professor left the tower.

✦

Thirteen

Algot Forslund held out his hat. Agnes thought it smelled bad, a mixture of smoke and something rotten, and quickly consigned it to the shelf. He wriggled out of his coat and hung it up all by himself.

She and the attorney were the same age but he looked considerably older. The change had come quickly, his posture had always been poor but his face had collapsed during the past year. The previously so fleshy and rosy cheeks now hung loose and gray in color.

Agnes sensed that it was not only the daily alcohol consumption that was the reason. He's sick, she was sure, but she felt indifferent in the presence of the bent man who passively stood and waited for her to open the door to the library. Forslund had never interested her, either young or old, sober or tipsy, so why should she start caring now?

These days Bertram von Ohler was his only client and he would visit the house four or five times a year. There were always some papers that had to be arranged. Agnes suspected it was the will that was up for discussion again. Now and then it would be adjusted, some detail added or removed. During the day the professor had been rooting in the "archive," as he called the old safe. Agnes knew, the only one besides the professor himself, where the key to the safe was stored: in an old tin can in the cellar.

She had to retrieve it, he usually did not dare make his way down the steps himself. The talk about her being able to rest awhile after lunch had evidently been immediately forgotten. He filled the afternoon with constant new instructions and orders and now she felt very tired. As always when she was forced to walk a lot the pains in her left hip also increased. She limped, which even the dim-sighted Forslund observed.

"What's the matter? Is he after you?" he said with a grin.

"Go right in," said Agnes, holding open the door.

The attorney turned into the library.

"Thanks, Agnes," said the professor. "We'll have a bite to eat in an hour. Or maybe half an hour," he corrected himself after taking a look at Forslund.

Was she herself in the will? She thought so. The professor had mentioned something several years ago. But since then it had been rewritten several times. Forslund would no doubt gladly remove her as a beneficiary. He had previously shown a certain interest in her, hinted that there were many rooms in the house where she could have a private legal consultation. During a certain stage of intoxication he always tried to grope her and when that didn't work he would change to verbal indecencies. She had always refused him, sometimes brusquely. But that was many years ago now. They had both withered a bit.

It struck her, while she made the final preparations before dinner, how little she cared about her assets. The professor changed his will every so often, while she herself barely knew what she had in the bank. She had talked about retiring but had not reflected on the financial side of it all.

She had always lived and eaten for free at Ohler's, her expenses were limited to clothes and little things. She also regularly sent a sum to Lutheran World Relief.

Did she have enough money to pay rent somewhere else? She didn't know. And what did an apartment cost? It had not felt necessary to investigate, the cottage on Gräsö had always been there as an alternative. But would Greta accept her moving in? And would she herself want to come back?

The odor of herring in mustard sauce always made her a little nauseated, yet she made a point of making it herself. Say what you will about Forslund, but herring he understood. Pickled herring with onions, regular pickled herring, the classic *glasmästarsill*, however long the parade was he could never get enough. He also praised her preserves at great length, so if it was for the herring alone they would make an excellent couple, she thought and smiled.

In the morning she had put a bottle of aquavit in the fridge. Now she put it in the freezer along with the schnapps glasses, so that they would be properly frosted. She set a hand towel over the pan of potatoes, arranged the plates with cucumbers and capers and supervised the sweet-pickled herring filet which in a creamy egg mixture was getting the right color in the oven.

Forslund always wanted to eat in the kitchen, it's suitable for herring, as he put it, and the professor accommodated him this time too. They arrived just as she was taking the filet out of the oven.

"Magnificent!" exclaimed Forslund, "Agnes is a jewel."

The sight of all the good things on the table, complemented by a couple bottles of Hof cold from the refrigerator, and the encounter with the smells in the kitchen made him mildly exhilarated.

The professor lingered by the door and observed her with a peculiar expression, as if he could not immediately recall who the woman in the kitchen was. Agnes registered his curious appearance out of the corner of her eye while she poured the first aquavit. The professor was too shaky nowadays. The attorney would take care of the refills himself.

"I'll be in the TV room, if you need anything," she said.

"Agnes should actually be here to celebrate," Forslund exclaimed. "That would probably—"

"Thanks!" the professor interrupted him, who seemed released from his blockage. "As usual it looks very appetizing. Thank you, Agnes."

"But I don't think anyone ever died from one glass of aquavit," Forslund continued, spearing a pickle with his fork.

"Agnes doesn't touch alcohol," said the professor, stepping aside so she could leave the kitchen.

She sank down on the couch and turned on the TV. She had her own TV in the little drawing room one flight up, and would have preferred to withdraw there, but it was understood that she should stay in the vicinity to be able to respond quickly.

The news had just started and it was a minor shock when the first thing she saw was a picture of the professor, a photograph that must have been twenty-five years old. At first she refused to really take in the picture, as if it did not depict the real Bertram von Ohler.

The news anchor began by saying something about the "massive criticism" that had struck the Academy of Sciences for its choice of prize winner. Agnes lowered the sound on the TV.

Then a journalist appeared standing in a large hall, in the background rows of chairs and a podium could be seen. The reporter squinted with one eye, and that distracted her for a moment, but his voice was sharp and clear as he accounted for the atmosphere among a group of scientists who were gathered for some meeting in Germany. He talked extremely quickly and so did the person he was interviewing, HORST BUBB read the text that appeared on screen, but Agnes understood well enough that Bertram von Ohler was taking a real beating.

At the end of the feature the news anchor said that the Academy of Sciences declined to comment on the criticism.

Then was a report from the United States on the crisis in the car industry.

Agnes remained sitting awhile without taking in anything of what was said, before she got up and went over to the liquor cabinet, took out a bottle and poured a centimeter of liqueur in a crystal glass that she had polished that morning.

Just as she brought the glass to her mouth and sensed the almost corrosive odor of alcohol rise up in her nose the phone rang.

She set down the glass. The portable phone was on the table and she answered after the second ring.

"Professor Ohler," said a voice more as a statement than a question.

"He's occupied at the moment," Agnes replied, "I'll have to ask you to call back tomorrow."

"My name is Liselott Karnehagen and I am calling from *Aftonbladet*." Agnes remained silent.

"There is no possibility—" Agnes persevered.

"We would really like a comment."

"From me?"

"And who are you? Some kind of secretary, or what?"

"No, really now!"

"Professor von Ohler seems to be a fraud—"

"That may be," said Agnes calmly, "but right now he's eating herring."

"Herring?"

"As I said, call back tomorrow," said Agnes, and ended the call by simply setting the phone down on the table.

It rang immediately again. Agnes quickly went out in the hall and pulled out the phone jack. She realized they had a rough time ahead of them.

By way of the connecting corridor that ran through half of the house she went up to the kitchen door. Forslund was doing all the talking but Agnes could not make out what he was saying. She considered knocking and asking whether everything was satisfactory but put that out of her head when she remembered the poured liqueur, went back to the TV room, and sank down on the couch.

She did not like that prize. Why should they start poking at the professor and bringing him to life? He was an old man and he'd had so much in his day that he didn't need anymore. She had read about the prize sum in the newspaper, inconceivable millions. That was probably why the lawyer had been summoned. Once again her own situation came to her. The professor had completely rejected her talk about retirement and she understood that very well. She was needed.

Fifty-five years, she thought, leaned her head back, and fell asleep at once with the glass in her hand.

✦

Fourteen

If he let go of the tabletop he would fall. He ought to open his eyes, that would alleviate it, but it was as if such a simple thing, raising two eyelids, was associated with a kind of uncertainty, perhaps fear. There was a pressure over his body, his legs felt like poles, his head was heavy as lead, and fear was coiling like snakes around his body.

I'll have to stand here until the end of time, he thought. Once he had seen a petrified human. The man's joints were stiff, the face immobile as a wooden mask, and the body cold and shiny like the belly of an oribi, the fish that played in the river below his house every spring. The man's wife said that at night he talked in words that no one understood. A strange language had crept into him and that was what frightened the villagers most. She left the village shortly after and went to live with one of her brothers. She did not want to be infected, and that was an argument that most understood and accepted. The man died after a few months. Later he became a story that made its way through the valley, in which his nighttime talk took on a different meaning, that it was God who was speaking through him. His wife was depicted as an evil woman who had abandoned her husband in a difficult time.

So fall or become petrified? That was his choice. He chose to fall. He let go and collapsed like a high-rise that had been primed with dynamite and then exploded.

A wave of relief washed away the fear. His one shoulder took a blow when it hit the floor but it did not hurt especially. Maybe the pain would come later. But the fear was gone, that was the main thing.

He dragged himself up onto all fours. He was thoroughly intoxicated, as drunk as he had been in decades. Yet his thoughts came to him as clear as crystal. He thought about how the associate professor had scolded him, and what shame he felt. He had abused the hospitality by trying to make himself important. A dreadful failure.

He tipped over and remained sitting on the floor with his legs stretched out in front of him. *All in all, I'm a failed character,* he thought, and at the same moment he became angry at himself for his self-pity.

He tried to think about the planting he had to complete. A few white azaleas were not to be found so late in the season, so instead he would have to be content with the rhododendron, three Cunningham's White, which he got for half price. But it was a vain attempt. The thoughts of Ohler constantly returned.

He wanted to throw one more stone, and another. His joking mention of a catapult was not just loose talk. He wanted to besiege the big house, drive the professor out into the light, exposed, ridiculed.

"Get up!"

The words were intended to be forceful but were heard mostly as an exhausted sigh, and he sneered.

He had seen the professor on the TV news and that had triggered the reaction to mix a toddy, something he seldom did. Unaccustomed as he was, a few glasses of the rum he had bought during his most recent visit in Germany had been enough to get him thoroughly intoxicated.

I'll kill the bastard, was his last thought before he tipped over and remained lying there.

✦

Fifteen

"Death threats?" Ottosson exclaimed. "That's going a bit far."

"That's how he understands it all," said Allan Fredriksson, scratching the back of his head for the third time.

"Do you have lice?" asked Sammy Nilsson.

Ann Lindell grinned and scratched herself in a motion that was supposed to resemble a monkey. This happened behind Fredriksson's back but he whirled around, as if he sensed that some mischief was going on.

"Nice, very entertaining," he said sarcastically.

Lindell gave him a nudge in the side.

"Okay," she said, "a skull in the mailbox."

"Plus a stone thrown the other day," said Fredriksson, waving a piece of paper. "And then quite a few articles in the newspaper. Today the Uppsala paper had something and evidently *Aktuellt* ran a feature yesterday."

"But death threats?" said Ottosson again.

It was noticeable that he wanted to set the whole thing aside, send the case right back to the uniformed police.

"Wohlin is very definite," Fredriksson continued. "This is still a Nobel Prize winner, an aristocratic professor we're dealing with."

Agne Wohlin had the title of superintendent and was a new star at the Uppsala Police Department. No one liked him, as you instinctively disliked newcomers, superintendents, and people from Dalsland. This last item Sammy Nilsson had added, no one really understood why. He had never spoken badly about Dalslanders before. There were no doubt few at Homicide who knew anyone from Dalsland, or could even point out the province on a map.

"This is a case for the uniformed police," said Sammy. "They can post a couple of bluecoats there, then it will be calm."

"Wohlin wants us to investigate the threat pattern."

"Something for SePo," Sammy attempted.

"*Us*," Fredriksson repeated.

Not me, thought Lindell, but that was exactly what Ottosson decided.

"Ann, you can handle the poor folks in Kåbo, drive out there and talk with the old man."

"But don't go down in the cellar," said Fredriksson.

A number of years earlier Ann Lindell had investigated a series of murders in the countryside outside Uppsala and then had reason to visit a villa in Kåbo, a visit that almost cost her her life. Since then she had not set foot in the area.

"I suppose it's the same block?"

"Don't think so," said Fredriksson, "although it is the same street."

Both of them seemed strangely unaware of the effect the talk about Kåbo had on her. Perhaps they thought she had left it behind her, but sometimes she still woke up at night, drenched in sweat, in her dreams transported back to a burning inferno.

Sammy put an arm around her shoulders.

"I'll go along," he said, pulling her away from a nodding Ottosson and a wildly scratching Fredriksson.

"What the hell can it be?" was the last thing Lindell heard Fredriksson say.

"Something is rotten in Denmark," Sammy observed in the elevator going down.

Lindell did not bother to ask what he meant. The whole morning had been slightly absurd. If she was to ask about everything she thought was strange she would not get anything else done.

Lindell assumed that the professor did not want uniformed police officers running around in his home, but still! It would be enough if Superintendent Wohlin went there himself, presented all his credentials in his most charming Dalarna dialect, and calmed the old man down, then everything would work out for the best.

"Was it Dalarna?"

"Dalsland," said Sammy.

As they drove out of the garage and up onto the Råby highway she told about her nightmare, which included everything from scratching rats and rotting corpses to smoke and consuming fire. She had not even talked about this with Brant, even though he was the one who was occasionally subjected to her nocturnal anxiety.

She realized while she was talking that she was being subjected to Ottosson's solicitude; for therapeutic reasons he simply wanted her to be confronted with the sight of the imposing villas and relive the events from that time, thinking that this would get her started, get her to talk. And it had succeeded beyond all expectations. She unburdened her mind, put words to the torments even before they arrived in Kåbo.

And Sammy was the right person for her to confide in. They were getting along better than ever. Lindell had even socialized a bit during the fall with the Nilsson family.

And there were not too many others to choose from, in a squad that was in the process of falling apart. Ottosson had announced that he would retire at the end of the year, withdraw to his cabin in Jumkil. Berglund had already quit, Haver was on long-term sick leave and would most likely not come back, and a couple of days ago Beatrice Andersson had dropped a bomb: she was going to get a divorce, resign, and move to Skåne. She had met a man, a farmer from the Östra Sönnarslöv area, and was going to "start over." It sounded like she was presenting a package from some agency, with forms, start-up subsidies, and follow-up.

"How the hell do you meet someone from Skåne?" Sammy Nilsson had asked.

"Through the Farmers Cooperative newsletter," Ottosson speculated.

"What's wrong with farmers?" Fredriksson hissed.

"I was talking about Skåne," said Nilsson, who was known for his almost racist attitude toward people from that province.

And clearly Dalsland had now also fallen into disfavor.

Ann Lindell hardly knew her way around the block west of Villavägen and she sensed that the terror she had felt five years ago had erased many of the memories. Where the Hindersten villa had once stood there was now a newly constructed, functionalism-inspired house.

"That time it was an associate professor, now it's a professor," said Sammy Nilsson with a smile. "Does that mean that—"

"We have both an associate professor and a professor," Lindell interrupted. "A neighbor is an associate professor and he's the one who's the villain in the drama, our Nobel Prize winner thinks."

"What do you mean? Is he the one who's threatening the professor's life?"

Lindell shrugged.

"We'll just have to see," she said in a tone that expressed her understanding of their mission.

In front of the house was a van from the local radio station and a couple of other cars.

"Journalists," Sammy moaned, "and then you're along. This is going to be really amusing."

They stopped behind the van. The journalist they already recognized, Göte Bengtsson. He was one of the fixtures on local radio.

When Lindell got out of the car he was standing on the sidewalk, with a wry smile. Dressed in a large parka, he looked like a shaggy bear.

"Reception committee," Lindell observed.

Göte Bengtsson nodded. He had a disarming talent for looking uninterested, a little disheveled and borderline indifferent, as if he had just been wakened and sent out on an assignment that barely intrigued him. But Lindell did not let herself be fooled.

"I see, Nobel Prize," he began grandiosely.

In the corner of her eye Lindell saw one of his colleagues approach. In the background a photographer could be seen.

"Personnel shortage," said Lindell, trying to put on an embarrassed but at the same time bored expression. The journalist, however, did not seem convinced.

"He's still alive," said Bengtsson, who knew very well what kind of cases she worked with normally.

"You are too," said Sammy Nilsson, who had joined them on the sidewalk and now voluntarily took on the task of trying to disarm Bengtsson's colleagues. He went up to them.

"Is this a new initiative, a kind of preventive activity from the homicide squad?" Bengtsson asked.

Lindell was cold and wished she had a parka too.

"Stylish shack," she said. "No, we're allocated here by quota, to get an idea of how the social cases in Kåbo are doing."

It was not a particularly funny remark, but Bengtsson smiled.

"I had a chat with our prize winner," he said. "He was extremely outspoken."

"That's nice," said Lindell with a smile. "Then you don't need me."

"A little later perhaps?" said Bengtsson.

Lindell nodded and smiled again.

Bengtsson smiled back, turned his head, and saw how Sammy Nilsson was backing away from the journalists with a dismissive gesture.

"Karnehagen from *Aftonbladet*," said Bengtsson, "and a new star from *Expressen*."

"Do you have any coffee with you?"

Bengtsson nodded toward his van.

Lindell, Bengtsson, and Nilsson then had their coffee in peace and quiet, talking about this and that, and Bengtsson's impending retirement.

On the sidewalk outside was the tabloid press.

"There are no excuses for the laxity you have shown. Two uniformed policemen came here and then nothing happens."

"What should we have done, do you think?" asked Sammy Nilsson. "Cordoned off the block, called in the marines?"

They had talked for ten minutes with Bertram von Ohler and both police officers felt they had no business being there.

The professor stared at Nilsson.

"Perhaps we can speak with your . . . employee," said Lindell.

"Why is that?"

"Perhaps she has seen or heard something of interest?"

"And what would that be?"

Lindell smiled. Nobel Prize winner, she thought.

"I don't want you to worry Agnes, she is extremely sensitive."

Agnes Andersson did not look at all worried. She was sitting straight-backed on the other side of the gigantic kitchen table, her hands folded in front of her. She mostly resembled an aged confirmand who was waiting for a question from Bible history. A question that she knew in advance and would manage splendidly.

"What an amazing kitchen," said Lindell, "so well organized."

"Thank you," said Agnes.

Lindell let her eyes sweep again over the walls and cabinets.

"How long have you worked here?"

"Fifty-five years. I came here in 1953."

There was something familiar about Agnes Andersson, thought Lindell. Had they met previously?

"As a young girl," Lindell noted, inspecting the woman before her a little more carefully.

How old could she be? Over seventy, at a guess. The protruding eyes looked fixedly at Lindell.

"Before, there was more to do," said Agnes, "and then there were more of us too. Now it's just the professor and me."

"But you can't very well clean the whole house yourself?"

"Oh yes, but three times a year my sister comes and helps out. At Christmas, in May when the apple trees are blooming, and now in the fall."

Lindell tried to imagine what it would be like to vacuum, dust, and mop fourteen rooms and kitchen, but couldn't. Just polishing all the copper forms that were hanging on the walls must take at least a week.

"My sister likes apple blossoms very much," the woman added.

Lindell tried to imagine what it might be like to have a sister who liked apple blossoms, but couldn't do that either.

"You must be a strong woman," said Lindell unexpectedly.

Agnes Andersson moved her head almost imperceptibly.

"I'll take a look in the garden," said Sammy, slipping out the kitchen door without waiting for any comment from Lindell.

"I mean, to run a household of this size basically alone."

"I'm used to it," said Agnes.

Lindell smiled, and to her surprise the woman answered with a smile.

"The professor must have quite a few guests too."

"Not anymore. He wants to take it a little easier."

"What do you think about what happened? I mean the stone-throwing and then the threat in the mailbox this morning."

"What should one think?" Agnes replied after a few seconds of reflection. "If you ask me I think it's just some rowdy kids, schoolboy pranks."

"Have there been threatening phone calls too?"

"Not that I know," said Agnes, and for the first time during the conversation she looked a trifle uncertain.

"You haven't noticed anything unusual recently?"

Agnes shook her head. Just then it occurred to her what made Agnes Andersson so familiar. It was the dialect she didn't really manage to conceal. Fifty-five years in Uppsala had rubbed off most of it but like a shadow from the past the Gräsö dialect was there.

"You weren't born in Uppsala, were you?"

"Gräsö," said Agnes.

Lindell wanted to ask if she knew Viola, but refrained. Obviously she knew Viola, probably everyone did on Gräsö, just like everyone knew, or knew of, Munkargrundarn and other features on the island.

Viola, whom she had gotten to know through Edvard Risberg, the man she met during a murder investigation ten years ago. He had gotten a divorce, moved to Gräsö, rented the top floor of Viola's old archipelago homestead, and he and Ann had started a relationship. Later, when she got pregnant with another man, the relationship fell apart. The biggest mistake of her life, she might think, always with a bad conscience, as her son Erik was her great joy. But Erik would have been Edvard's too, that was a thought Ann could not let go of and suffered from. One night's lack of judgment and she was punished by losing the man she loved so deeply.

She knew that she would never experience that passion again. Edvard was there like a thorn in her heart. She had talked with Anders Brant about him, but always in that relaxed way you are expected to do where old relationships are concerned. Perhaps he understood anyway that he could never fully replace Edvard?

Reminded about Viola by Agnes's dialect, however faint, was to travel along a painful path. It was like looking out through a train window and reliving a beautiful, familiar landscape but not being given the opportunity to stop and get out and experience it close up once again. She would never be able to sleep with Edvard again. Never feel him cuddle up next to her. Never hear Viola rummaging in the kitchen on the ground floor, making morning coffee and sandwiches for her and Edvard.

Agnes was observing her. Ann felt caught and made an effort to come back to the present.

"Can you imagine anyone who wishes the professor harm?"

"That would be Bunde then, the neighbor," said Agnes, tossing her head. "He's the one who has an article in *Upsala Nya* today. The associate professor, he lives one house over, is probably not too pleased with the professor, but he wouldn't hurt a fly. He's a man of peace. He's the one who has the high tower you see. He grows olives and a lot of other things."

Ann turned her head and through the window she glimpsed a glass cupola. She knew that the associate professor had been a colleague of Bertram von Ohler. The professor had pointed out the associate professor as the instigator of the article in the newspaper, and that although Torben Bunde wrote it, that did not affect the matter. The associate professor was surely behind the skull in the mailbox too, Ohler thought.

Lindell had not read the article that Agnes was talking about, not even noticed it when she quickly leafed through the newspaper that morning. It was Göte Bengtsson who mentioned it and said that it actually did not add anything new, and was more an account of what was being said in Germany and other places. Bunde was well informed according to Bengtsson and unusually temperate, but could not keep from slipping in a few spiteful remarks in the last paragraph about what a duck pond Sweden was, and in an ingenious way Bunde made Professor von Ohler a victim of provincial narrow-mindedness. Being known at a regional hospital in Sweden does not necessarily mean that you should be rewarded with the Nobel Prize, he had concluded.

Bengtsson had pointed out where the author of the article lived and Ann Lindell had on several occasions seen a face visible in the windows.

"A real wasp's nest," she let out.

Agnes smiled carefully.

"And then we have the Germans," she continued, and Lindell saw how the old woman was becoming increasingly exhilarated, her eyes glistened, her hands came up from the table and she underscored each word with cautious gestures.

"The Germans have never liked the professor. And vice versa."

She told about the article that had been published in some German magazine and how the professor had become hopping mad, first carrying on "like a brigand," then collapsing on the library couch, stunned and silent, barely responsive.

"I was worried for a while, thought about calling his daughter. He is an old man after all and his heart can give out at any time."

Lindell nodded as if she completely understood Agnes's analysis.

"But perhaps Birgitta would make everything worse," said Agnes in a gruff voice.

There was something of Viola in the woman. Perhaps some kind of female Gräsö gene? The thought amused Lindell and she smiled carefully.

"There are two sons too, I've understood."

Agnes smacked her lips.

"Abraham and Carl," she said. "I watched them grow up. I shined their shoes."

Lindell let the words sink in before she continued.

"Perhaps you'll think I'm impertinent, but what is he like as an employer?"

"I take care of myself," said Agnes.

"But the professor too, right?"

"That may be," Agnes replied, and Lindell did not know what she should believe, whether the gruffness was directed at her or at the professor.

She heard voices from the yard and thought she could identify Sammy's, but was not sure.

"I should thank you," she said.

"It was nothing," said Agnes, getting up.

Lindell did the same. They remained standing a moment on each side of the table.

"I'll use the kitchen exit, like my associate. Maybe I can take a few apples?"

Agnes rounded the table, opened a drawer, and took out a plastic bag which she gave to Lindell.

"You probably know that Viola is not well," Agnes said suddenly, when Lindell was standing with her hand on the doorknob.

She stared at Agnes.

"How did you know—"

"My sister Greta keeps track of everything," Agnes explained.

"You knew that I—"

"You're the police officer from Uppsala who associated with Edvard, yes. I recognized your name. I've known Viola my whole life. I've met Edvard too. A good person."

Lindell bowed her head and got an impulse to hide her face with the plastic bag.

"She's very weak," said Agnes. "Greta went to see her yesterday. Viola doesn't want to go to the hospital. Edvard will be with her. He's like a son."

Lindell nodded, incapable of saying anything.

"I'll call Greta and tell her that you send greetings to Viola," Agnes decided.

"Thanks," whispered Lindell. "I didn't know."

She opened the door and stepped out into the garden. The wind took hold of the plastic bag and it fluttered away before it got stuck on a branch.

Lindell saw Sammy Nilsson standing by the boundary of the lot talking with a man in the neighboring yard. Laughter was heard. It was Sammy's specialty, easy talk while at the same time taking in a little information.

Ann pulled down the bag, hesitated before the various apples. There were yellow-green oblong ones, another variety was bright red, while a third was blotchy and vaguely conical. She was enticed by the red ones, reached out and picked a few.

She filled the whole bag with a mixture of each variety, before she stopped. She was actually at work and was surely being observed by the neighbors. She set down the bag, leaning it against a trunk, and went over to Sammy.

The man he was conversing with was red-cheeked and actually somewhat red-eyed too. Lindell suspected that it was because the wind on this side of the house was blowing firmly.

"Now I know everything about spruce needles," said Sammy.

Lindell did not understand what he meant and had no desire to know either, but she nodded toward the man on the other side of the fence. He nodded back and gave her a long look, as if he recognized her but could not place the face.

"Shall we get going?"

"Nice to meet you," said Sammy, and Lindell was getting mortally tired of all the heartiness.

"Perhaps we have to talk a little with the associate professor too," she said irritated when they had walked a few meters.

"What's with you? Was she surly, the domestic servant?"

"Not at all," Lindell said.

"My old man was almost pure sunshine," said Sammy.

"That's nice. Did he have anything to offer? What do you mean, almost?"

"He said that he knew of the professor, but no more than that. But then he said something that made me wonder, that Ohler has always been an oppressor, vermin. Those are really strong words."

"Agnes knows Viola and Edvard on Gräsö," said Lindell.

"I'll be damned! It's a small world."

"Gräsö is small," said Lindell.

"I wonder what he meant by vermin?"

"Viola is really ill."

"Go out and see her then," said Sammy thoughtlessly.

Yes, maybe I should do that, she thought. *She would probably be happy. I'm sure I would cry the whole time and Viola would be the one who would have to console.*

"Shall we go see the associate professor?"

Sammy nodded and cast a glance backward, before they rounded the corner of the house. Yet another car was now parked on the street.

"We'll have to bring Moberg here," said Sammy.

Anthony Moberg was a particularly zealous traffic cop, with zero social skills and the one who used the most parking ticket forms in the whole department, perhaps in the whole country.

"Shall we see the associate professor?" Lindell repeated in such an expressionless voice that Sammy stopped and turned toward her.

"Forget about Gräsö now," he said, without being able to conceal his irritation.

"Okay, I'll cheer up," said Lindell, giving him a crooked smile. "It's just such a shock to be reminded."

"Shock," muttered Sammy Nilsson, but he seemed appeased and jogged over toward the journalists who now were thronging by the gate in full force, except for Bengtsson.

"We'll do the phone trick," he mumbled.

He opened the gate and smiled at the assembled press.

"Ann Lindell will tell you a little," he said, slinking off.

She swept her eyes over the flock before she started to perform her spiel.

"Yes, as you know we have received reports that Professor von Ohler has been subjected to a number of villainies"—where did she get that word from?—"and because he has received so much attention, both in Sweden and abroad, in connection with the Nobel Prize, we obviously take seriously—"

"What does Professor von Ohler think about this?" asked Liselott Karnehagen, the woman from *Aftonbladet*, taking out her pocket recorder.

"What does he *think*?"

Karnehagen nodded eagerly.

"You'll have to ask him that," said Lindell.

At the same moment a shrill whistle was heard. They all turned around. Sammy was standing by the associate professor's gate gesturing. With exaggerated movements he pointed at his cell phone.

"Excuse me," said Lindell, pushing her way forward, "evidently there's a call I have to take."

She set off at a rapid pace and reached the associate professor's gate before the throng of journalists realized what had happened. Göte Bengtsson started his van and rolled off, giving a thumb's-up as he passed Lindell and Nilsson.

"Associate Professor Gregor Johansson," Lindell noted on her pad, and it struck her that he was the first associate professor she had spoken with. The one she had encountered previously was in a state of decomposition.

Something also smelled in the living associate professor's house, not rotten, but she got a faint sense of the untidy, the unaired.

"Why don't we go up in the tower," said Johansson.

Sammy and Lindell gave each other a look. Neither of them wanted a lecture on orchids or some other exciting species, but they could not say no, the man was obviously delighted at the thought of letting their conversation take place under glass. Perhaps he wanted to show them how well he had arranged it? He radiated loneliness and Lindell had nothing against keeping him company for a while.

"That would be exciting," said Sammy.

They climbed up, the associate professor in the lead, eagerly talking about when and how he had his tower constructed, while Lindell thought about Viola. Was she on her deathbed? Agnes's choice of words might suggest that. She was not a person who exaggerated, dramatized about death, Lindell was sure of that. Agnes seemed to possess a kind of stripped-down, unsentimental attitude to hers and other people's lives, just like Viola. So when she said, "Edvard will be with her" it could mean that the end was near for the old woman.

Lindell sighed. Sammy gave her a worried look and reached out his hand to support her as she climbed up into the tower.

"Yes, I must say, the view is good," he said.

The associate professor nodded.

"For the annual fireworks in the Botanical Gardens I usually sit here with a glass of wine."

"What beautiful plants!" Lindell exclaimed. "And an olive tree! Do you see, Sammy? Olives! And lemons. I don't think I've ever seen anything like it."

Pride made the associate professor's skinny cheeks twitch. It was obvious that he didn't know how to react to this enthusiastic and wholehearted praise.

"That was kind," he was finally able to say.

Lindell was happy that they had taken the trouble to come up. The tower gave an overview of the block. This is where the drama is playing out, she thought, amused and slightly energized. The former colleague and now bitter enemy, the associate professor who apparently calmly observes everything from above: the neighbor Bunde, whom they had only glimpsed like a moray in its hole, prepared to strike again with its sharp teeth at any moment; the red-eyed gardener in the neighboring yard who with his tirade about "vermin" and "oppressors" was the strange bird in this academic wasp's nest; the "Germans," this frightening people who were only jealous that they did not have a Nobel Prize to either award or receive; Agnes, with a half century of experiences, with slow cooking and shiny copper pans, who certainly knew more about Bertram von Ohler than he did himself.

And as the cherry on the cake, someone who with more tangible methods amuses himself by throwing stones and placing a cranium—a real-life skull, as Ottosson had expressed it—mounted on a fence post next to the professor's mailbox.

"This stone-throwing, what do you think about that?" Sammy Nilsson abruptly interrupted the associate professor's lecture about succulents.

The associate professor was startled. He looked at Sammy Nilsson in a way that expressed a wounded fatigue, as if the police had abused his confidence.

"I don't think anything," he said.

"You haven't seen or heard anything?"

Gregor Johansson shook his head.

"Have you talked with the gardener, Haller? You seem to have a good deal in common," said Sammy, pointing down toward the man. "He called Ohler vermin, what could he mean by that?"

"No idea," said the associate professor.

"Have you discussed the professor and the prize with him?"

"Just in passing," the associate professor answered.

"Do you share that understanding, about Ohler as vermin?"

"If that were the case, I would be very careful about airing such opinions."

"Wise," said Sammy Nilsson. "But now we have to be going. Nice to get a little perspective on existence."

"What the hell are succulents?" Sammy exclaimed as they were getting in the car.

"What the hell did you mean by being so contrary? He was a friendly old man."

The throng of journalists was standing in a semicircle in front of Ohler's steps. On the steps stood the professor. The whole thing resembled a press conference at the White House.

"Yes, old, and perhaps friendly, definitely to us, but I think there's some shit there. I thought Haller hinted at a few things. He stood surrounded by dirt and a number of stones that he had dug up, did you see that? He also said something about 'there is more ammunition for anyone who is interested.' He stank of booze, did you notice that? And he talked about the associate professor as his 'brother-in-arms,' what did he mean by that?"

Lindell leaned her head back and closed her eyes and immediately after that her ears. She did not want to hear more about associate professors and skulls. They would write a report, then turn their attention to essentials.

The essentials proved to be a sixty-year-old garage owner and member of the Home Guard in the Almunge area who had gotten tired of his wife and then of himself.

The wife was tied up with her back to a chopping block in the woodshed, shot once in the head and once in the chest. The walls of the shed were covered with dried blood, brain matter, and bone chips.

The man was on his back a couple of meters outside the woodshed. Half of his skull was missing. By his side was a hunting rifle.

It was a neighbor who found them. He had heard the shots and "immediately understood" that something was wrong.

"It's to defend his home," said Sammy Nilsson, kicking at the foundation of a tank that was on the yard.

After the first attack of nausea, he vomited in the woodshed. He had been seized by fury and yelled at the man who was lying at his feet.

Lindell had been forced to pull him away from the dead man.

"We don't know what happened," she said.

"He tied her up," said Sammy.

That she could not deny and therefore did not say anything. She was also nauseated, partly by the sight of the dead, partly from the smell of diesel.

"Let's move away a little," she said, taking Sammy by the arm.

They walked in silence. There was not much they could do now, the technicians would have to perform their duties first. Lindell was struck by the dramatic difference between the villa in Kåbo and the farm in Almunge. Ottosson called just when they had left the associate professor and driven up to the main road. One moment among the bigwigs and the next in front of two dead people in a little village in the country, the man obviously unhappy, evil, or crazy, or all three at once. With the woman bound and terrified in the presence of her husband, Lindell thought this was obviously an uncommonly brutal sight that indicated a kind of planning, and she understood Sammy's rage. But he was too blocked to start reasoning, so she had to do it for herself.

Perhaps he "only" wanted to scare her by tying her up, but then the sequence of events got out of control? But why in the woodshed? Had it started as a silly quarrel? Probably they would never find out. They had not, after a quick check in the house, found any letter or message that might cast the least bit of light on the background to what happened. The only thing they discovered that suggested a drama was a torn-open box of bullets on the kitchen table. Some bullets had rolled onto the floor.

Could it be a double murder? The question had to be asked, even if Lindell realized it was not very likely.

It took an hour for the technicians to arrive. During that time Sammy and Lindell questioned the neighbors, most of them elderly, who lived closest. They were obviously shocked, the village was small, everyone knew everyone. No one could give a reasonable explanation for the whole thing. As far as the neighbors knew, the man had never before threatened or abused his wife.

"They seemed to be like most folks," said one of them, who had recently moved into an older, half-dilapidated shack. "I got help from him to fix the roof. He was a real hard worker, rarely allowed himself a break."

"She was not particularly talkative but thoughtful," said a very pregnant woman who lived two houses away. "We used to bake together."

When they left her she was crying uncontrollably and Lindell felt like a villain.

"I think he didn't have much work after the summer," the nearest neighbor, a farmer, mentioned. "Maybe he got depressed? We had talked about him helping me with the fertilizing. Now I'll have to find someone else and it's not that easy."

Lindell had experienced this many times before, how people close to the eye of the storm got hung up on everyday details about the dead.

"Depressed" was a word that turned up again and again in Lindell's thoughts, while they poked around the farm. Fredriksson and Beatrice, who had joined them half an hour before, went through the house. Fredriksson looked moderately amused, he always wanted to be outdoors, but the itching seemed to have stopped. When he disappeared into the house Lindell saw that the hair on the back of his neck was sticky from some yellow-white cream.

All in all, the farm looked a little depressing, careless in some way. Perhaps the season contributed to the impression?

There were no children to notify. According to an uncertain piece of information, the man had a half-sister "up north." According to the neigh-bors, the couple otherwise never talked about any relatives.

"If there are any relatives, then *they* certainly won't talk about the dead, especially not about the old bastard," said Sammy, who seemed unusually bitter and restless.

Or the other way around, thought Lindell. Now perhaps the family can really talk rubbish. But she did not say anything so as not to add further fuel to the fire.

On the way home Lindell fell asleep in the car. That was not unusual. She had a talent for dropping off after a period of tension. Others got wound up, Lindell fell asleep.

Sammy woke her before the Gnista roundabout.

"Are you going home or to day care?"

"No, I have to get the bicycle," said Lindell.

She looked at the clock and determined that she had plenty of time to pick up Erik.

"A day on the job," she said, as they turned down into the garage under the police station.

Sammy gave her a quick glance and mumbled something.

✦

Sixteen

"Who has access to skulls?"

Sammy Nilsson's question was tossed out unexpectedly before the morning gathering had formally been opened. All eyes were aimed at him, the majority very surprised. Yesterday's incident with Ohler was not the sort of thing they dealt with in Homicide. The newspaper had not revealed what the threats against the professor were, other than that a stone had been thrown at the house.

"Grave diggers," said Fredriksson.

"Doctors," Sammy Nilsson answered himself.

"You can't rule out the associate professor," said Lindell with a smile.

"The old man is cunning," said Sammy. "He and that gardener have cooked something up, I'm dead sure of it."

"And what would that be?" asked Ottosson, who looked amused.

Perhaps he thought it was liberating for a change to make small talk about somewhat less dreadful crimes than murder.

"I don't know," said Sammy, "but I think that the gardener threw the stone and the associate professor set out the skull."

"The criminals are just getting older and older," said Lindell in a dejected voice.

Sammy smiled and she understood that he had been able to shake off yesterday's irritation, which had actually been an expression of powerlessness.

"I see," said Ottosson. "Shall we get started?"

"Is there any alternative?" Fredriksson asked drily.

"Pick mushrooms, maybe," said Sammy.

Fredriksson's thoughts shifted immediately to the autumn chanterelles.

Ottosson began the meeting. "Almunge! There is nothing that indicates anything other than murder and then suicide. The deed appears to have been done without premeditation, as it is so nicely called. As Allan already pointed out last evening"—Lindell looked up, had Fredriksson worked overtime?—"the woman was probably hanging up laundry. On the laundry line at the end of the house a number of garments were hanging and in a basket on the ground there were more clothes, damp."

"Perhaps it was the husband who was hanging laundry?" Pedersén threw out. He was one of the new ones, someone about whom Lindell had not yet formed a clear impression.

"The woman had clothespins stuck in her waistband, but as usual don't rule anything out," said Ottosson.

They could rule out most of it, thought Lindell, who was tired of all the clichés, even the ones she made use of.

She felt a kind of nausea creeping up. Perhaps it was the information about the clothespins in the waistband that triggered the reaction? Being murdered in the middle of such an everyday chore, dragged away and tied up to a chopping block, underscored the capriciousness and made it all stand out as even more bestial. "Disloyal" was a word that occurred to her. You don't murder someone who is hanging up your wash.

Lindell lost herself in thoughts about what Alice Eleonora Sigvardsson was thinking when she was hanging up her blouses, her husband's

underwear and shirts. Did she suspect anything? Had they quarreled that
morning?

Otherwise no new serious crimes had been reported; the fact was
that the past few weeks had been unusually calm. It had given them some
breathing room and several of the ongoing investigations got more attention and in several cases were closed. The hooligans have taken an early
and long fall break, Hill, the other newcomer, wisecracked.

As the meeting continued Lindell was very preoccupied as she listened
to what was being said; she was not called on a single time either. From
Almunge her thoughts flew back to Gräsö. Before yesterday's visit it had
been several weeks. She almost had a bad conscience for not having thought
about Edvard for such a long time, and thereby not about Viola either. It
had happened before, during periods with relative harmony in her life, that
the memories subsided.

When she and Sammy discussed it, he maintained that the bad conscience was due to the fact that she did not allow herself to be happy. To
him Edvard was a dead end, always had been. For a while Ann got the idea
that Sammy was jealous, but that was unlikely. Sammy always seemed
satisfied with his family life.

Now she had Anders. Since the adventure in Brazil he had changed, was
no longer so dead certain. Mostly he stayed at her place; they had never
talked about moving in together, but more and more of his things, especially books and CDs, were ending up in her apartment. She actually had
nothing against it. It was not the things, wherever they physically were, that
were decisive. But she was wary, it was like walking on newly formed ice,
a cliché that she never liked before but that she thought described the feeling well. They still had to fumble their way forward.

He was still physically fragile after being badly knifed earlier in the year.
Sometimes Ann got the idea that he exaggerated his weakness, that he
wanted to be frail and pitiful. Or else the recovery from his mental fragil-

ity was delayed. He was not in balance, that was obvious, and Ann was moved by his attempts to sometimes seem stronger than he was in reality.

The experiences in Brazil, first as witness to a murder and then battered by a bus, had left their marks. She also realized that the breakup with the woman he met there had dominated his mood. He said nothing specific but she understood by his evasiveness that he was very upset. It did not come out whether it was he or she who had taken the initiative to separate, even if he hinted that she was the one who had been hurt most. But that could just as well be a way for him to safeguard his vanity. Who wants to be abandoned?

Ann decided not to poke her nose into it. When she realized that he was two-timing her, she kept Billie Holiday's recording of "Don't Explain" in her mind: Don't explain, just come back. That was how desperate she was. Then she had been prepared to swallow a lot. And she did, asked no questions, made no accusations. He was the one who got to determine at what pace the story would be revealed. And fragments were still coming out, piece by piece. But the more time passed, the less urgent the story felt to Ann.

He was with her now, not in Brazil or somewhere else. On the contrary, occasionally he almost got clingy. He offered her warmth and skin. He was considerate, sweet to Erik, who seemingly without difficulty accepted him as his stepfather. They were doing well together. Quarrels were avoided by Anders taking a step back, unimaginable before, as if he wanted to try a new tactic. He was accommodating but maintained his silence as a shield of integrity.

Was *she* too accommodating? That was something that Görel, her girl-friend, always maintained. Görel wanted to *know*, she wanted a complete confession, she wanted to see him crawl. When Ann defended herself she was told that she was too submissive. And—this was Görel's point—this behavior would punish her in the long run. If Anders Brant now stood out as an honest man, there would come a time when his deceitful tempera-ment flared up again, and then Ann would be, if not powerless, then in any event not as well armed. But she could not believe in the image of Anders as a slumbering monster. She herself had acted deceitfully toward Edvard and knew that life could not be lived according to an instruction book with one hundred percent morality and rationality as a guide. Sometimes you got caught. No one else needed to pronounce the punishment, you managed that well enough on your own.

"You have to think about yourself, don't let yourself be fooled," Görel said so often that Ann was getting tired of her nagging. Sometimes she got the feeling that her friend preferred an unhappy Ann, a single Ann, an Ann who sought consolation, but that was such a strange conclusion that Ann suppressed it. Why should Görel, who had always supported her over the years, harbor such thoughts?

She had told Anders about Edvard, about her betrayal, and about the long rehabilitation, that was the word she used, to come back, to dare to believe that she would meet another man. She did it without ulterior motives, she didn't want to make him feel guilty, just give a factual picture of herself and their circumstances.

He had listened patiently, asked a few questions, but after that did not comment on what she said. Even so she sensed he was grateful that she wanted to tell him.

And now Edvard would be on the table again. It was necessary. She had decided to go out to the island and visit Viola before it was too late. If Edvard chose to lie low that was his business, she would steel herself and get through it. There was no other choice. It had been eight years since they were together. It would be silly if she could not see him after such a long time.

It struck her that perhaps he was living with a woman. She felt her cheeks burning. Sammy, who was always attentive, made a gesture with one hand. She did not know how to interpret it, so she just nodded back and tried to look content.

The meeting was over. Everyone exhaled and left as fast as they could. Only Ottosson lingered as usual, as did Lindell. It was a habit they'd had for a long time, a kind of post-meeting, filled with familiarity. Sometimes it was only about work, other times about private things and then mostly about Ann's life, but most often it was a mixture.

The others on the squad had accepted these brief conferences, realized that the bond between the chief and Lindell was somewhat special. What made her colleagues feel well-disposed or indulgent to Ann was that she never used her status as favorite to appropriate benefits for herself.

It was just this relationship, their slightly peculiar relationship, that Ann now brought up.

"Who am I going to make small talk with after the end of the year?"

Ottosson smiled, but said nothing. He picked up his papers. They both knew that there was no answer. Instead he picked up another thread.

"I was thinking about this business with the professor. Could it be someone who was wrongly treated once upon a time? He worked at University Hospital, right? Someone who wants to get revenge, who has fumed about it a long time and now when the old man has gotten some notoriety wants to mess with him a little."

"I think he worked as a researcher. He probably didn't have much to do with the general public. Seeing patients, performing operations and that. He's a virologist. Viruses."

Ottosson nodded.

"And that was probably a good thing," Lindell added.

"I see, he's one of those."

Now it was her turn to nod.

"Have you talked with Ola at all?"

"Not for a couple of weeks," said Lindell. "When he was in Stockholm visiting someone."

"A lady?"

"Hard to believe."

At one time, Lindell had felt attracted to Ola Haver. It was not long after the separation from Edvard. Now, in retrospect, she had a hard time understanding why.

"Is he coming back?" asked Ottosson.

"Don't think so."

"He doesn't want to talk with me. The last time he hung up. So he's probably coming back when I'm gone."

Ottosson sounded sincerely worried. He was not self-pitying, instead sad that perhaps he had said or done something that upset Haver.

"No," said Lindell. "He's angry, not at you personally but at the department in general and you'll have to take the blame since you're the boss. He's angry at life, at Rebecka, at everything and everyone."

Ottosson observed her.

"There are many who are angry these days," he said a bit cryptically.

"Complaints?"

"No," said Ottosson. "Sometimes you wish that more people complained."

"Go visit our Nobel Prize winner," Lindell encouraged him. "He complains about most everything."

After a few minutes Lindell left. She felt a certain impatience and she knew why. She wanted to call Gräsö.

✦

Seventeen

The notes from Africa no longer interested him. He had long intended to edit the scattered paragraphs into a coherent text. Obviously a lot would have to be deleted, but there was enough that held up to closer inspection.

Now he didn't know. Small observations of nature by a white man in a black country, what would that be good for? Miss Elly would have been immensely amused, he smiled at the memory of her merciless laughter. He read a couple of sentences: "I know nothing about fireflies. That worries me." Miss Elly would have choked.

No, I'll throw the piles of papers in the garbage can, he decided, but changed his mind at the same moment. What if his mother had thought the same way and actually thrown away her diaries? Then he would be suspended in ignorance of who she really was, and above all he would never have gotten an answer to questions he had wondered about ever since childhood. Perhaps the answers came a bit late, but he experienced a great warmth at the sight of his mother's primitive scribbling.

But on the other hand, he had no children who would read and understand in retrospect. They never had any children. That was why Miss Elly died, there was no other explanation. Her shame at being a barren cow was too great. Her despair hollowed her out until only a dry skin remained. She weighed nothing when she passed away. He carried her casket alone on one shoulder.

So who would read his notes? He had no ambition to stand out as intelligent, because he had never seen himself that way. He was good at a number of things, he could track, haul wood, imitate bird calls, likewise lay an acid-soil bed and a whole lot more. None of this was especially remarkable. The birds sang better than he did. Millions of people in Africa could track, but he had been given a talent that not many white people had, Miss Elly thought. In that area she was impressed by his skills. Otherwise his experiences could be sorted under the "everyday" category.

He harbored no ambitions to be an author either. He had never read that much; during the years in Africa there had simply been a lack of books. At his uncle's in Windhoek there were only German novels of miserable quality and pornography of even lower quality. Then, in the northern provinces, he never experienced any need for books.

If he had at least been agitated when he jotted down his lines, then perhaps it would be instructive or at least readable for a wider audience. Strangely enough, though, he thought in retrospect, the notes were chemically free from comments about what was happening in the country. Not even when the resistance struggle intensified and the armed groups went past, sometimes only gangs of boys from the high plateaus equipped with a few automatic rifles, did it leave any traces in his writing. He had not hesitated a moment about where his sympathies were; many times he had ended up in arguments with other whites, not least the Haller family in the capital, but none of this appeared in his writings, not a single expression of anger.

In his texts animals and nature dominated, skies, stars and desert sand, rain that fell or was absent, mooing, bellowing, and shrieks in the night, sunrises so beautiful that he wept with gratitude.

A few lines about Miss Elly. *If I had written more about her and love any-*

way, he thought, *I could have filled however many pages. No, instead I wrote about fireflies. No wonder she laughed.*

The conclusion was that what was most interesting to others, most universally applicable or exciting in a more conventional sense, was lacking.

But perhaps, he concluded his train of thought, perhaps in the future could there be a person, in Sweden or in Namibia, who would find the text interesting? The problem was how this person would get hold of his notes. That was an insurmountable problem. When he died the text would die with him.

He should let chance decide! As part of his estate, his typed-out African meditations would be neatly collected. Those to whom the task fell of cleaning up after him would have to decide. Either the papers would end up in a black garbage bag along with old vouchers, warranties for the toaster, and everything else he had collected, or else the finder would sit down and start browsing, perhaps enticed by the exotic photo on the front page depicting Miss Elly sitting on the skull of a hippopotamus, and after a couple of pages would say to his assistant, "This is really interesting." Then the other person, tired of the first person's passivity, would encourage him to take the papers home and continue reading there.

That is what would happen when the text started to have a life of its own. What would happen then no one could know. The number of possibilities made him dizzy.

He laughed, stirred a little absentmindedly the bowl of pasta he was cooking, and thought about the police officers he had met earlier in the day. The man, Nilsson he had introduced himself as, stood out as a cheerful fellow. Or was he just pretending? No, Karsten thought to himself, he seemed genuinely pleasant, open and talkative. But the woman who came up later looked like seven years of famine.

She had inspected him suspiciously. Perhaps she despised people who dug? Or else she was angry at her colleague, thought that he was wasting time, and then let her displeasure spill over on him.

What surprised Karsten was the information that new threats had been made against the professor. What the threats consisted of Nilsson would not say, other than that it concerned something that was placed by the mailbox. No, Karsten had not seen anything, he was fully occupied with excavating and could not possibly perceive what was happening in the neighboring yards, especially on the other side of the houses. The policeman seemed content with that.

It was obvious that the professor was being attacked from several directions. The morning's article in the newspaper spoke for itself. The academic feuding was a fact, and clearly not only in Sweden. It serves him right, thought Karsten contentedly, taking the pot from the stove and pouring the pasta into the colander, rinsing it with cold water, adding a little butter, and tilting it up onto the plate.

But who had set something by the gate, and what? You might think it was a bomb, the way the police were acting.

The meat sauce, bought ready-made, was not especially good, but he still shoveled it in with good appetite. Perhaps the associate professor knew more? He decided to look him up. There was a witch alder waiting for him, after all.

He picked up his workbook, opened to a new page, and noted how many hours he had put in at Lundquist's, how many kilometers he drove during the day and how much he had spent on plants. Everything had to be noted for later accounting, but also for his own sake.

There was a certain joy in this, browsing back in the workbooks, recalling things large and small, plantings or stone paving that he was especially pleased with, which customers had been grateful, or for that matter who had complained. The latter were, however, clearly in the minority.

It struck him that this was as good a diary as any. Since his return to Sweden he had filled a combined thirty-eight workbooks. All were lined up on the bookshelf.

He was a lonely man, it had gradually occurred to him. Not because he thought about himself and his own situation that much but because he observed other people. He saw how they sought each other out, clumped together, terrified to have dinner at a restaurant on their own or sit on a park bench down in the City Garden and philosophize, read a book or simply casually watch people passing by. Not to mention going to a concert or a play alone. Everyone tried to look as if they were waiting for an acquaintance, looking at their watches, taking out their cell phones, conversing with someone or at least pretending to converse.

That was foreign to him. He was usually most content being by himself. Recently, however, a new type of worry had come over him, perhaps triggered by his mother's death. He became dazed by the new thought that the loner's existence was in opposition to the very idea of life, the African thought and attitude to life that he was so familiar with, where loneliness was considered an illness.

For it occurred to him, late in life it might seem, that everything he did was measured not only against his own conceptions but also other people's dreams and needs. Of course your own satisfaction counted for a lot, but still it was a little sad now: Lundquist was out of town, he had no one to talk with, show his progress to. Even if most of his customers were ignorant, and downright thankful not to have to think and decide on something, they were still polite, pretending to be interested or impressed by the progress in their gardens.

Now he was groping along, in principle sure of his business, he knew every species and its characteristics and needs, but subjected to the vacuum of loneliness he was listless and perplexed. The notes of the workbook became hours and kronor, nothing more.

He was a solitary person who erected monuments that people barely noticed.

The dishes were soon done and there were hours until it was time to go to bed. He sat down in the sparsely furnished living room and continued thinking. He was not particularly good at it, he was a man of action, but the recent years' practice in brooding was starting to produce results. He was getting ever more persistent and capable. *Just so I don't get like Father*, he thought, *who could sit for hours staring into space.*

Karsten understood early on that it was the war that was raging in his father. The eighth of May 1945 meant peace but not the end of the war. He was marching as long as he lived inside himself the long way from East Prussia to Stralsund, over and over again.

On lampposts and provisional gallows to the right the "traitors" were hanging and to the left the "Nazi swine" were swaying in the wind. Their tongues were swollen. Often they had pissed and shit on themselves. Birds were sitting on their shoulders. Flies buzzed. At their feet were dogs.

Between them marched columns of the destitute, hungry, terrified, stinking, apathetic, wounded, dying. Westward. Karsten was in this parade of human wreckage too, secured to his father's body with a belt from a German soldier. Karsten still had the belt with the eagle.

He remembered nothing himself, he was an infant. What was he fed on? A mystery. "On love," said his father, who then burst into tears; Karsten saw how he struggled to hold it back. He hugged Karsten, then age fourteen, so hard it hurt. He still felt that grip, almost fifty years later.

Karsten Haller smiled. What strength, he thought. What love that surrounded him. The gratitude of his parents' energy and consideration shot up like laughter.

He understood that he had turned his thoughts around. It was here that the skill showed itself. Only a couple of years ago it would have gone in the other direction, right toward the abyss. Nowadays he could stop and reset his course. The happy memories took over.

He stood up, went over to the window. On the other side of the street was a woman who usually had dinner at this time. She was perhaps in her forties, had moved in a year ago. Karsten thought she was divorced. No children were ever seen. Her kitchen table was lit up by a red lamp, shaped like a funnel. It was like a painting: the gentle light, the woman with small, deliberate movements, she always ate slowly, always alone, sometimes she browsed in a magazine.

He observed her awhile, let his eyes rest. It was like at Okanga, the southern water hole, where he also used to stand concealed for a half hour or so and study the animals that came to drink.

✦

Eighteen

The low-built church was shrouded in haze. On the cemetery wall out toward the road sat an old man dangling his legs. It was such a peculiar sight that Ann got the idea that something was not right. It was dark and a little raw, it had rained hard.

As she drove past the man turned his head and followed her with his eyes. She was driving very slowly and could see that he was smiling. She accelerated up the rise and turned left, passed the store, and was struck by a sensation of dizziness. So many years ago. She tried to figure out exactly to the day how long it was, but gave up at once. During the drive there she had decided to live in the present, not let herself be dragged down into a morass of guilt and wasted chances.

Should she have brought Erik with her? It only struck her now, with just a few kilometers left. Viola certainly would have appreciated that. But probably not Edvard.

Ann had said that she would be back no later than nine. Now it was ten past six. She had checked the ferry schedules. She would have to leave Viola's no later than seven thirty.

She did not need to hesitate about the way. She had driven here many times as if intoxicated, filled with expectation and desire, sometimes in jubilant joie de vivre. And the fact was that despite her intention the old feeling took hold of her. She felt it purely physically as a thrill through her whole body.

She opened the window, as if to blow out all the thoughts that were circulating in the car. The wind had picked up, due west, she noticed. She thought about Edvard and his musings about weather and wind, how he drew her into his speculations. At the start of his time on the island he was a little uncertain, accustomed as he was to inland weather phenomena, a farm worker's observations of the outlook for precipitation or clearing. But as he became more sure, Viola, and above all the old neighbor Viktor, also taught him a great deal about the idiosyncrasies of archipelago weather.

The side road down to Viola's had been widened. That was surely thanks to Edvard. He had always complained about the road. Viola seldom left her farm and experienced no great need for a good road. Edvard on the other hand commuted to his job as a construction worker and was of a different opinion. Ann wondered whether he was still in that industry. She knew nothing about his present life.

There were two cars in the farmyard. One was a pickup, probably Edvard's, thought Ann. Behind it was hidden a Corolla that was at least twenty-five years old. *I should have called,* it struck her when she caught sight of the car. Perhaps he was living with someone? That was not an impossibility, more likely probable. He was surely still an attractive man, of which there was a shortage on the island.

She got out on shaking legs, prepared to throw herself back in the car at any moment and take off. Steeled herself to look relaxed. She realized that Edvard had already heard the car, unless his hearing had gotten even worse.

There were lights on in the kitchen, in the parlor, and one flight up. Viola's bedroom—Ann assumed that the old woman was bedridden—faced out toward the sea.

When she was a few meters from the glassed-in porch, and noticed that all the door and window frames were freshly painted, the door opened. Edvard. He had not turned on the light, perhaps he had stood and watched her for a few moments, uncertain whether he was mistaken. But to her his shape was so familiar that she would recognize it among thousands.

"You," was all he said.

"Me," said Anna.

You and me, she thought.

"I heard that Viola was ill."

He nodded, perhaps he was waiting for a continuation. Was the shock so great that he was incapable of saying anything? Perhaps his disgust at her unexpected visit made him mute?

"Do you have . . . company?"

The question was unbelievably silly, she realized that immediately, but she could not get herself to put it another way.

"Yes, a buddy of Viola's is here," said Edvard, nodding toward the Toyota. "She'll be leaving soon."

She sensed that he understood her embarrassment. Buddy, she thought, and could not help smiling a little. Viola's buddy.

"How is she doing?"

He was still standing with his hand on the doorknob. Perhaps he didn't want to let her in.

"She's very weak," he said.

Ann heard from his voice that he was tired.

"You've fixed the road," she said.

He nodded.

"And painted the porch."

"Yes, a lot has happened since the last time," he said, and she could not determine whether he was teasing or amused at her remarks.

"Nice," said Ann, "very nice," and nodded eagerly as if she wanted to underscore that she thought everything seemed to be in tip-top shape with the side road, the house, Edvard, and life.

"Come in," he said curtly, leaving the door and disappearing into the house.

She followed him as if he were an executioner and these were her last steps up onto the scaffold.

The smell was the same. In the kitchen to the left as usual it was sparkling clean. Ann suspected that Edvard had help, he never cleaned up completely himself, there was always something left on the counter, a cup on the table or crumbs on a cutting board. Perhaps there was another woman in the house?

To the right were the stairs up to Edvard's room, worn by his feet, not repainted since last time.

Edvard walked straight ahead. He was limping a little. The hair on the back of his head was perhaps a little thinner, otherwise he looked like he always was.

He stopped and waited for her before he pushed open the door to Viola's room.

"You have a visitor," he said, taking a step to the left and making room for Ann.

The room was lit only by a table lamp in the corner. Viola was laying like a dowager, submerged in a sea of blankets in the gigantic bed. Ann remembered that she was always cold and in the winter often had double blankets. It smelled of cleanser and coffee.

Her cheeks were skinnier than ever. The thin, white hair was even thinner and whiter. Immediately when Ann came into the room she opened her eyes and fixed her with her gaze like the way she did the first time they met.

"Ann, my own policewoman," the old woman croaked, making an effort to pull her arms out of the covers.

Ann went up to the bed and placed her hand on Viola's cold cheek. They looked at each other.

"I knew it," the old woman said.

Ann fought back the tears. This was such a valuable moment that instinctively she did not want to throw away a single second by sobbing and weeping. She wanted to have a clear gaze, be just as strong as Viola had always been.

"I got your greeting," said Viola.

A discreet cough was heard from the unlit part of the room. Ann turned her head and there sat an elderly woman on a chair. Ann realized immediately that this must be the sister of the Nobel Prize winner's housekeeper. Despite the darkness it was not hard to make out the resemblance, not least the slightly protruding eyes that now observed her with a mournful expression.

Ann got up to quickly introduce herself so that the woman could then leave her and Viola in peace. She did not want to have a funeral singer sitting in the room.

Perhaps Ann still harbored a wish that it would be only Viola, Edvard, and her in the house. Like before.

The woman got on her feet surprisingly quickly and greeted Ann with a nod.

"I'll be in the kitchen," she said. "Perhaps you'd like a cup later?"

She did not wait for an answer but instead left quickly and quietly. All that lingered behind her was a faint odor of sweat. Edvard followed her out of the room and closed the door very carefully behind him.

Ann sat down on the chair that was placed on the other side of the bed.

"You didn't bring the boy with you?"

Ann shook her head and realized her mistake when she saw the cross frown on the old woman's furrowed face. Sometimes she had considered Viola a kind of paternal grandmother, a replacement for the one Erik would never have, but out of pure selfishness she had not brought him with her. She had been afraid of Edvard's reaction, ashamed to display the physical evidence of their capsized love story. Because it really had been a story, full of desire and tenderness. But Erik would have been his child and no one else's.

She ought to have put herself above this, overlooked Edvard's possible animosity and her own embarrassment, and introduced her son to his "grandmother." She would have liked that, Ann realized now. Perhaps she considered Ann the daughter she never had.

Ann, who had been the unfaithful one, the one who betrayed her Edvard, was now forgiven. She understood that and a sense of longing shot through her, making her feel that all the bad things could be made undone. An impossible wish, a dead end. She was taken back for a moment or two to another life, to a different sort of love than what she experienced with Anders Brant.

"Next time," said Ann. "Do you want to see a photo of Erik?"

The old woman shook her head, and this did not surprise Ann. She had never seen a single photograph in the house.

"It takes a rickety old woman to get you to drag yourself here," said Viola, regaining in her voice a little of the ironic astringency that was her trademark.

"If you knew how I've longed to be here," said Ann quietly.

"Edvard is in the woodshed," said Viola. "He goes there when he gets nervous. So he won't hear us."

"How are you?"

"I want to die at home," said Viola, and Ann knew that there was no point in protesting, but instead nodded and squeezed the old woman's claw-like hand.

"I've done my part, always taken care of myself, haven't been a burden to anyone. I was born when the bells were ringing in the war and I'm leaving in evil times. You should know how afraid they were of the Russians here on the island. We didn't know any better. Can you understand how badly they steered us? But here on the island we didn't care that much. The old men sat in Stockholm and gave orders, but we took care of ourselves," she ended the harangue with a grin.

It was Viola's showpiece, the incompetence and lack of common sense of anyone from Stockholm, whether it was the government or summer visitors. It was an understanding she shared with generations of refractory islanders.

"Does it hurt?"

The old woman shook her head.

"It aches a little in my hip, but it's done that a long time."

Ann could not really understand why Viola was preparing to die, she seemed the same. She had been thin as a rake as long as Ann had known her, and Ann had heard the complaints about her hip before. The explanation came immediately.

"Viktor passed away," said Viola.

"No," Ann exclaimed, squeezing the old woman's hand.

"Three weeks on Monday," said Viola. "He was buried a week ago. There were a hundred and twenty people at the funeral."

Viktor had been Viola's life partner. They never had a regular relationship. It hadn't turned out that way, Viola said one time when Ann asked, but they had been schoolmates in the 1920s, neighbors their whole life, and saw each other basically every day. It was Viktor who came over, helped her with small chores. They had sat in her kitchen for eighty years.

"We never got engaged," said Viola, "but he was a fine man. We were born the same year. He just dropped dead. He was going down to the lake to make sure that Edvard brought his boat up."

"So Viktor had his boat in the water?"

Viola chuckled.

"He and Edvard were out all the time. That was the life for Viktor. He was so fond of Edvard, that they could go out."

How I've missed this! Ann thought desperately.

"That he was," said Ann, "a fine man."

"He used to talk about you," said Viola. "Most of all when he'd had a drop."

"I have longed to be here," Ann let slip again.

"You should have been here," said Viola. "But it's not too late yet."

Don't say that! Ann wanted to cry out. *Don't entice me with a life that no longer exists!* But she didn't say anything. If Viola wanted to believe that Ann could come back, that's the way it was.

"He's not seeing anyone?"

Viola snorted.

"He'll be like Viktor, the old bachelor here in the village," and Viola made it sound like it was Ann's business to change that.

"But didn't he . . . ?" Ann persisted.

She wanted to know. She wanted to hear the old woman say that of course there had been women, and hint that perhaps there was someone he was seeing now.

The response was another snort.

"I've seen you in a picture in the newspaper," said Viola. "Edvard usually reads out loud when there's a story."

Ann could see them in the twilight at the kitchen table. Edvard with his reading glasses and Viola with her eyes toward the farmyard.

"And then a woman adds a little charm," said Viola, who never stopped being amazed that women could be police officers. "It's like an extra . . . but listen . . ."

She fell silent and closed her eyes, lying so still that Ann got scared. The covers did not move, her hand was cold.

"Bye-bye, Ann," Viola said suddenly, opening her eyes. "Now I'm going to sleep a little, I'm so happy we had some time to talk. Take care of yourself and Erik. Do well."

Ann felt Viola grasp her hand. She squeezed back. Their eyes met. Viola smiled her usual old smile before she closed her eyes again. Ann sat awhile before she carefully released her hand and got up.

She closed the door behind her, but regretted it immediately and opened it again. Perhaps Viola would call for something. She took a last look at the old woman and then let her eyes slowly register what was in the room. She got the impulse to take something with her.

In the kitchen it was quiet. The woman, Ann recalled that her name was Greta, was sitting at the kitchen table with a coffee cup in front of her. Edvard was nowhere in sight.

"I set out a cup for you too," said Greta.

Ann looked at the clock, there was still time to exchange a few words. She declined the coffee but sat down.

"I didn't know that Viktor had passed away," she said. "I really would have liked to be at the funeral."

"Edvard was pallbearer. There'll be another one soon," said Greta. "Viola wants to follow Viktor, but I'm sure you understood that."

Ann nodded. She could not be upset by the woman's frank manner. That's just the way it was, so why pretend?

"I've met you before," said Ann.

"I've known Viola my whole life. She took care of us sometimes, Agnes and me, when we were little. Yes, I ran into you when you were going with Edvard, but then you only had eyes for him."

"And then your sister," Ann said. "The world really is small."

"So what is happening at Ohler's?"

Ann was happy to be able to talk about something besides her time on Gräsö and told what had happened with the Nobel Prize winner. She suspected that Greta wanted to have a different version than her sister's. Greta listened without interrupting her and then sat silent for some time. Ann recognized the atmosphere from many interrogations, there was something bothering the woman.

"It's no wonder that people wish him harm," Greta said at last.

"What do you mean?"

"May God forgive me, but he is a bad person."

She pushed aside the coffee cup and looked out the window. Ann followed her eyes, she was afraid that Edvard was approaching.

"Perhaps I should check on Viola," said Greta.

"She's sleeping," said Ann. "I can tell that something is bothering you. Are you worried about your sister?"

"No, not anymore," said Greta with bitterness twisting her mouth. "They have always treated people like whores, everyone who worked there."

"You too?"

Greta nodded. With her fingers she twined a thread that was hanging loose from a small lace tablecloth. Ann guessed that she was the one who put it on top of the oilcloth.

"I got away," she said. "But Anna didn't. Do you know that she lived with Viola for a while?"

"Who is Anna?"

Greta looked up in surprise.

"My oldest sister. She had to live here. Our parents were very strict. They couldn't bear that Anna gave notice at Ohler's, so when she came back to the island she was not welcome. Papa was convinced that she had behaved badly and had to quit for that reason. So he sent me as a replacement to Ohler's. I was only fourteen. It was during the war. I lasted for nine long years. Then it was Agnes's turn."

"What had Anna done?"

"Nothing. Absolutely nothing. Anna was the most peaceful creature you could imagine."

"So she had to stay here?"

"Viola took pity on her. She never forgave Papa. Or Mama either. Viola said that a mother who did not defend her children was not a true Christian. Anna lived here almost a year. She did not visit Mama and Papa a single time. It's only a kilometer or so through the pasture and Lövgren's hill."

Greta told about God's Army and how her father had preached in his own house, condemned his daughter as faithless.

"The congregation revived during the war, people were worried, and then they got Anna to think about. It's always good to have some sinner who you know about, who you can condemn and lament over. Agnes said that it never smelled of brimstone as much as then. She was always afraid, she was just a little girl. And Anna had always been so kind to her, but then suddenly she became the devil incarnate. I avoided hearing that myself. I cried myself to sleep in the maid's chamber at Ohler's."

"What happened to Anna then?"

"She moved from the island. Went south."

Ann guessed that Anna was dead. The thread from the cloth had now definitely come loose and Greta wrapped it slowly around her left index finger. It was a gesture of absentminded playfulness that contradicted the seriousness that marked her face.

"Did Anna forgive her parents?"

Greta slowly shook her head.

"Not that I know of," she said.

"You had no contact?"

"I know that she wrote to Viola," said Greta. "Anna was eternally grateful to her for the support she got when she came back from the Ohlers."

She unwound the thread from her finger and looked hastily up.

"Do you think there are people who wish Ohler harm?"

Ann felt a sting of bad conscience that she had apparently so quickly seemed to leave Anna to her fate, but Greta appeared almost relieved.

"I firmly believe that," she said. "Those kinds of bigwigs always make enemies."

"Has Agnes mentioned anything? I understand that you don't want to gossip, but we have a difficult situation," said Ann deliberately vaguely.

"I think you also have a difficult situation," said Greta, pursing her lips.

"What do you mean?"

"It's written all over you. You came here to see Viola, but you're shaky as an aspen leaf because of Edvard. And now you're playing cops and robbers awhile to stop thinking about Edvard."

Ann's cheeks turned bright red.

"Yes, it's true," she said. "You'll have to excuse me."

Of course she's right, thought Ann, and cursed her own insensitivity. She was playing policewoman in a dying woman's kitchen, while the great love of her life was chopping wood simply to avoid being confronted with her.

"I am like an aspen leaf," she said. "But now I'll drive home and leave you in peace."

It sounded more self-pitying than she intended.

"Agnes hasn't said anything," said Greta. "I know everything and I despise that house and, may God forgive me, the whole family. I don't understand how Agnes endures. I go there to help her. She has gotten so tired."

Ann got up. The tension made her tremble.

"Thanks, Greta," she said. "I'm glad that I came here. I got to talk with Viola awhile. Perhaps you think I'm insensitive for coming here, but Viola was like a mother to me too."

Greta gave her a quick glance and Ann saw the surprise in her eyes.

"And then I got to see Edvard, that he seems to be doing well. And got to talk with you awhile too."

Ann extended her hand across the table and in that way also forced Greta to get up. They shook hands and Ann left the kitchen, closing the veranda door behind her. It had cleared up and the stars were sparkling.

Like before, she thought, but took care not to stay on the farmyard staring at the sky. Edvard was nowhere in sight. She hesitated a few moments before she got in the car.

She drove down the hill toward the ferry, passed the church, and checked whether the old man was still sitting on the wall, which he was. Everything was as it should be on the island. As the fifth and final car she rolled on board. Immediately the gate closed behind her and the ferry departed.

Thoughtfully she remained sitting a few seconds before she put on the hand brake, got out of the car, and went up to the railing. She let out a sob in sorrow, but also felt pride that she managed the encounter with Edvard so well. The mainland came ever closer, she wished she could have stood at the railing longer.

She got an impulse to call home but refrained. For one thing she knew that Anders and Erik got along well together, and for another she was unwilling to break the enchantment at finding herself on the Road Administration's ungainly, clumsy ferry.

It struck her that this series of events and emotions that were layered over each other in a single house, Viola's, expressed everything there was to say about life. A single house. One of thousands, millions.

Viola had experienced almost a hundred years of sorrows and joy by turn. People came and went in her house. Viktor her whole life. Edvard who by chance happened to rent a room and stayed. Anna who in the 1940s got a sanctuary, and then herself fifty or sixty years later.

"Anna," she mumbled. "Anna and Ann."

The thud of the ferry against the abutment made her wipe away the tears from her cheeks with the back of her hand. If she could only blow her nose, the way Edvard used to do! Just keep on blowing, then everything was cleared out.

I managed it! she thought, and drove off the ferry. Viola was her next thought. *Now you will pass away. Edvard will carry you, just as he carried Viktor.* She suddenly pictured Edvard, felt his hands.

She was exploding with loss and absence, and could only barely steer to the side and stop the car.

I didn't manage it!

The rest of the drive to Uppsala was a reprise of a previous trip many years earlier. That time when everything was over. Convulsively she held on to the steering wheel and guided the car in a headwind toward the southwest.

✦

Nineteen

The uneasiness gave way as he dug. At nine he took a break, put the spade into the ground and sat down on a rickety garden chair that he leaned up against the wall. He had coffee, ate a sandwich, and enjoyed the October sun that had just found its way onto Lundquist's lot.

In front of him was his work, the hole he had excavated. A new grave. To avoid removing the excavated clay soil, he had used it to form a little bow-shaped ridge at the one edge. He had previously carted in lighter, more humus-filled soil, which he tipped into a neat pile on the lawn alongside the excavation.

In the hole he would plant a magnolia, which stood in a garbage bag against the wall. Alongside were three sacks of compost. As ground cover he would use wintergreen, an unimaginative choice perhaps, but a safe bet, hardy and invasive as it was. And he appreciated its blue flowers. The magnolia was a Wada's Memory, one of the best white-blooming varieties. It would all be complemented with a few Himalayan windflowers and, as a companion to the magnolia, the witch alder from the neighbor. He would also dig down a few yellow stars-of-Bethlehem. Spring dominance with an element of sparkling autumn fire, that was the intention.

What a joy it was just to be able to look at his work, and actually be able to touch it. A bus driver had every reason to be proud of his job, his trips, but purely physically there wasn't much to show afterward. A teacher might feel satisfaction when her pupils understood what she was talking about, but there was nothing tangible that testified to her exertions.

A landscaper on the other hand could return to his workplace five, ten, or fifty years later and see that the result of his work was there, a stair, a wall, a horse chestnut, or whatever it was, and many times more magnificent than the design. A stone worn by feet, rain, and wind became lovelier with the years, a striped maple's full beauty did not appear until after a couple of decades.

Whether the magnolia would be alive in fifty years was uncertain, but it would bloom splendidly every spring in any event as long as he himself was alive and certainly many years after.

He thought he heard pounding from the professor's house. A window opened and he saw the elderly woman, whom he assumed was domestic help, hook it fast. She must have a lot to do now, he thought, and let his eyes sweep across the façade with all its windows, eighteen in all and those on only the back side of the house.

His mother had written about how laborious it was to clean all the windows in the house, even if there were several who helped out. Three times a year the ritual had to be gone through. Now it was probably less often, he assumed. They looked gray and shabby.

The thoughts of his mother and thereby the Ohler clan made him uneasy. With a little effort he got on his feet, he was getting more and more stiff. He stared at the massive house, tried to imagine his mother there. In her diaries she had laconically yet vividly described the routines, her coworkers, and the gentry. There was also an element of sensationalism when she described the intrigues and gossip that always arose in a big household. But Karsten did not think that was strange, she had been young and inexperienced.

The notes from the first few months were filled with wonder at the life in Carl von Ohler's home. She described the toilets as if they were marvels and the number of exclamation points when she told how many sheets, crystal glasses, and table settings there were in the house testified to her excitement.

But soon the exclamation points in the diaries would have a different connotation.

Karsten Heller was seized by a desire to see the house from inside. He wanted to walk on the stairs where his mother had walked, see the gigantic bookcases in the library that she so solemnly described, and take a look in the kitchen. But that was impossible. He would never be let in, whatever pretext he resorted to.

He could in principle force his way in, or sneak in. He smiled to himself. Break in but without intention to steal. What could that be classified as? Breaking and entering perhaps?

The woman in the window reminded him of his mother's fate and also made him aware of the continuity. Even today women served at Ohler's, exactly like sixty or seventy years ago, and he wondered how many had come and gone over the years. How many there were who had had experiences similar to his mother.

He had not followed the political squabbling about domestic services and maid's deduction very closely, but after finding his mother's diaries the debate had a different connotation for him. The books were a unique testimony by a woman in the most subordinate position you can imagine and the feeling that he was the one who had to make the text known was growing ever stronger. It would be a contrasting image to the national Nobel Prize frenzy and bombastic tributes. He readily admitted that there was a large measure of desire for revenge in this wish to expose the Ohler family.

He was returned to reality by a signal from his cell phone. It was Roffe from the nursery he usually used who reported that two flats of wintergreen were now ready for pick up. Would twenty-eight plants be enough? He cast a glance across the surface. Since he made the order he had expanded the flower bed by a couple of square meters. Sure, he thought, I'll spread them out, they'll quickly grow together.

It fell into place: the magnolia, perennials, and then the witch alder. He picked up an Ingrid Marie apple and chewed meditatively. He decided to wait for twilight before he went to work.

✦

Twenty

Ann Lindell was on a stroll through her old investigations, that was how she experienced it. She had never seen such a dull period before. The crooks really had taken a fall vacation. She could pick a little absentmindedly at what was now on her desk, including a number of cases that were very well-seasoned. Fortunately the folders were not starting to smell like old cheese; instead they were drying out, shrinking, and sinking deeper and deeper into a dusty forgetfulness. But she had a three-year-old rape in English Park that she could not let go of, even if she realized that the prospects for success were not particularly good.

On the other hand she had a knifing at a bar in the center of town. She ought to do something about that. It looked like a dispute in criminal circles, as the local newspaper called it. The chances of solving the case were moderately good. There was presumably someone out there who would profit from the perpetrator going away for a few years. Perhaps she ought to dig a little more? There was a tip about a Ludwig Ohrman, who should be questioned. She stared at his list of credits. Not a nice guy, she could see that.

She pushed aside his CV and became lost in thoughts about yesterday's outing to Gräsö. It had left a bad taste in her mouth. She regretted not having said goodbye to Edvard. She had been uncertain whether she could cope with a strained good-bye on the farmyard and instead sneaked off with the thought of calling him later. But that did not seem like a good idea either. She simply could not muster the courage. She was afraid of his judgment. Had he put it all behind him, forgiven her? She was also afraid of her own reaction. She did not want a romantic nostalgia trip back in time to destroy everything she had built up with such effort. Edvard was history. Sure, he still had that magnetic influence over her, she had felt it immediately, but now she had a new life to live. Being thrown back several years was not an alternative.

"That's that," she said, and suspected that this was how an old drug abuser must feel when, despite the yearning, he turned down an invitation for a shot. Shaky, but also pleased with himself.

Ludwig Ohrman would have to wait, she decided. It would be Savoy, the café where she had solved a number of troublesome knots, both personal and professional, where she would celebrate with one of their special pastries.

It turned out to be a princess pastry. The marzipan made her smile. Perhaps some experience in childhood. Sometimes when she got to go with her father on his rounds with the beverage truck in the areas around Ödeshög and Vadstena they took a break at some pastry shop. Ann realized in retrospect that what she thought was a generous gesture from her father was not as extravagant as it seemed. They were no doubt treated. He had actually delivered soft drinks in the area for twenty years.

It was unusually peaceful in the café, she was the only customer until an elderly woman laboriously made her way to a table and sat down. After her a teenage girl—a vocational student, Lindell suspected—came with a tray in her hand and set a cup of coffee with a Danish pastry in front of the old woman. There must be at least seventy years between them.

Lindell recognized the old woman. They had met several times at Savoy. She got more and more decrepit every time, but her mind was razor sharp. She had previously related that she had worked as a hydrologist, an uncommon profession for a woman when her career started in the 1940s.

"So now we have a Nobel Prize winner," the woman said suddenly, pointing with a bony finger at the newspaper spread out in front of her.

"Yes, that's nice," said Lindell.

The elderly woman took a bite of her Danish. Flakes rained down on the table.

"Maybe not so nice," she said. "I knew his father," she continued after taking another bite. "He operated on me. Age nineteen. He was skillful, very skillful. Surgeon. Burst appendix."

Lindell nodded. Now she remembered the woman's abrupt way of communicating.

"Good friend of my father. They were in some kind of society during the war. Papa was Scottish. But the son," said the woman, striking her hand against the newspaper, "was a real piece of shit. Even then."

Lindell was a little surprised at her candor and choice of words.

"How is that?"

"It's past the statute of limitations," said the old woman, hacking her dentures pleasurably into the center of the Danish.

Lindell's curiosity was aroused but it was impossible to go further. Two younger women with three children came in and sat down at the only round table in the place, which seemed to have become a gathering place for young mothers in that part of town, a kind of open preschool. A circumstance that Lindell was not particularly amused by.

"Legally anyway," the woman said, wiping her mouth meticulously.

The mothers gave each other an amused look. Lindell suspected that they took the old woman for a senile crone who was talking to herself.

One of the children was spraying orange juice over the floor.

"Is it a good idea for him to pour the juice?" Lindell asked.

"But Willie! You're not allowed to do that," said one of the women, and made no sign of cleaning up after little Wilhelm, but instead continued talking with her girlfriend, while the boy tore a roll to pieces over the table.

Lindell sighed, the old woman likewise. They got up at the same time as if at a given signal and went out together. Lindell was grateful that Linnea Blank, as she now recalled the old woman's name, did not comment on Wilhelm and his mother.

"What you said about it being past the statute of limitations made me curious. You do know that I'm a police officer," said Lindell with a smile.

The woman arranged her coat. Lindell got an impulse to pick off a couple flakes of Danish that were on the collar.

"I had a girlfriend," said Linnea Blank after she had buttoned all the way up. "She went out with Bertram. It was going to come to a sad end. I don't need to say more than that."

"How is that? Did he mistreat her?"

Linnea looked around. Lindell discovered that her one eye was covered with a gray film. Probably she was blind in that eye.

"He was good-looking. Came home in a uniform. This was during the war."

Lindell tried to imagine Bertram von Ohler as good-looking. It didn't work.

"But he was mean," said Linnea. "Now I have to be off. Goodbye! I'm sure we'll meet again soon."

A few years earlier Linnea Blank had been featured in *Upsala Nya Tidning*, Lindell remembered. The article told about a long, exciting career, with assignments in Turkey and India. She had been active besides in the peace movement in the 1950s and later in the struggle against apartheid. As an eighty-year-old she had taken part in the hydrological world congress in Nairobi and given a lecture on the subject "Water and Peace."

Lindell watched her. The judgment on the "Nobel guy," as Sammy called

Ohler, was hard and relentless. Greta had much the same attitude. Had he abused Linnea's girlfriend or simply been "mean" in general?

She got in the car, made a U-turn and took Ringgatan east at high speed. Outside Sverkerskolan she became 2,400 kronor poorer.

✦

Twenty-one

There was life and activity at the Ohler house. Even laughter. When Liisa Lehtonen let out her cackle for the first time Agnes did a double take. It had been a long time. Now she was compelled to leave the kitchen and peek through the chink of the door to the hall.

Hanging wallpaper was clearly a pleasurable job. For the Finnish woman anyway. Birgitta von Ohler was obviously of a different opinion. From the kitchen Agnes could hear her muttering, which sometime rose to more loud-voiced objections. But Birgitta had to accept the consequences. She was the one who had taken the initiative for the renovations. She had managed to convince Bertram with the argument that in any event the first impression of the house should be light.

"Now it feels like stepping into a crypt," she had maintained.

Expressed a little insensitively, thought Agnes, but she silently agreed with her. The old wallpaper must have been hanging for thirty-five years and even when it was new it had not made anyone happy. The pattern was dark leaves of some vague sort, perhaps grapevines, against an even darker background.

Now the hall would be lightened up with a light cream-colored paper with elements of barely visible, light-blue lines. Agnes thought the sight of the heaps of plastic-covered widths and all the working material was almost indecent, a feeling that was hard to explain. Perhaps it was because it had been so long since anything new had been brought into the house. Everything had settled into a quiet rut where she and the professor had become increasingly worn in increasingly worn surroundings. For that reason she perceived Liisa's loud laughter as almost improper, like laughing out loud in a hospital ward of dying patients.

Couldn't they have waited until Bertram died? was Agnes's next blasphemous thought while she sliced leeks. She suspected that it was Birgitta who would take over the house when the professor was gone. She had hinted at something along those lines, and even said that Agnes could go on living in the house as long as she wanted, "no matter what happened." The only thing that could happen was that the old man would drop down and die. Or perhaps it would happen in the opposite order, she'd go first and then the professor?

She sighed heavily, even though she was content cooking for more than just the professor and herself, neither of them particularly interested in food any longer.

As far as she knew he was in the study. He would spend the day answering letters, he said in the morning. But not that many letters had arrived, she thought, that it would take the whole day to write responses. But it's all the same, he kept calm and she could catch her breath a little.

Birgitta's voice from the hall sounded more and more whiny. Agnes thought it was due to fatigue, she had looked out of sorts already that morning, but Liisa had hinted that Birgitta was simply upset that she did not get to accompany her boss to Baltimore, which he had more or less promised her. That would have to be as it was. Birgitta liked leek au gratin and that she would get.

She let go of the thoughts about the family, let the knife work over the cutting board and sliced up the last leek, then greased a casserole dish and noted at the same time that the oven had reached 175 degrees. The leek au gratin was only one of the dishes for lunch. Birgitta had bought mackerel, which Agnes would grill. With that boiled potatoes and a cold sauce with a touch of curry flavoring. A green salad would complement the whole thing.

As she leaned over to put in the casserole she saw the reflection of her face flutter like a shadow in the oven window, and happened to think about Greta. Her sister had called earlier that morning and told about the police-woman's visit and said that she thought Ann Lindell seemed pleasant. Based on the little she had seen, Agnes was prepared to agree.

Greta had reported that Viola was getting steadily worse. She mostly slept and during her waking moments she did not say much. Edvard tried to feed her, but she mostly refused. He had only gotten a little porridge into her.

Agnes understood that it was a matter of days, perhaps hours, before Viola would be gone for good. This pained her. Viola had always been a fixed point, someone to hold on to. During the worst time, after Anna came back, Agnes had secretly gone over to Viola as often as she could.

Her father's fanaticism had taken on an increasingly threatening tone. The sermons in the home were not relieved by the good news from the continent. Not even the end of the war made him dampen his pessimism and Judgment Day prophecies. Then Viola became the rescue for ten-year-old Agnes.

During all of Agnes's teenage years their contact continued and was interrupted only by her move to town in 1953. Viola did all she could to de-christianize Agnes, she understood that completely later on. Or in any case Viola wanted to sweep away the fear of God that she loathed so sincerely. God should be a nice fellow, nothing else, was Viola's opinion. Agnes had been influenced and her father's authority had gradually been undermined.

It could not be denied that sometimes she compared her father Aron to the professor. Their capricious moods and will to dominance were common denominators, likewise their vocal resources—in any event, when the professor was younger.

She had been reconciled with her father. Now Agnes was afraid of neither God nor Bertram von Ohler. He was a piece of meat and bone that staggered around the house, nothing more. The reluctant respect she once felt was completely gone. If anything she felt contempt, sometimes even loathing.

It was Greta who pointed that out, saying something to the effect that now and then Agnes looked at her employer with hate in her eyes. Agnes had indignantly dismissed it, but of course it was that way, although she had a hard time admitting it even to herself.

Hate, she thought, standing by the window toward the back side of the house, was that what made Anna leave the island the second time? She was living with Viola and waiting in vain for her parents to restore her to favor, but they barely noticed their daughter. She might just as well have been on the other side of the globe. After a year Anna left and was never heard from again.

What was it that created these awful emotions? Perhaps Viola knew? Or Greta? But she never said anything about Anna. It was as if she never existed.

The regret at the loss of her sister had always rested like a black clump inside Agnes, and the sorrow at having lost her had increased over the years. What she could not understand was why she should be punished, she was only a child, ten or eleven years old, who loved her sister. Anna could have sent a card, shown that she was not angry at Agnes. But nothing.

Anna had always been the happy one, unlike her sisters not only in terms of appearance but also in her disposition. She was the one who came up with mischief and lightened the mood in the home. Despite her father's protests she could sometimes hum popular songs that she picked up from the radio at her neighbor, perhaps at Viktor's.

In Lundquist's yard the gardener worked on. Now he was pruning lilacs and other bushes. It was about time, thought Agnes, it was drab and dark back there.

Perhaps she should ask him if he could prune the fruit trees? It was a long time since that had been done. The professor would surely have no objections.

Shame! It was shame that drove her parents to such implacability. This idea had occurred to her before, but now it seemed obvious. It was something Liisa had talked about when they were having morning coffee. She had read an article about a mother who kept her mentally disabled daughter locked up in the cellar her whole life. When she was asked why, the only explanation she had given was that she was ashamed of showing her daughter to the outside world.

Shame. Anna had left her position even though Aron Andersson promised that she would serve with Professor Carl von Ohler. That was why he had so quickly sent Greta there as a replacement. You don't disappoint the powers that be, whether they are heavenly or earthly. For that reason Anna had been punished in this cruel way, outlawed from the family. But was that the only reason?

Agnes sighed. She envied the gardener. He stood with a saw in his hand observing his work. She had studied him on several occasions. He always worked alone. Perhaps that was why she felt a certain affinity with him?

Then he suddenly turned around and it looked as if he was staring right toward the kitchen window where she stood. Agnes quickly stepped back.

In order to justify her curiosity—he must have seen her—she decided to exchange a few words with him. She pulled on her boots, hung the old coat over her shoulders, and went out.

She saw that he noticed her at once and set a course toward the corner of the lot. He came up to meet her.

"Excuse me," Agnes began, "I saw that you were outside."

"Yes, I am most of the time," said the man with a smile.

"I was thinking . . . it looks so nice there where you've pruned, and perhaps you might want to look over our overgrown bushes too."

The man let his eyes travel over the professor's yard.

"There are lots of things that are neglected," Agnes continued. "The trees too for that matter."

He had taken off his work gloves and set them up on Bunde's fence. There was something thoughtful in his features. He appeared to hesitate, as if he did not know how he should respond to the offer.

"Maybe you don't have time?"

"Time lives a life of its own," the gardener said.

Agnes stared at him with surprise.

"You don't rule over it," he added.

Agnes shook her head.

"What's the matter?"

He reached out one hand, as if he thought she would fall down over the fence.

"You're as pale as a sheet."

Agnes backed up a couple of steps.

"What did you say?"

"That you're pale."

She turned around and walked quickly back to the house.

✦

Twenty-two

The rear of Ohler's house was in darkness. No lights were on and the many overgrown apple trees effectively blocked the sparse light from the neighboring lots. Only two windows were illuminated, but they were at the other end of the house.

Karsten Haller had changed his mind several times while he waited for it to get dark. He would get up from his hiding place to leave Lundquist's yard and go home, and then sit down again on the upside-down bucket he was using as a chair. It was an idiotic idea, he understood that, but once it had taken hold he had a hard time letting common sense decide.

Now and then he had been startled when an apple fell with a dull thud to the ground. Otherwise it was eerily quiet. Even the organ music from the neighbor had fallen silent.

He pushed aside a few branches in the brushy thicket where he had hidden to keep an eye out. The light in yet another window had been turned off. He looked at his watch. Both the professor and the old housekeeper certainly must go to bed early. He had realized that she was not, as he thought at first, home assistance from outside, but that she lived in the house. He drew that conclusion after their conversation earlier in the day when she offered him work in the professor's garden. What surprised him was her strange reaction to something he had said. She looked as if she had seen a ghost.

An hour ago she had gone around and drawn the curtains in what he thought was the library.

Another half hour, he thought, letting go of the branches. He was very tired. Hungry besides. But since his time in Etosha he was used to sitting for long hours on shift simply biding his time. He had developed a kind of mental technique for sinking into a trance that could be immediately broken when required. He made use of that capability now. He saw and heard but was taking it easy, resting.

What did he want to achieve with his expedition? He had repeatedly asked himself that question, but was not able to give any complete and unambiguous answer. Sure, he wanted to see the environment, the home where his mother worked and which changed her life forever and thereby also affected his, that was true. But curiosity could never be a reason for breaking into another person's residence.

He suspected a deeper motivation. It was a thought that he did not dare let out, not even vaguely formulate into a complete sentence. "Damage"— he had been content to summarize the vague motivation to sneak his way in under cover of darkness. He thought he knew how to conduct himself. Once inside the house he would have to see what that might lead to.

When half an hour had passed he got up, picked up the bolt cutters, left the bushes, and walked quickly over to the fence. He had decided to make his way over to Ohler's by way of the organ man's lot. That maneuver was the riskiest. For a short time he would be visible, with only a currant bush that could partially conceal him. He waited, but everything was calm except for a dog barking in the distance. He quickly climbed over the fence, disappeared crouching behind the bush, then ran a couple of meters and squeezed through the hedge onto the professor's lot.

He caught his breath. Several seconds had passed. He had scratched himself on the face and it stung. It bled a little, but he was not worried about the injury. He was used to such things.

It was perhaps ten meters up to the house. He could move in deep shadow except for where a narrow band of faint light came in from the street. He let his heart quiet down before he made a run for it.

He pressed himself against the wall, slipped carefully up to the cellar access he had aimed for. It was a classic old design with two doors that raised up. Perhaps in the past they had brought in wood and coal this way. An iron rod sat over the doors, secured with a padlock. Cutting open the lock with the powerful bolt cutters was a moment's work. He put it in his pocket and then lifted away the iron rod, opened one door, and slipped down. The stairway was narrow and steep. He listened but heard nothing, then turned on the flashlight which he had covered with a cloth so that it only shone with a thin beam. Along the side of the stairs ran a slide that confirmed his theory that the cellar doors had been an intake for fuel.

The door into the cellar was unlocked. When he opened it he was met by an odor of paint. He let the flashlight play across floor and walls, then took the cloth off the flashlight so he could form an impression of how the room looked. Sure enough, along one wall cans of paints were stacked.

A passage led into the inside of the cellar. On either side openings could be seen. He passed a space that was almost completely filled by an old oil furnace. Next was a spacious laundry room with a large, obsolete semiautomatic washing machine, a couple of stainless-steel rinse tubs and a dryer of a centrifuge type he remembered from his childhood. The laundry room had surely not been used for many years.

He could picture his mother lugging wash back and forth in the passage. She had always been slender, but tough when it came to physical work.

At the far end was a storeroom for old garden furniture and other leftover rubbish and at the end of the passage a door. He opened it and was met by a landscape of furniture, boxes piled on each other, antique trunks and much else. From the ceiling garment bags and chandeliers were hanging. On the opposite wall a stairway led up to a door.

He looked around and quickly determined that he was in luck. All the windows were covered with black paint. He could turn on the lights without anyone seeing from outside. The switch was most likely at the top of the stairs. He made his way there and turned on the lights. The cellar was bathed in a clinical white glow.

Here his mother had undergone an abortion in 1944.

He could spot where the operation occurred. In her diary she described the pipes that ran along the ceiling above the place where it all happened—the rape, the conception, as well as the expulsion of the ten-week-old fetus. Two pipes that ran parallel along the entire long side and the bed had stood where the one pipe suddenly turned off. It all tallied. Perhaps the bed that stood not far from there was the same one? A solid piece of furniture in some kind of dark wood.

It was Bertram von Ohler who committed the rape, but for the abortion he had help from his father, the renowned skillful gynecologist Carl von Ohler, and Bertram had served as his assistant.

Two days later Anna Andersson had turned twenty.

Karsten Haller went down the stairs and collapsed on the bottom step. He wept. Was this what he had wanted to see? Was it the cellar that subconsciously had been his goal?

Suddenly steps were heard that echoed from the house. Karsten got up quickly and took a few steps up the stairs, but realized that he would never make it up in time to turn off the lights. The steps were heard more and more clearly. Instead he ran back down in the cellar and looked around for someplace to hide. The door to the cellar opened and he positioned himself behind some hanging garment bags.

He tried to breathe calmly. The bags smelled of mothballs. He had bumped into one of them and it rocked slowly on its hook. He reached out his hand to stop the movement.

Careful steps were heard from the stairs. In a gap between the bags he glimpsed first a pair of legs, then the trunk, and finally Professor von Ohler's dogged face. He recognized him from the newspaper. Karsten suspected,

considering the strained expression, that the stairs were a worry for the Nobel Prize winner.

Where did the professor intend to go? What was he doing in the cellar?
It did not seem normal, staggering down into a cellar this late. It was past
ten. Karsten peeked out. They were perhaps seven or eight meters from each
other. If Ohler were to turn in behind the massive dining room chairs that
were to the right of Karsten, there was a great risk that he would be discovered. A narrow corridor, surrounded by moving boxes, led straight up to
the hiding place.

The old man shuffled along, supported himself against something and
muttered angrily. He was coming closer and closer. By the chairs he turned
and in doing so came into the corridor. Haller held his breath. What should
he do? Silence the old man and run away? He had an advantage and that
was the element of surprise. True, the cellar was illuminated but with a
quick charge out of the cellar, the same way he had come, the professor
would perhaps not even have time to realize what happened, much less create an impression of the fugitive's appearance.

He would fling himself forward, bump into the old man so that he fell
over the boxes and then take to his heels.

Suddenly the professor stopped. Karsten heard a rattling, metal against
metal. The old man was muttering something again and with his feet dragging went back toward the stairs. It took him a minute to make his way up
to the door. Karsten could see how he rested between every other step and
he heard the labored breathing.

The light was turned off and the door up to the house closed.
Karsten exhaled. The beating of his heart slowed down somewhat. His
armpits and palms were soaked with sweat. The sense of unreality made
him collapse on a trunk. He had found himself perhaps two meters from
his mother's tormentor, the rapist and illegal abortionist Bertram von
Ohler.

What had the old man been doing in the cellar? The whole thing seemed
suspicious. That clanging of metal could mean only one thing: The professor

had left something behind in the cellar, a metal object, most likely a smaller item.

Karsten waited for ten minutes before he once again slipped up the stairs and turned on the lights. He followed the professor's path, turned by the chairs and took the narrow corridor between the boxes, searching with his eyes for an explanation.

In a carton, one tab of which was open, he found the answer. In the bottom of an old can that had once contained a kilo of ground coffee was a sturdy key and two smaller ones, connected with a ring.

Karsten Haller immediately saw where they would lead. To a Hauptmann safe. He had seen a similar set of keys at his uncle's office in Windhoek. Hauptmann was one of the more well-known manufacturers of safes during the interwar period, and according to his uncle the most reliable producer. Karsten recognized the *H* that formed the bit of the key.

According to Uncle Helmuth this was a foolproof safe with triple-locking mechanism made of the most refined Krupp steel.

Karsten fished up the keys and weighed them in his hand. He smiled. *Uncle Helmuth,* he thought, *you and your safe, whose contents you so anxiously guarded: an old revolver, a bundle of South African rand and an even thicker pack of American dollars, the family photos from Germany, and a stack of pornographic pictures. You thought no one knew that you were a relatively rich man and that, despite your racist rhetoric, you had a certain fondness for pictures of young black boys.* But Karsten had figured out where the key was. One day when his uncle was out on the farm in Bero he had opened to check what it was that Helmuth so carefully concealed from the rest of the family.

He chuckled to himself. He now knew how he could injure Ohler. A man who panting and on shaky legs made his way down into the cellar at ten thirty at night, like Uncle Helmuth used to do, had important things in his safe, perhaps secrets. In Ohler's case it was probably not pedophile photos or weapons, but certainly valuable documents and perhaps money.

Where was the safe? Should he make his way up into the house and start searching? He looked at the keys that were in his work glove. Snooping in the cellar was one thing, but sneaking around in the house something else altogether. For such an expedition he must prepare himself better. More flexible gloves, lighter shoes, a smaller flashlight, and a small bag, if he found anything interesting to take with him.

He looked one last time up toward the pipes in the ceiling and carefully put the keys back in the coffee can. He had transformed himself from gardener to burglar. The thought exhilarated him.

✦

Twenty-three

The bank clerk was embarrassed. That was easy for Sammy Nilsson to see, but it did not make him any more kindly disposed.

"You cancelled the loan because Sigvardsson was 'careless'?"

"Could you please tone it down a little?"

"Tone it down? The hell I will! And there's no neglect here, is there? Not in your fine bank accounts, no, no. How much have you embezzled with your so-called good advice? How much has she taken for herself in bonuses, the old witch in management?"

Emanuel Roos was perhaps twenty-five years old. He had certainly encountered dissatisfied and sometimes angry customers, but he had probably never been confronted with a furious policeman, who was spitting out his contempt.

"Perhaps Sigvardsson read about that in the local rag before he shot his wife and himself. Have you ever heard of financial stress?"

Roos nodded eagerly, happy to be able to answer a question affirmatively.

"Then you know that's what you get when you don't have money, don't have a job, and at the same time the bank cancels all of your loans. Do you think the stress goes down when you find out that the same bank is showering its managers with millions of kronor in a bonus program?"

Roos shook his head.

"That you put up with it," said Sammy Nilsson, with contempt in his voice.

"There's not much I can do," Roos objected.

"The best would be if you did as little as possible!"

"I can't possibly—"

"That is your signature." Sammy Nilsson hissed at him, waving a piece of paper.

"We have to follow the regulations."

The policeman stared at the bank clerk, turned on his heels, and left the place in long strides. Lindell, who was taking the opportunity to do some errands in town, had just joined him at the bank, in time to hear the final exchange. She took a breath, sighed, and followed. Sammy Nilsson was waiting for her on the sidewalk.

Lindell did not need to say or ask anything to understand, Sammy had lectured on the way to the bank. It was best to keep quiet, she thought, and followed her colleague.

Sometimes he lost his head. It was as if a fuse blew and then it was hard to get him to calm down. She remembered the investigation when a whole family from Bangladesh was burned inside their home in Svartbäcken, how manic he had become when he had familiarized himself with their background and how work in the textile factories was conducted. The woman had been active in some kind of union and forced to flee from her country, only to fall victim to a racist arsonist. That time Ottosson had been forced to crack down to put an end to Sammy's lectures and aggressive attitude.

He was sitting with his hands on the steering wheel as Lindell got into the car. She shared his indignation but considered it totally meaningless to take out his fury on an individual bank employee. Perhaps it would have happened anyway. Perhaps the letter from the bank had been the triggering factor that made the otherwise sensible garage owner reach for the moose rifle. This did not concern enormous amounts. Another person, in better balance, would probably have tried to find a solution, but for Bo Lennart Sigvardsson this was the last straw.

"Shall we roll?" she said at last.

Sammy started the car.

"Excuse me," he said.

"It's okay," said Lindell.

"Sometimes I get so angry."

"I know. That's why I like you."

He turned his head and looked at her before he put the car in first gear. The car took off.

"You can drive me home," said Lindell. "Anders is supposed to pick Erik up."

"Is it working out?"

Lindell understood that he meant her relationship with Anders Brant. Sammy had followed the drama from close up earlier in the year: the journalist's return home from Brazil and the solving of two murders that Brant was indirectly involved in. He was also the one who supported her when everything fell apart, when she discovered Brant's infidelity.

"It's moving forward," she said.

"A knife wound like that is nothing to fool around with," said Sammy. "It takes time."

"It's in his head too," said Lindell. "There's too much brooding. He's ashamed of it and tries to cheer himself up. It's almost touching. Erik is the one who can really get him going. You should see!"

Sammy smiled. Ann likewise, as much at the thought of coming home as that she had such a colleague and friend.

He dropped her off outside her building. It still felt a little exciting to have a new apartment. She was comfortable, and it was close to most everything. In a different way than before she could go out and have a glass of wine, go to a movie or listen to music at Hijazz or Pub 19. Now it didn't happen that often anyway, but simply the thought that it was possible made life a little lighter and happier.

Before she went home she slipped into the convenience store, picked up a newspaper and some candy for herself. Her increasing desire for sweets worried her a little. Perhaps it was also because she was living with Anders that she had gained weight. She was now eating better, and more, they indulged themselves in good cheese and a lot of other things that obviously had to go somewhere. Anders could put away any amount without it leaving any noticeable traces.

Ann was met by a jubilant son and a somewhat more subdued man. Erik had a lot to tell as usual. He literally bubbled up with information about everything that had happened since they last saw each other. Mostly it was about numbers and all sorts of mathematical questions. Quite unexpectedly, and from Ann's perspective equally incomprehensibly, Erik had developed a passion for numbers and along with it mathematics.

Despite her fatigue she could not help but smile at his eagerness. She was sitting at the kitchen table and behind her back Anders was preparing dinner, while on the other side of the table Erik added, divided, and subtracted at a furious speed. In front of him he had a pad of graph paper and in his hand a pencil. Perhaps it was the absent—and for Erik completely unknown—father who had given his son this math gene? thought Ann. He was an engineer, or at any rate introduced himself as one the only time he and Ann met.

Erik was like a player piano. "That's nice" alternating with "that's interesting" was all she needed to put in. She wondered to herself what Anders thought about the improbable torrent of words, he who always maintained a person's right to silence.

"What's it going to be?" she managed to interject when Erik paused for a few seconds.

"An experiment," Anders answered. "A Turkish dish with ground beef."

"Cabbage rolls?"

"Something along those lines," said Anders, turning around, "but not like Mother's."

"Yummy," said Ann, and smiled at him, but she felt a sting of irritation at being reminded of her mother, even if that had not been his intention.

Her parents constantly gave her a bad conscience. It was now over a year since she visited them in Ödeshög. Her mother's lamentations were becoming increasingly intense. Although she usually phoned once a week, Ann seldom called, and there were basically three recurring subjects: her father's increasing senility, Ann's lack of interest in her parents, and last but not least illnesses and death within their shrinking circle of acquaintances.

Ann sometimes caught herself loathing her own mother. Her father was out of range. He was muddled, had been for a long time, and Ann could no longer be angry at him. Why she felt such antipathy and sometimes outright hatred she did not understand. Her upbringing had not been any more difficult than other people's and she had fled Ödeshög as soon as it was at all possible.

Perhaps it was the lack of joy? Life stood out as so heavy for her mother, as if positive ideas and cheerful memories were forbidden, almost unseemly. For her there was always something negative to latch onto. Ann realized that it was not easy for her mother, caring for a senile person was no story with a happy ending, even if her father was not aggressive like many others with dementia. But her mother's downhearted attitude toward life went back many years, long before her husband became confused and sick.

One reason for Ann's irritation and disinclination to visit her parents was that she recognized herself in her mother. It was hard to admit that to herself but, yes, she too had this trait of despondency and pessimism inside her. An inheritance she would have happily done without.

She did everything to struggle against this personality trait, kept an eye on herself, was aware of the signals for approaching melancholy and destructiveness. It was a struggle, but for the first time in many years she felt she had a proper advantage in the match. Erik, young as he was, was a great help. She did not understand how she would have managed through the difficult time without him. And now Anders, who loved her. She wanted to believe that, she wanted to believe in his quiet assurances.

Perhaps she was the one who could break *his* scourge. She thought so sometimes, when the helpless, tormented face he had worn since his return gave way to the smile that made him beautiful, charming, and active.

For active he could be, both when they made love and when he discussed the state of things in the world.

She shook off these thoughts. Erik had given up and left the kitchen without her noticing. Ann told about the Nobel Prize winner, tried to give a picture of the block in Kåbo where everyone seemed to be lying in wait for each other, and emphasized the comic aspects.

Anders sat down across from her. She pulled his hand to her, picked off a bit of onion skin that was caught on his wrist, and then looked him in the eyes.

"I like you very much," she said.

He smiled and got that embarrassed look. She held his eyes, did not let him get away. Now she was strong.

"I like you," she repeated.

He swallowed. *Say that you love me,* she thought. Now she was weak. A minute passed.

"The cabbage rolls," he said, pulling back his hand and getting up from the table.

Ann felt a chill spread through her body, the ice-cold of uncertainty that mercilessly brushed aside joy and hope.

But before Anders put the pan in the oven he burrowed his face into the back of her neck and hair and put his arms around her. He mumbled something that Ann could not make out. But that didn't matter.

✦

Twenty-four

Liisa Lehtonen and Birgitta von Ohler had returned to finish the wallpapering. Agnes had to admit that it seemed to be turning out very nicely. The hall looked more inviting. The professor had mumbled something inaudible before he disappeared into his study. The three women took that as approval.

Liisa was the one in command, she was happy to give orders and took for granted that her opinion should prevail as indisputable. It was a character trait that Agnes had great difficulty with. She was actually accustomed to the professor's manner, but thought it was somehow unbecoming in a woman who in such an obvious, almost physical way took the initiative and kept it.

Perhaps it was Birgitta's complaisance that irritated Agnes most. Birgitta who otherwise held her ground well simply acted wishy-washy, though for what reason Agnes did not comprehend. The Finnish woman was not that terrifying. Besides, it was Ohler's house, so she ought to be a little more respectful, Agnes thought.

She sat down on a chair and listened distractedly to the discussion—perhaps they should take the opportunity to move the furniture in the hall too? She was tired. The night had been difficult. The aches in her hip had tormented her. In addition, the thoughts about the gardener circled like a restless nocturnal bird in her head. The statement he had made about time—that it lives a life of its own and that you cannot rule over it—had shaken her up considerably. It was more than sixty years since she last heard that expression. It was Anna who said it. She often used it to describe how small people were; in any case that was how Agnes understood it, that people did not rule over their own fate.

Her father had heard her say it once and got angry. For him such vague expressions of human wisdom were completely reprehensible. It was God who ruled in everything, over time as well, therefore it could not live a life of its own. It was perhaps due to her father's fury that Agnes remembered the whole thing so well. Where Anna got the expression from she did not know. Perhaps from Viola, who was full of proverbs and sayings? Or perhaps from Viktor?

It might be a coincidence that the gardener used that particular expression. But Agnes did not believe in chance. Perhaps he was from Roslagen, even Gräsö? Or perhaps the saying was more common than she had thought. Speculating about time was a very human trait.

No matter how that was, she felt ill at ease. Was it the memory of Aron's indignation, her terror in the presence of his anger and God's wrath that called forth the uneasiness? He had thundered in her childhood, not least over Anna's lack of faith, how she deserted the Ohler house and thereby brought shame on her parental home.

Thoughts of Anna had always come and gone. The absence and uncertainty had often been hard to endure. She and Greta never discussed the fact that they had not heard from their sister in more than half a century. What had become of her? Was she still alive?

Could she go over again and ask the gardener a direct question, whether he possibly came from Gräsö? No, that would seem impertinent. It would be better to inquire through Associate Professor Johansson. She knew him and harbored great respect for him. He was upright, as her father Aron would have said. The associate professor would take her question the right way, not as a sign of curiosity or desire to snoop.

"What do you think, Agnes?" the Finnish woman interrupted her musings.

Liisa Lehtonen was standing by the old dresser, measuring its width with her hands.

"It will be fine," said Agnes. "You decide."

She got up laboriously from the chair.

"I think I have to go down to the pharmacy," she said.

Birgitta looked at her inquisitively.

"The professor's prescription," Agnes clarified. "And then I need a few pain tablets."

"Do you have aches?"

Yes, what do you think, was on the tip of Agnes's tongue but she only nodded. Birgitta came up to her. She was dressed in a yellow overall and had tied a scarf around her head.

She put on a worried face, but Agnes suspected that Birgitta mostly saw an opportunity to interrupt Liisa's lesson in interior decorating.

"It's the usual," said Agnes. "No worries."

"Do you want me to drive you into town?"

"No, not at all. I also need to go down to Luthagen and order a little meat."

"You can call," said Birgitta.

"It's not the same," said Agnes. "I want to talk with Jansson himself."

In reality she wanted to get out of the house for a while, get some air and shake off the increasing feeling of discomfort of the past few days. Take the opportunity to steal a little extra time for herself now when the professor was taken care of. Perhaps walk a little in town, have a cup of coffee at Landings?

Birgitta smiled at her. *She is probably the only one besides Greta who is going to miss me,* thought Agnes, but despite that she could not rouse the old feeling of sympathy. Not even when Birgitta put her arm around her and insisted that she would really like to drive Agnes into town, that it was no trouble at all.

"I've made lunch," said Agnes. "All you need to do is warm it up a little. The salad is in the refrigerator."

As usual there was always duty to resort to when Birgitta got too affectionate. It amused her, because she knew that Birgitta always felt a little discomfort at being taken care of, above all in the presence of others. She preferred to present herself as equal with Agnes and became overly considerate.

Birgitta looked hurt. Liisa Lehtonen urged them on, the last few widths had to be put up. Agnes left the two of them, went upstairs to put on something warm and get her handbag.

She saw him immediately. He was raking leaves. Agnes could not help but smile. The associate professor's leaf raking was legendary in the neighborhood. He had once explained to her how valuable leaves are, how they promoted growth. She believed him. His garden was the evidence.

As she approached he straightened up a little and Agnes was convinced that if he had been wearing a hat he would have raised it in a stylish gesture.

"Taking a walk?" he said in an inquisitive tone.

Agnes stopped. He came up to the fence.

"I just have a few errands. And it's so nice to get out a little."

They chatted awhile about this and that, commented on how terrifying earthquakes are—thousands of people had died somewhere in Asia the day before—but both carefully avoided mentioning anything about the professor.

"I've been thinking about the garden," she said when they had both fallen silent. "It's starting to look too dreary. Lundquist has had help and I exchanged a few words with the gardener. What do you think about him, can he be trusted? You can judge such things."

"I definitely think so," the associate professor testified. "He seems serious."

"Do you know who he is? I thought he seemed so familiar."

"No," said the associate professor. "I've never met him before."

"Perhaps he's from along the coast?"

"No idea," said the associate professor. "We've only talked a few times, but I immediately got the impression that he knows his business."

"Hardworking too," said Agnes in order to round off and conclude the question in a kind of harmony, something that she and the associate professor always seemed to achieve when they spoke.

The associate professor nodded and smiled. They parted and Agnes walked toward Norbyvägen to take the bus into town.

During the walk she decided to actually ask the gardener if he came from the coast. The decision revived her. True, the week had been full of gloomy thoughts but also involved a growing sense of energy. It was as if the professor's awakening from his static existence meant that she too found new ways of thinking about old ideas. The statement, so shocking to the professor, that she was going to retire was not just a loosely tossed out thought but a manifestation of how a slumbering idea had taken firmer form.

Now the thought of leaving her position and moving back to the island did not seem quite as unreal. After fifty-five years she could not, like Anna, be accused of faithlessness if she left the Ohler house, could she?

The bus came and she got on. It was the calm driver, the one who always waited until she sat down before he started up again. She smiled at him.

Agnes felt uncommonly satisfied, as if her thoughts were freed after years of constraint. It felt as if she was sitting in bus number 811 en route to the rock at Tall-Anna's. There she would get off, thank the driver for their final trip together, and start the laborious ascent.

✦

Twenty-five

All the tools were at the site, he would not be picking up any more material during the day and therefore he could leave the car at home. But the main reason he took the bicycle was that it was not a good idea to leave his car parked on the street in front of Lundquist's house during the evening. The neighbors would surely wonder what the gardener was doing there so late.

To be on the safe side he took the bicycle with him to the back side of the house and pushed it in between a couple of bushes.

Now the only thing to do was wait for darkness. He sat in the same spot as before, in some bushes he had waited to prune. In his pockets he had a flashlight, rubber gloves, and a black garbage bag, running shoes on his feet. He was prepared. He smiled to himself, pleased at his own initiative.

He was also forced to hurry, because if he had understood Lundquist correctly he would be returning to Uppsala in three days. And then the opportunity disappeared to have the bushes as a base for excursions into enemy territory. That was how he perceived it: He was entering the enemy country.

The night before he had browsed in his mother's diaries to refresh his memory and strengthen himself. He was not really clear what the purpose of a second break-in was, other than to search for the safe. For nostalgic reasons he wanted to see one like it again, but above all to investigate what it contained.

But this lack of structure did not worry him, it would sort itself out. Once inside the house a kind of dynamic would arise and decisions would stand out as obvious. The starting point was "injury." Revenge, if you will. That was a word he was not unfamiliar with.

"Anna," he whispered, "you should see me now."

He was amused by the thought that she was observing him from her heaven. He was not convinced that his mother would be that enthusiastic about his idea. On the contrary, she would be terrified.

He thought something rustled and turned his head. His eyes fixed on the bicycle and he happened to think of his father. His father never got a driver's license, but instead always bicycled to his job at Barnängen's soap factory in Alvik on the outskirts of Stockholm. For many years he was responsible for two old-fashioned machines that spit out small hotel soaps.

The rustling returned. He guessed that it was a blackbird and smiled to himself. Blackbird and him, two figures in the late evening.

Right after ten o'clock he got up, massaged the stiff muscles in his thigh and peered out into the darkness. There were lights on in more windows than yesterday evening, but everything seemed equally calm. Kåbo had settled down to rest.

The sound of a car was heard at a distance, perhaps as far as away as on Norbyvägen. The blue-hued light from the associate professor's tower cast a ghost-like glow over the neighbor's house and backyard.

Perhaps it was this, the Etosha tension—he could find no better way to put it—that was the driving force? Able to remain stock-still, listen, sniff like an animal in the wind, try to understand what was happening right then, patiently waiting out everything that could constitute a threat or obstacle, be the one who made the wisest decision, to strike or get away. Survive. He pushed aside the branches soundlessly and scouted one last time before he took off.

After a few seconds he was at the cellar entrance, opened the door enough that he could slink in and close it soundlessly behind him. He took a deep breath to free himself from the tension.

Once down in the cellar he let the flashlight play across the furniture and everything else that stood in an unorganized mess. He realized that it was the combined excess of generations that was down there. Much of it was probably old and useless while some was certainly antique and valuable. He withstood the impulse to start poking around—he had loved to stroll around at the market on Windhoek Platz to search for pearls in a sea of junk and scrap—and instead went immediately to the passage with all the boxes to check whether the keys were there.

He grinned as he picked up the key ring. Then he suddenly became thoughtful. The first time he broke into the cellar could be explained by curiosity, but now he was taking a step over a boundary that could not be explained away as an innocent visit.

"Well, what of it?" he mumbled, in an attempt to reinforce the feeling that he was morally superior to the owner of the house, that a break-in was a trifle in relation to the crimes that had been committed here earlier.

He sat down on an old armchair, turned off the flashlight, and prepared to wait. He had decided to make his way up into the house right after midnight.

It was pitch-black but that did not worry him. While others were afraid of the dark and saw various imagined dangers in the deep shadows, the deep night also constituted a shield for him.

Miss Elly had sometimes called him "the cat" for his capacity to smoothly move in darkness. He understood that it was a compliment. In reality it was one of the reasons that she loved him, that apparently he melted in unimpeded with the African reality.

With his thoughts in Africa he fell asleep and woke up with a start, for a moment unaware of where he was. He turned on the flashlight, looked at his watch, and discovered that he had slept for almost two hours.

The house was silent. The stairs creaked slightly. The tension increased with every step. It struck him that perhaps the door was locked but he exhaled when it opened without difficulty. He turned off the flashlight and peeked out. He had come up into the house under a stairway.

In the pale light from the street the details gradually emerged in what he understood was the hall. As long as he stayed on the ground floor he certainly did not need to be worried. He assumed that the bedrooms were one flight up. With cautious steps he opened the first door, one of four in the hall. A long passage stretched out ahead of him. He realized now that the house was considerably larger than he thought. He did not dare turn on the flashlight for fear that the light could be seen from outside.

After ten minutes he found the Hauptmann safe squeezed into a corner behind the last door in the corridor. In the middle of the room was a billiard table. There was a twinge of excitement when he saw that the safe was the same model as his uncle's. Karsten remembered the numbers 51 so well, embossed in the middle of the trademark that decorated the sturdy door of the safe.

He took out the keys. He remembered the order, first the middle one, then the small key down to the left and finally the big one in the centrally located lock. It creaked as he turned the last key. Uncle Helmuth never would have tolerated such a racket, he thought.

After very slowly opening the door, careful not to create the slightest commotion, he turned on the flashlight and shone it into the safe. On the top shelf, where Helmuth stored the pictures of young black boys, a half dozen folders were stacked. As he reached out his hand to take out the top one a sound was suddenly heard from the top floor. He froze and instinctively turned off the flashlight.

The sound of steps was transmitted and Karsten Heller got the feeling that the ceiling was vibrating. He peeked upward. The sound decreased. He waited on tenterhooks. Was someone on their way down? Half a minute passed. A minute. He carefully wiped the sweat from his forehead. The odor of the rubber glove nauseated him. He suddenly regretted his outing.

Then came the reassuring explanation: a toilet flushed and there was a roar for several seconds in a pipe invisible to Karsten. He had to suppress a laugh of relief and turned on the flashlight again. He realized that either the professor or the housekeeper had relieved their bladder and now were on their way back to bed.

Close, he thought, but still not. He put the flashlight in his mouth to have both hands free and lifted down all the folders. He put them on the billiard table, retrieved a chair, and sat down.

The topmost folder was of no interest. He quickly browsed through the papers, a number of them yellow with age, and found that they all dealt with an association he had never heard of, the Gregorious Brothers. Probably a fraternal order.

The following folders were equally uninteresting. There were various documents from University Hospital, deeds of conveyance, contracts and so on.

He started to despair of finding anything exciting when from the sixth and final folder he pulled out a will. He quickly browsed through it and as good as immediately saw his mother's maiden name. "Anna Andersson" it said, clear and obvious. He was forced to set the will aside a moment.

He took the flashlight out of his mouth, looked around and discovered a flower pot with a sadly neglected hibiscus, got up and spit out the saliva that had collected in his mouth.

What was he to believe? Perhaps it was another Anna Andersson? It was not exactly an uncommon name. There was only one way to find out, to read on, regardless of where it might lead.

He found the section again and read: "To Miss Anna Andersson, who was in service in the house for a few years in the nineteen forties, I bequest 100,000 (one hundred thousand) kronor."

It was immediately clear to him that he would inherit from Professor von Ohler.

His surprise was no less when he read the continuation: "To Miss Greta

Andersson I bequeath 200,000 (two hundred thousand) kronor. To Miss Agnes Andersson, number three in the group of sisters and whose time of service now exceeds fifty years, I bequest 300,000 (three hundred thousand) kronor."

And right after that the parting shot: "Should I survive one or all of the misses Andersson, then the respective amounts return to the estate."

Now the inheritance was not as obvious, but what surprised him the most was the word "now." That meant reasonably that the woman he had seen working in the house was this Agnes Anderson, "number three in the group of sisters." In other words, she was his aunt!

He checked when the will was drawn up and found that it was only two days old.

For a long time he sat staring into space. He could have expected anything at all, but not this. He had been given a family.

He read the will again, determined that the amounts Ohler bequeathed to the Andersson sisters were an insignificant fraction of what he owned in total in properties, securities, and cash bank deposits. This was shown by the appendices that were attached to the will. A major item among the agricultural properties was a farm outside Eslöv, which the Ohlers had apparently rented out since the early 1900s to the same farm family. Bertram von Ohler was determined that this would also apply in the future.

But there were also other farms mentioned, including half a dozen in eastern Småland and two in the areas around Bålsta.

The shares were distributed among some two dozen Swedish companies. The largest individual entry was in Alfa Laval with 180,000 shares, but the holdings in SKF, Handelsbanken, various pharmaceutical manufacturers, and forestry companies were also significant. The strangest information was a fifty-percent ownership of a car garage in Nybro, Johansson Brothers Welding and Forging.

A numbing enumeration of companies and figures. Page up and page down that testified to a financial power that was hard to imagine. This was no chance lottery winning but instead columns of riches that had accumulated over many years, perhaps centuries, Karsten Heller suspected.

He was dispirited, melancholy in a way that he did not completely understand. Not just at the discovery that extraordinarily enough his mother was mentioned but rather over the massive weight that the will expressed. There was no mercy, that was how he experienced it. Pure and sheer power. How could you object to such wealth? It stood out as a massive colossus of granite, obvious and imperturbable. The Ohler family had succeeded, to put it simply. To oppose it was to air your envy, nothing else.

He gathered up the papers into a package, not caring whether they were in the right order, pushed it all down into the folder and nonchalantly tossed it into the safe. The remaining contents he had not been concerned with so far, but now he crouched down to investigate what was on the other shelves. He picked a little absentmindedly for a while in the piles of papers, which appeared to be letters. But under everything he glimpsed something that he recognized from his uncle's safe: bills. In a shoebox were bundles of five-hundred-kronor notes, held together by rubber bands. He rooted in the box and picked up a bundle.

Money doesn't smell, it was said, but that wasn't quite true—Karsten remembered the story about the hotel in San Francisco that washed and ironed the guests' currency—the professor's money smelled greasy and musty.

There must be a dozen bundles. Half a fortune, all in five-hundred-kronor notes. He wondered how much it could be, surely half a million, maybe more.

He pocketed the bundle without really thinking about it, then got up, numbed by all the wealth and not least by the will. He closed the safe.

A hundred thousand kronor his mother would have gotten. That was the amount that Ohler thought was suitable to pay for a ruined life. She had never really recovered from the rape. It was not about forgiveness, Karsten understood that when he read her diaries. Sure, you could try to forgive even the cruelest actions, but the wound was so deep that it could never possibly heal. His mother had been deprived of so much, not only her virginity, but above all a kind of faith in the future. She had always, as long as Karsten could remember, lacked faith in herself, always expressed an anxious worry that perhaps things wouldn't go well, that any temporary happiness sooner or later would be ended.

He only realized now that the reason for her anxiety perhaps had its background in what played out in Ohler's cellar in 1944. While she was alive he had often been irritated at her vacillation and nervousness. Now he regretted that deeply. If he had only known!

She had never recovered from the loss of the fetus either, even though it was the result of an assault. She had written something about that: "It was my chance to have a child of my own." Those were words that hurt. In his late teens Karsten found out that Anna was not his biological mother. It had been a cataclysmic piece of news but still did not constitute a terrifying shock. He had always felt surrounded by Anna's and Horst's love and concern, so the message did not basically disturb his trust in them. At the same time his parents told him that Anna had adopted him.

When he read the diaries and his mother's words about "a child of my own" he had been angry and heartbroken to begin with, but gradually the anger had subsided. He understood her longing and boundless despair that the abortion also made her sterile. In reality the circumstances enlarged the image of his mother as the considerate and loving person she had always been. She had never uttered even the slightest little comment that could have made him feel sidelined or a kind of substitute for a "real" child.

He leaned his head against the safe, whose steel was not cool. On the contrary, it burned his forehead.

One hundred thousand kronor for a rape. A domestic servant's virginity, future life, and peace of mind.

Anna Andersson. Anna Haller. Raped, dead, and buried.

Someone called, woke him out of his daze. It was Miss Elly, his companion. She was calling as usual for justice. He raised his head, looked up toward the ceiling, burrowing his gaze through the brown-stained paneling and screamed with Miss Elly.

He started going like a warrior through the house, firmly determined to administer justice, but stopped suddenly when he came out in the hall. It was too simple to kill the professor, it struck him. He wanted to create greater damage than that. Then the old man could die in shame and disgrace.

Perhaps it was the thought that he had been given an aunt, perhaps two, that made him calm down. They could fill out his mother's life story about her childhood and youth, a period in her life she never talked about.

The return through the cellar out into the fresh air went quickly. He was no longer afraid of being seen, whether from inside the house or by the neighbors. *What of it,* he thought rashly, *I'm the one who's sitting with the strong cards.*

He jumped over the fence, took his bicycle, pulled it out onto the street, and disappeared from the block.

✦

Twenty-six

It was with mixed emotions Agnes noted that Birgitta and Liisa Lehtonen had decided to spend the night in the house. After finishing the wallpapering they shared a couple bottles of wine and then decided to continue the renovation work the following day.

Cleaning and mess—dust and garbage to take care of—Agnes had thought the evening before, but now at the breakfast table having the two women there felt refreshing. The Finnish woman was in an unusually good mood besides and entertained the others with hilarious episodes from the time she was active as a competitive shooter.

The professor preferred to have breakfast in the dining room and had then withdrawn to his study.

"Did you hear all the commotion last night?" asked Birgitta. "Were you the one who was up?"

She looked with a curious expression at Agnes, who realized that Birgitta saw a chance to ventilate her theories about night sleep, the position of the planets, and inner harmony. Agnes denied having left her bed.

"I usually sleep like a log," she said. "You know that."

"And then someone screamed," said Birgitta. "But that was probably Daddy having a nightmare."

Agnes had also heard the scream but was convinced it was not the professor, the scream had come from the ground floor. She thought Birgitta and Liisa had quarreled, and fell back asleep almost immediately.

"Maybe it was a ghost," Liisa suggested. "Strange things do happen here in the house. And probably always have. What was his name, that chauffeur who worked here long ago that we saw a year or so ago?"

"I don't remember," said Birgitta.

"Don't be that way, of course you remember!"

Birgitta shook her head.

"What was it? Something short, like Malm or Berg," Liisa forged ahead. "Maybe we can ask Bertram? He must know."

"Wiik," said Birgitta.

"That's it!" Liisa exclaimed. "He maintained that you could hear someone sighing and moaning in the cellar."

Agnes saw that Birgitta was becoming more and more irritated.

"What was that?" she asked.

"It was before your time," said Birgitta, "and the old man was ancient and gaga when we saw him."

"I think he was as clear as anything," said Liisa with an unconcerned expression. "He maintained that awful things had happened in the house."

"Talk," Birgitta said.

Now there was not just irritation but also discomfort in her face.

"When was that?" asked Agnes.

"During the war," said Liisa. "He claimed that he was fired by the old Ohler. That he knew about things that—"

"Stop now!" Birgitta screamed suddenly and started sobbing. "I don't want to hear a rehash of untrue old rumors. It's enough with all the new untruths."

"What do you mean?"

Liisa's voice sounded unusually melodic. Agnes sensed the breakdown. From a pleasant conversation at the kitchen table to a stormy quarrel. She had experienced it before. There was something in the Finnish woman's voice that called forth these recurring eruptions.

But this time Birgitta's customary vehement reaction and the accompanying escalated dispute did not appear. Instead she leaned her head in her hands and Liisa mumbled something that could be understood as an apology.

Agnes had listened to and observed it all with increasing astonishment. She had never heard mention of any Wiik who might have worked in the house. Whatever the story was about, untruthful rumors or not, they must have been buried deep in the hidden chambers of the house. Rumors had a habit of propagating among the employees, sometimes for generations. There were few circumstances that the servants did not know about. Here was evidently a case that had been effectively hushed up. Agnes understood that it meant several things: The rumor was completely or at least mainly true; it concerned something sensational; and the servants had been properly frightened and certainly warned. Her coworkers during the early 1950s, who surely would have known who Wiik was, had kept their mouths shut, probably out of fear of losing their positions.

It struck Agnes that perhaps it was about homosexuality. Did the old professor have a relationship with Wiik, perhaps exploit him? That could explain the Finnish woman's hectoring—she loved to mercilessly swoop down on all forms of double standards and fear of deviant sexual behavior. Agnes had been astonished many times at her frankness.

But now Liisa too fell silent, surely out of consideration for Birgitta, who calmed down and wiped away the tears with the back of one hand. The other hand held Liisa's.

Agnes got up from the table and started clearing. Experience told her that the two women would withdraw for a while. That was not something she had an opinion about any longer.

"We're going to rest a little," said Birgitta.

The two women left the kitchen. They could at least say thank you, thought Agnes, but more out of old habit than because she was actually displeased. Nor did the fact that they disappeared to "rest" right after breakfast surprise her.

She picked up and did the dishes at the same time as she kept an eye on whether the gardener would show up. Perhaps he was working on the front side of Lundquist's lot? She had become more and more curious about the man, although the connection to Anna was too vague for words. A saying, a few words, no more than that. But still, the uncertainty about who he was and where he came from was there, and it worried her more than she wanted to admit to herself.

The house was silent. She recalled a time when there was life and movement. Birgitta and her friends especially could make a racket. And then Dagmar, "the professor's wife," as she was called by the employees, she could also live it up so that it resounded in the whole house. Above all when the drinking started getting more serious. At night Agnes could sometimes hear her tripping across the floor, the sound of the liquor cabinet being opened, then a short silence—when Agnes could imagine how Dagmar was bringing the bottle to her mouth and taking a few swallows—followed by a contented "ahh." And then the tripping back to the bedroom. Sometimes she vomited early in the morning. Agnes was always the one who had to tidy up.

Strangely enough the professor never realized the extent of his wife's boozing, but on the other hand there was a lot at that time that he didn't notice. He lived for his research, showing his family and home only a preoccupied, duty-bound interest.

Everyone knew that he was unfaithful. There was talk of a younger woman who worked at the hospital whom he, like an old-fashioned benefactor, supported with an apartment and certainly other things too. Agnes suspected that his trips to Italy did not have that much to do with his work but instead were outings together with his mistress, or "the piece" as the cook called her.

Dagmar was deeply unhappy. Everyone in the household realized that, but no one actually showed any pity on her. The professor's wife took out her frustration on the servants, she was spiteful and unfair. The professor could be obstinate and really mean.

Their quarrels poisoned existence for everyone. When Dagmar died after a heart attack, Palmér, who used to come and potter around in the garden, adjust the furnace, and take care of other practical tasks, summed up everyone's opinion when he said, "It was probably all for the best that she was called home" and made a gesture with his hand to show in which direction he thought that Dagmar von Ohler's new "home" was.

She was written out of the story with ease and with relief, but so many years later Agnes was prepared to partly reconsider her judgment of Dagmar. She was probably driven to drinking and ill temper. Agnes could also recall a considerably more obliging and friendly woman.

Why these mental outings back in time? It only made her depressed and slowed her down. But was it perhaps her own departure, her own "calling home" that was approaching, and which therefore evoked this review of memories? She needed to melt down all her recollections, all the fifty-five years in service, into a manageable clump, in order to be able to take bus 811.

She would get off at the state liquor store in Öregrund, buy a bottle of liqueur of the kind she knew Greta drank in secret, then go down the hill by the ICA grocery store, past the square and the loathsome snack bars that were housed in the old boathouses, to come at last to the ferry landing. From the ferry she would dump the black clump in the water and see how it disappeared in the depths.

This time there would be no Fredell that she could share the transit with, and at Lidbäck's no old mare would be standing there to talk to. But everything would be the same. She would walk home at a calm pace, this time without getting pneumonia.

She was going home! Home to Gräsön! It was like a revelation. She smiled to herself and automatically ran the dishcloth over the already shining counter, while she looked out into the garden. The few apples that were still hanging in the trees rocked alarmingly vehemently in the strong wind. It was a pity if the fruit were to go to waste so she decided to pick the last ones and make a few more apple cakes. One they could have today and the rest could be frozen. Those the professor could chew on in his solitude, she thought, with a tingling sense of mischief.

✦

Twenty-seven

The phone call came at the same time as before, right after the morning meeting. Edvard Risberg had learned when there was a point in calling if you wanted to get hold of her.

"Hi, I just wanted to say that Viola is dying," were his introductory words.

He had never had the talent for softening his messages. Ann Lindell sank down on her chair but sat up just as quickly again.

"Is it that bad?"

"Yes," answered Edvard.

His voice testified to great fatigue.

"I'm coming," she said, and ended the call.

She went into Ottosson's office and reported that she was going to drive to Gräsö. He looked up from some papers on the desk, mutely gave his approval by nodding and waving his hand. She had not expected any objections either and was already on her way out of the room.

Fortunately she had taken the car to work and was out on the street after only a couple of minutes. *I don't care if I get another ticket,* she thought, and put on the gas as she turned out on Vaksalagatan and headed for the coast.

But at Jälla she slowed down anyway, her associates were usually there, she knew that. She passed the towns one after another: Rasbo, Alunda, Gimo and Hökhuvud, at Börstil she turned left and passed the exit to Östhammar exactly thirty-two minutes after she had left the city behind her. Then it was six minutes to the turnoff toward Öregrund—she had always hated the speed limit at Norrskedika—and from there it was just as long to Öregrund and the ferry.

"That was quick," Edvard noted when he opened the door.

In daylight he looked more worn-out. Keeping watch by Viola's bed was probably a factor, she thought.

"She's awake."

Ann nodded and withstood the impulse to hug him. Like the time before he turned around without ceremony and disappeared into the corridor toward Viola's bedroom. Ann followed in his wake, steeling herself for what was waiting. In the corner of her eye she glimpsed Greta in the kitchen.

Viola was now, if possible, even thinner. She raised one hand in welcome. Or else it was to shoo Edvard out, because he immediately left the room and closed the door behind him.

"Shaky," she said in a hoarse voice, as Ann sat down by the edge of the bed.

Ann nodded and took Viola's hand in hers. All that was heard was the wind that howled around the house and made the thin curtains slowly shake.

"I'm pleased and content," said Viola suddenly, "and everything will be fine with the house."

Ann nodded and thought she understood what Viola meant. She had lived a long life and Edvard would stay on in the house. Perhaps one of his two sons would take over after him, something the old woman had mentioned long ago. Ann knew that Viola loathed the thought that the house would be torn down or taken over by summer visitors.

"It was lucky that Edvard showed up," said Ann.

"He has been a great joy to me. He and Viktor."

For the first time ever Ann heard how Viola's voice broke with emotion and she had a hard time holding back the tears.

"I'm the oldest person on the island, I've seen people come and go. Had my health. So I can't complain."

"But you have complained," said Ann with a smile. "You've complained about the hens, about Stockholmers and the chimney-sweep, the weather, the shopkeeper in Öregrund, the Road Administration, and God knows what else."

"You have to have a little fun," said Viola. "Greta has promised to look after Edvard a little. He's sensitive."

"He'll manage," Ann assured her.

"Of course he'll manage," Viola hissed, "but it can be good to talk with someone sometimes."

Ann understood that Viola had instructed Greta to go over to see Edvard occasionally. What he would think about that was uncertain.

"You can come and visit too. He needs company."

Ann wondered about Viola's comment, her words about Edvard's "sensitivity"—did that mean he wasn't doing well? Or was it a way to try to put her together with Edvard?

"Maybe I'll do that," she said.

"I think a little sea air will do you good."

Ann simply nodded, disinclined to continue on the present track. And it was as if Viola understood that, because after a few moments of silence she changed subject.

"Another thing," she said. "About Anna. I heard that Greta and you had talked. Anna Andersson came to me. It was at the end of the war, but I was doing pretty well. Perhaps you don't know it, but at that time Viktor smuggled quite a bit and I kept the books, you might say. He was never good at numbers. And then he was too nice. So Anna was here, her parents didn't want to hear about her. Shameful, but that's the way it was."

Now it was as if the old Viola had returned. The shaky voice was gone and her eyes shone like before.

"She was bleeding when she came. I wanted to bring Åkerman here, the doctor from the mainland, but that was not to be discussed. She bled for a week."

Ann sensed where Anna Andersson was bleeding from but asked anyway to be a hundred-percent sure. Viola told that Anna was trying to hide the bloody sanitary napkins but it was futile for her to try to hide her miserable condition.

"The girl was scared to death. She knew nothing about life and her own body. And it's clear, with those parents who believed in the immaculate conception, she was poorly prepared. I forced her to eat food made from animal blood. Viktor had to butcher. He did not ask but surely understood what the girl needed. That's how it was then! Now you know how things were in those fine families."

"What happened?"

"Anna never wanted to tell and when someone doesn't want to talk of their own free will you shouldn't force them. What has to come out will come out in time. The main thing then was that she got healthy and strong. Right?"

Ann nodded, but in her mind she could not keep from speculating about what had happened.

"What is so strange—"

"Yes!" exclaimed Viola, as if she had read Ann's thoughts. "Greta went to town and that riffraff. And then Agnes. Anna was very unhappy when Greta left. Her sister was just a girl-child."

The "girl-child" was now sitting in the kitchen. She must have turned on the coffeemaker, because it was starting to smell like coffee.

"What happened to Anna?"

Viola did not answer immediately but instead seemed submerged in thoughts about what had happened more than sixty years ago, or else she had simply used up the last of her strength. Ann was getting increasingly worried.

"How are you? Do you want to rest a little?"

"Rest," the old woman hissed. "No, I don't want to rest."

"What happened to Anna?" Ann repeated.

"She went to Stockholm, got work as a housekeeper, and later she started working at a soap factory. She managed well, got married to a Haller, he came from Germany but he was no Nazi because of that."

Ann laughed and Viola glared furiously at her.

"But she could never have any more children."

Viola's words confirmed what Ann had guessed: that Ann had gotten pregnant, had a miscarriage, and then fled to the island.

"But the German had a child from before. A cute little thing, but so skinny, Anna came here and showed him when he was four or five years old. She took on the little guy as if he was her own. She made it through. Now she's gone. Even so she was younger than me. Where the boy went I don't know. To Africa, I think."

Ann sniffled. Viola's brief, almost brusque account of a woman's life and fate touched something inside Ann that she did not want to be reminded of. The story had created images that emerged and overlapped each other. There was the picture of Anna and her despair, the skinny little boy, but also Ann and Erik. And then this island. This house, this Edvard.

The sea, she thought, *the sea that Edvard always talked about, maybe that's what I miss? Sea air, as Viola put it. Away with all these idiotic thoughts. My life is working. I don't need a sea to stare out over like Edvard. I don't need him.* She gasped for breath, filled by a bubbling anxiety but also by determination that she too would "make it through."

"Now you know," said Viola, "you who are so curious by nature."

Ann tried to smile. Once again it struck her with what finesse Viola could manage things. And what strength she showed, even now, when according to Edvard she was at death's door, which Ann doubted, however. Even if Viola was worn-out she was not exactly tottering on the edge of the grave.

As if to contradict this Viola hiccoughed and for a moment opened her eyes wide as if she had something in her throat.

"Help me up a little," she said in a cawing voice.

Ann got up, took hold under her arms, and raised Viola up so that she was sitting almost upright in bed.

"Now we'll say good-bye," Viola decided.

Ann leaned over, pressing her cheek against Viola's. The old woman definitely did not smell of sickness and death, but rather soap and perhaps a splash of perfume. Ann felt great warmth for Greta, she was surely the one who provided for Viola, keeping her clean and nice-smelling to the end. Ann felt the skinny arms about her body and could not stop the tears any longer.

The old woman hiccoughed again and Ann released herself from her grasp. They looked at each other.

"Good-bye now," said Viola.

"Good-bye," said Ann, squeezing Viola's cool, skinny hand.

She stood in the farmyard staring upward where a few scattered clouds glided along in an otherwise blue sky. This was how it could be to say farewell, she thought. Without torment and only a pinch of anxiety, otherwise great gratitude for how magnificent life could be, for being part of it, getting to share and then separate, with death like a considerate relative.

Ann was no longer crying, but knew that more tears would come later. She stood submerged in memories when she heard the veranda door open behind her. She turned around and in a strange way she was expecting it to be Viola standing there with her scarf around her head, her worn coat, and cut-off rubber boots on her feet.

But of course it was Edvard. He looked searchingly at her, as if he wanted to check how she was feeling.

"What a woman she is," said Ann.

Edvard nodded. Only now did Ann see how tense he was.

"I guess I'll be leaving," she said.

"Ann," he got out, stepping down from the stairs.

Don't come closer, she thought. But he did. She could not flee when he had that expression on his face. He stood before her. *Don't touch me,* she thought. But he did, took hold of her and pulled her to him.

"Ann," he whispered, "it's you."

He felt like before. Smelled like before. She felt how something was loosening. An inner valve was opened and out streamed everything that had accumulated since their breakup: all the thoughts about a reunion, hopes and disappointments; all the glasses of wine she drank just to be able to sleep; all the tears she had shed, and like a stinking stream now this mess rushed through and out of her body. Only resolve and anger remained.

She pushed him away from her.

"No, Edvard, it's not that way anymore."

He shrank a little, like a surprised animal who is unexpectedly struck by a projectile, if not directly fatal, then still one that made him shake with the insight that this was the beginning of the end.

"You know that too," she continued quickly, because she didn't want to hear his assurances and explanations. "You're sad now and need someone. But I'm not the one you need."

"Yes," he whispered doggedly. "It's been that way since you left the island."

She wanted to let out her anger that he had waited so many damn years before he came out with this but she held back so as not to worsen his obvious suffering. He had enough with his despair that Viola had decided to die.

"I'm leaving now," she said, suddenly struck by the thought that behind her anger perhaps love was lurking.

True, that was not very likely. The feeling that they had come to a definitive end was strong. But stranger things had happened in the history of the world, so she decided to shut down everything and make herself inaccessible. She simply didn't want to be there anymore. She wanted to leave the island and go home to Erik and Anders.

She stroked him across the cheek—a gesture that she regretted afterwards—and then walked quickly to her car, jumped in and drove off, leaving the farm and Edvard behind her. In the rearview mirror Edvard could be seen for a moment before his figure was blocked by stones and juniper shrubs.

✦

Twenty-eight

He had dreamed about money. But mainly about Africa. And then not only about Miss Elly but so much more, the whole continent had streamed into his body like a pleasurable potpourri of beautiful images. Laughter and howls were heard in a landscape bathed in sun, where then twilight came creeping with coolness and surprisingly quickly everything was in shadow and darkness.

It was a good dream with many fine details, and a few that were funny. If he had been staying at the camp Christian and John would have listened to his account with great delight. They would have nodded energetically and persuaded Karsten to expand on the story. John would have giggled at his inimitable way when it came to Miss Elly and love. He loved to hear Karsten's words about his "best sister," as John had always called her.

Karsten got up to make breakfast and decide how he should organize the day, but the thoughts of Africa would not leave him in peace. Were John and Christian still at the camp or had other guides and trackers come, younger and faster? He did not want to believe that. No one could beat John where felines were concerned, and Christian knew everything about rhinoceroses.

He had coffee in a melancholy emotional state of joy and loss. Should he go back? *Could* he go back? The questions would come up now and then but so far he had rejected all thoughts of leaving Sweden. Now suddenly the idea of selling the little he owned, packing up and buying a one-way ticket, seemed fully feasible.

He did not want to live in Windhoek, but a little house in Shiwo he could probably find. Miss Elly's relatives were there. They would welcome him with song and swallow him whole.

The money he set aside would perhaps be enough for the trip, a patch of ground and a house, but not much more. Miss Elly's family would not hesitate a moment to support him, in reality they would demand to do so, but he did not want to live off of others, above all not those who were worse off than himself.

Karsten knew where this was heading. The image of the shoe box with money was burning on his retinas, in the dream the bundles had been his. He had been sitting on the veranda with the box at his feet conversing with his good friend Mr. Green, a thirty-centimeter-long lizard with a brown head and a shimmering green thorax that changed to turquoise toward the tail. His wife was an identical color, just as curious as her mate but careful and guarded in everything she undertook.

Mr. Green had let his tongue play—Karsten assumed that the lizard also sensed the smell of money—and approached slowly and sniffed at the shoe box. It had quite unexpectedly raised itself on its hind legs and leaned over the edge of the box and inspected the contents. And then something really unexpected happened. Mr. Green had seemed to sneer with his broad lizard mouth and triumphantly did a thumbs-up to his lizard wife as if to say: Here there are resources.

Karsten was awakened by his own laughter. Mr. Green had a talent for always putting him in a good mood. At times of melancholy and loneliness the lizard had been a friend to rely on.

Should he too do the thumbs-up? Should he take Mr. Green's contented expression as a sign?

He finished breakfast in a quandary and with a growing sense of irritation. It was just past six o'clock in the morning so he did not need to feel stressed but hurried away anyway. He needed to leave the apartment, put his body to work, it was the only way to relieve the discomfort.

What remained at Lundquist's was to cut down the birch tree on the front side and then clean up after himself. The birch was not particularly large but was in an awkward location. If he were to cut down the tree in one piece there would not be much room to spare, and there was a risk that it would fall over the fence toward the street, so he had decided to lop off the top first. For that maneuver he needed the ladder and was therefore forced to take the car and trailer.

He drove to the minimal storeroom in Boländerna where he stored his tools. He rented the storeroom from a sheet-metal shop. While he rooted among his things—there was no point in taking off too early—he heard the sheet-metal workers arrive. It was Hedlund and Oskarsson, as usual joking loudly with each other. Karsten became a little envious. The loneliness felt even stronger. He stopped a moment, stood quietly in the darkness of the shed and thought about Africa.

When the voices had died away he left the storeroom, unhitched the ladder from the hooks on the wall, and strapped it onto the trailer. He had already packed saw, oil, and fuel. It was time to finish the work in Kåbo.

The birch was soon dispatched, taken down and sawn into manageable pieces that he stacked in an old bicycle storage area that the homeowner used as a woodshed. Lundquist had explained that he would gladly chop the wood himself; he needed a little exercise, he said. Karsten could do nothing but agree in silence. Lundquist was alarmingly fat.

Everything had gone as planned and when he got in the car the sun was peeking out. He smiled quietly to himself and turned the ignition key.

After driving away he regretted that he had not thrown one more stone onto Ohler's roof and slowed down, but realized immediately the silliness in returning to carry out such a solely self-indulgent action.

On the other hand, there was one thing he had neglected and that was saying good-bye to Johansson. He turned around the block and parked outside the associate professor's house.

He found him by the compost sitting in a wheelbarrow.

"I got a little tired. I'm a little out of sorts actually."

Karsten saw how embarrassed Gregor Johansson was. He must have felt caught just sitting and idling.

"No, don't get up, it's all right. Well, is this the last grass-cutting for the year?"

Johansson nodded. Karsten crouched down and leaned his back against the compost.

"So you're done now?" said Johansson.

"Yes, the last is done. The birch is down. It feels good."

"And what is waiting now?"

Africa, thought Karsten. He had a desire to recount his dream, but the box of five-hundred-kronor bills would be hard to explain. And Mr. Green perhaps would stand out as slightly too fantastic a lizard for anyone who had never met him.

"I'm going to cut down a couple of maple trees in Årsta, then I'll have to see. Once again thanks for the witch alder."

"It was nothing. Maybe you can come by in the spring. Or sooner," Johansson hastened to add.

"I'd like to do that. I still have to look after Lundquist's garden next year."

At the same moment it occurred to him that he was lying to the associate professor. He would never set foot at Lundquist's again. It didn't feel right. He wanted to say goodbye to the associate professor in a better way.

"Maybe I can come by the day after tomorrow? I have a couple of gardening books that might interest you. Duplicates."

He wanted to give the associate professor something. He wanted to explain himself, tell him something about Africa. Not just disappear from this belated friend.

"Gladly," the associate professor answered. "Come for midmorning coffee."

They separated at the gate. What Karsten could not suspect was that they would never meet again.

✦

Twenty-nine

"Birgitta, I want you to speak with the professor."

Agnes had gotten up and hung her apron on the backside of the kitchen door. Birgitta and Liisa were still sitting at the table.

"Give your notice?"

Birgitta looked completely speechless.

"Yes, isn't that what you say?"

Liisa nodded and smiled.

"That's exactly what you say," she said, and despite her agitation Agnes could see the contented look on the Finnish woman's face.

"But why?"

Birgitta's question was simple but hard to answer. Agnes did not really know herself. She thought she had formulated the reasons to herself. But now she just felt deathly tired of the professor's carping and irritation. If he had won a prize he should be satisfied. Yet he had become even grumpier. She was also tired of the house, and she didn't know exactly why.

She missed the sea, she could also mention as a reason, but that sounded too pompous and strange, and not particularly believable besides. She had actually lived in town for more than fifty years and never expressed any longing for something so vague as a view of "the sea."

If she were to say something about the rock at Tall-Anna's, where you could see so far, the professor would laugh out loud. Birgitta perhaps would not laugh but become worried and take it as a result of confusion. For her everything outside the pruned garden had constituted a threatening disorder since childhood.

"I want to be a pensioner," said Agnes.

Liisa Lehtonen laughed heartily.

"Damn it, you're right about that!" she hooted. "Be a happy pensioner!"

Birgitta looked at Liisa in amazement.

"This isn't funny," she said. "Do you understand what worries there will be?"

"For dear Bertram, you mean?"

"For all of us," said Birgitta.

"I am actually over seventy," said Agnes.

They had eaten supper and Agnes had as usual cleared the table and loaded the dishwasher. The professor had retired. Liisa suggested they play cards, something that Agnes never did, except for Old Maid when the Ohler children were small.

No, she did not want to play cards. She did not want to do anything whatsoever other than go up to her room and call Greta. Her sister was the only one who would understand.

"Can I quit after this week?"

"Normally you give one month's notice," said Liisa, who had stopped laughing.

"You'll perk up, right now you're just worn-out," said Birgitta, and Agnes understood that Birgitta was only repeating what the professor had said.

"Yes, that can easily happen here," said Agnes, who felt that she had violated the established rules of the game.

There was so much involved in that simple sentence that neither Birgitta nor Liisa could say anything. It was as if the women in the kitchen were struck by an insight. Perhaps not the same one, but all three were silent for a few moments to take in and be able to properly handle what had happened. A new situation had commenced in the Ohler house.

It was Liisa who broke the silence, perhaps it was all the years of mental training that came in handy.

"We'll call for a company to come in and clean the whole house, make it sparkling clean and then come back every week. Agnes will be the supervisor."

"Good!" Birgitta exclaimed, who became enthusiastic as soon as she understood the import of the suggestion.

Agnes listened with growing impatience. She simply wanted to get away from it all. Didn't they understand that?

Just then the bell rang. Birgitta fell silent. Liisa looked up with a surprised, slightly frightened look on her face, as if she did not understand what was jangling.

"The study," Agnes said mechanically, and reached out her hand for the white apron she used outside the kitchen, but immediately let her hand fall, took a deep breath, and then let out the air with a sigh.

"I'll take it," said Birgitta, in a futile attempt to rescue the situation, for in that moment everyone realized that there was not a company in the whole world that could replace Agnes Andersson.

Birgitta left the kitchen. Liisa got up and went over to the kitchen entrance. Agnes studied the slender body and the short hair, tried to imagine her and Birgitta together. It didn't work. It was as incomprehensible as so much else in the Ohler family.

"Now the last leaves are falling," said Liisa abruptly, who had never commented on the garden before. She turned her head and looked at Agnes.

"Yes," said Agnes, "it's fall."

My last apple cake, she thought.

"Maybe what's happening is just as well," said Liisa, but did not specify what she meant, whether that concerned the inexorable arrival of autumn or the fact that Agnes wanted to leave the household.

"When I was competing I used to think about sex," Liisa went on. "It's the opposite of what all the experts recommend; it's calm you should try to achieve, a kind of peace that actually doesn't exist. That's what you aim for. I did the opposite, worked myself up. In my first Olympics, in 1984 in Los Angeles, I met a competitor from South Korea, we fell in love at first sight and met in secret. Then we met in the finals. I glanced at her and I wet my panties. Since then I always think about her at critical moments. I won in Los Angeles. She won on the home field four years later. That seems right, doesn't it?"

Why is she telling me all this? Agnes thought with surprise. *Does she want to shock me, or what?* She was forced to turn around to conceal her disapproval.

"Now I'm thinking about the Korean," said Liisa.

Agnes whirled around.

"Do you know what?" she exclaimed. "Now that's enough of your vulgarities. And this is no firing range or Olympic Games. And wipe that grin off your face!"

"It's there to cheer you up."

The Finnish woman's scornful tone and her own fury made Agnes leave the kitchen. *Never again,* she thought, *will I cook for that bitch.* She took the stairs like when she was young and was forced to catch her breath when she came up to the second floor.

Birgitta came out of the study at the far end of the corridor. She was crying. Agnes went in the opposite direction, slipped into the little drawing room, and closed the door behind her with a feeling of having escaped from a swarm of angry bees.

She collapsed in an armchair that had remained from years ago. The last daylight had disappeared and the room was in darkness. She closed her eyes. In her mind the house on the island emerged. She could picture Greta, how she had her coffee, and quietly felt the twilight in the kitchen and then went into the old drawing room, turned on the table lamp and the sconces on the wall, switched on the TV and settled in.

Agnes did not understand the curious attachment she felt for Greta. They had never been particularly close, but now the cottage and her sister stood out in a light shimmer that perhaps was not completely grounded in reality. The cottage was crooked and drafty, cold in the winter, the kitchen was old-fashioned, and her sister was often peevish and incommunicative.

But none of that mattered. She wanted to go home. She also wanted to settle down on the couch in front of the TV.

She did not know what Greta would think about having company, but there was no turning back. With that conviction she got up, turned on the ceiling light, went over to the telephone, and dialed the number to the island. Her sister answered after a couple of rings, which meant she had not yet sat down in front of the TV.

Agnes told her quite briefly and without superfluous comment that she would be quitting at Ohler's and coming out to the island within a couple of days. She said nothing about the future, if her intention was to stay for good or if the visit was to be seen as an interim stop before she got something of her own.

To her great surprise Greta had no comment but instead simply asked if Agnes needed help. Perhaps Viktor's cousin's grandson Ronald could come with his big car so that Agnes could take everything with her? After a moment of hesitation Agnes accepted the offer and they decided that Ronald, if he was able, would come on Saturday morning. Greta insisted that she herself would show up during the day tomorrow to help pack. Agnes understood that Greta also wanted to see the house one last time.

Agnes's hand was shaking when she hung up the phone. Something awful was in the process of happening, she felt it in her whole body. During the call with her sister she had taken great pains not to let her inner tension be known, but now she let out the worry and anxiety. She was forced to lay down, only to get up a short time later and restlessly wander around the room. At any moment the bell might ring, or perhaps more likely, Birgitta would knock and in her gentlest voice ask if everything was all right.

But they left her in peace. The whole house seemed to be holding its breath. Her decision to give notice had shaken things up properly.

It struck her as she stood looking out over the dark garden that Greta's suggestion to come into town was also a way to support her little sister. Greta surely sensed that it was not a completely painless maneuver to leave the professor. The tension in her stomach remained but the trembling decreased somewhat. She was holding steady.

The lights were on at Bunde's, likewise at the associate professor's, but at Lundquist's it was dark. She wondered for a while about the gardener but not for long, for why should she care about the professor's apple trees and bushes? And his remark about time was not so astounding, it was surely more common than she had thought.

Instead, in her thoughts she planned her packing. She had not accumulated much and that was just as well. Ronald would carry it out to the car in a jiffy. The thought made her smile. How quickly they would disappear. Before the others really understood what had happened, she would be sitting perched in the passenger seat alongside Ronald in his gigantic car. Greta would do all the talking from the backseat. Ronald would as always sit silently. They had last met at Viktor's funeral and she happened to think about everyone who had gathered at Gräsö Church. The majority she recognized, the others Greta had identified. Stronger than ever she felt that she wanted to go home to the island.

For the first time in many years, perhaps decades, she lingered in her drawing room for an entire evening and went to bed without having asked whether the professor wanted something before bedtime.

✦

Thirty

Friday was going to be rainy. It was pouring down already early in the morning. Karsten Haller cancelled all plans for tree pruning. The maples in Ärsta would still be there after the weekend. And if they weren't it didn't matter to him.

Instead he took the bus down to the city to visit a travel agency on Drottninggatan. There he had been well treated before, and he felt that a friendly reception was even more important this time. Perhaps he would never need the services of a travel agency again. He was on the point of leaving the country and now every human contact and every transaction had significance. These were the memories he would carry with him and he did not want to have bitter thoughts now at the end.

He stepped into the agency's office with a smile and half an hour later he stepped out with a smile.

He walked along the street with the quiet exhilaration of a person who has just made a life-altering decision—a mixture of reverence, euphoria, and an absolute conviction of having chosen the right path. But despite the light-heartedness, every step, every thought, was of the greatest importance. Even the rain drumming against his umbrella seemed to have a message. For Karsten Haller rain was something good, it made the semidesert bloom and fish that had been lying still, apparently dead, in the mud of the rivers waken to life. But even the absence of rain could be good. Then the animals flocked by the few waterholes. The clouds of dust on the horizon heralded migrating hordes of grass-eaters.

Now he was not stirring up much dust on Fyristorg. It was still raining intensely. He had decided to exchange the bundle of five-hundred-kronor bills from Ohler's safe. It went more smoothly than he thought.

"Have a nice trip," the young woman behind the security glass chirped, as she pushed over the yellow packet of money.

He had said something about visiting his relatives in the United States, with a vague sense that he had to justify his transaction. LUDMILLA, as it said on the woman's name tag, did not think there was anything strange about his wanting to exchange twenty-five thousand kronor to American dollars.

Crime is encouraged, he thought, smiling back, left the premises and headed for the next exchange office, which was in a shopping arcade.

There it went just as smoothly. He quickly stuffed the money in the inside pocket of his jacket and set a course for the exit. When he caught sight of his own mirror image outside a store he did a double take; he looked like he had shoplifted something. He slowed down and looked around. Did someone perhaps think that he was behaving strangely? But no one seemed to take any notice. A teenager bumped into him, but did not apologize, on the contrary he glared at Karsten as if to say "Get out of the way, old man."

He went into the pharmacy in the next arcade. He was sweating but did not want to unbutton his jacket. Now he realized that the theft was irrevocable.

He picked up aspirin and sunscreen. In the line to the register he suddenly became fretful. He wanted to shove the other customers to the side, throw a couple of hundreds at the clerk, and rush away.

Once out on the street he made the decision that he'd been tossing around ever since the last visit to Ohler: He would return and steal the rest of the bundles in the safe. Why should the rapist have so much, and in a couple of months a few million more in prize money?

He hailed a taxi that was passing. He wanted to get home as quickly as possible, get away from the people, the clamor in the stores, and the noise on the streets.

The taxi driver was black and Karsten took that as a good sign. During the ride he leaned back, closed his eyes, and the images from Namibia came to him. He smiled. Everything was falling into place. The old man would be punished. He would let himself be swallowed up by the interior of Africa. He opened his eyes. The rain was lashing against the windows of the taxi. It's spring in Etosha now, he thought.

✦

Thirty-one

"Do you remember Evert Gustavsson?"

Agnes was staring at her sister. She did not understand how Greta could make small talk the way she had done most of the time since she came to the house. She shook her head.

"You must. Evert was part of the congregation. Father was lighthouse keeper before he went to sea again. He was torpedoed."

Now Agnes remembered. Evert had been in love with Anna in that innocent way, surely never expressed but obvious to anyone and everyone. When Aron became increasingly fierce in his attacks against his own daughter Evert left the congregation; the visits became less frequent and then finally stopped completely.

"He died this week," Greta reported.

Agnes sighed. Death was one of the few things that could really liven up her sister.

"He collapsed. Just like Father."

They were packing. Greta carefully folded up her sister's clothes and placed them in garbage bags that she had been sensible enough to buy on the way. She had also brought with her a couple of shopping bags and a suitcase, borrowed from Ronald, and in it Agnes packed small things she had collected over the years.

She was grateful anyway for her sister's carefree talk. Greta seemed to be taking it lightly that Agnes so unexpectedly and hastily was going to leave Ohler and Uppsala. It made the leaving less troublesome.

Greta had also taken the worst blows with the professor, because at first he refused to believe Agnes when she told him that she was going to leave for good the following day. It was only when Greta showed up that he realized the seriousness and started blustering about breach of contract. Then Agnes chose to go upstairs, although she overheard Greta's impudent reminder that the Master and Servant Acts had been repealed. The professor's response consisted of an inarticulate roar, after which they continued to quarrel for quite some time. It did not stop until Birgitta started crying loudly.

Greta surprised her. Agnes would be eternally grateful for her unconditional support.

"What if he'd married Anna?" Greta continued her monologue on Evert Gustavsson. "Then they would have stayed on the island. Evert was a builder later, you know that?"

Agnes stopped. In her hand she was holding a silk cloth she had received once from the old professor's wife. She sensed that Greta's talk about Anna was because they were now in the process of ending an era that had been started by their big sister. But it felt unpleasant anyway. Anna had not been heard from in all these years.

She considered herself betrayed, Agnes understood that, but she thought that was unjust. She had only been a child and Greta a teenager, and they had not judged Anna. It was Aron and the congregation that rejected her.

"Why didn't she ever call or write?" Greta asked, as if she was reading Agnes's thoughts.

"She couldn't bear to," Agnes maintained. "The wound was too deep. It never healed."

"We'll never know," said Greta sadly.

"We'll never know," repeated Agnes, who thought that the wound still persisted. The time when Anna lived with Viola was the period that they could remember with a certain measure of joy. Anna had been happy the times the little sisters defied their father's prohibition and sneaked over to Viola. But then, when Anna disappeared from the island, all contact ended.

They looked at each other. This unexpected openness between them, airing a mystery they had actually never discussed, filled Agnes with a number of conflicting thoughts. She realized that they only had each other, and her sister had surely realized the same thing. Hence her support and involvement in the move.

She threw the cloth in the garbage bag.

"Are you going to throw it away?"

"I got it from Lydia," said Agnes.

"I know, I got one like it. She must have found some excess inventory."

Agnes smiled mournfully. Perhaps Anna got a cloth too? she thought, turning around to hide her emotion.

Packing Agnes's belongings did not take long. They made the revolutionary decision not to clean the bedroom and drawing room, *Birgitta could just as well do that*, Greta thought.

Instead they sat down in front of the TV. They were both waiting for Birgitta to show up. The professor would never humble himself to knock on the door. He had not, as far as Agnes could remember, set foot in the drawing room since it was transformed into her living room.

Birgitta came after half an hour. Quite certainly she had listened through the door and heard that the TV was on. She knocked and opened the door at the same moment. Her attempt to look unconcerned made an almost comic impression, or else she had been tricked by the sound of the TV, thought they had canceled the plans for retirement and now were staring at TV. But when she caught sight of the suitcase and the garbage bags Birgitta turned pale and the mask fell.

"Is this the thanks we get, Agnes?" she whimpered in a broken voice.

The crushed expression and the outstretched arms—Agnes happened to think of a biblical figure depicted in the illustrated scriptures of her childhood—completed the spectacle of a theatrical composition, presented to create a bad conscience, nothing else. Birgitta no doubt understood at that moment that Operation Persuasion was meaningless. If nothing else Greta's discouraging expression and posture vouched for that. The sister was also the one who answered.

"Thanks for what?"

Birgitta took a few quick steps into the room. Agnes knew what was coming. The spitting image of Papa Bertram. Now the heavy artillery is waiting.

But she did not have her father's perseverance, because after only a couple of minutes she fell silent, apparently drained. The final argument was that she was really the one who had arranged that Agnes got access to the drawing room.

"And how many domestic servants can live so regally?" she concluded the tirade.

Agnes stared at Birgitta. She remembered a ten-year-old girl who came running into the kitchen to seek shelter or consolation, or was simply eager to tell something, perhaps with a schoolbook or a drawing in hand. She remembered their chat in the kitchen only a few days ago.

Neither of the sisters commented on Birgitta's outburst, which was followed by increasingly loud and uncontrolled sobbing. Agnes withstood the impulse to get up, but said something to the effect that it would surely work out. Greta glowered. Clearly she had firmly decided not to lift so much as a little finger for Birgitta.

At the same moment Liisa Lehtonen stepped into the drawing room, which reinforced the image of a scene where yet another actor made an entrance. But she had no lines, only gave the sisters a furious look before she placed her arm around Birgitta's shoulders and led her out of the room. If the Finnish woman had had a pistol in her hand they would have been shot, thought Agnes.

"That was one round," Greta commented, getting up, going over to the door, and closing it with a bang.

Agnes saw that she was very content, presumably because they had stood up so well. She herself was shaken. She wanted to cry but did not really understand why. Preferably she would have left the house immediately, disappeared, but Ronald was not coming until the next morning. How she would be able to make her way down the stairs, through the hall, and out the front door she did not know. Would she say goodbye to the professor? After all, they had shared a roof for more than half a century. Would he shake her hand and thank her for the time that had passed or would he just make a fuss? Would she look around with a sense of loss? There were so many questions, so many emotions tumbling over one another that she could simply hide her face and sob.

"We'll soon be out of here," said Greta. "You know that gratitude has never been the Ohlers' strong suit. We don't need to feel ashamed. We've done what's been asked of us, and then some."

Agnes straightened her back a little and removed her hands from her face. Of course that's how it was. All three of them, Anna, Greta, and herself, had done good work. Still she felt a guilty conscience. She was deserting. Should she have waited perhaps until after the Nobel Prize ceremony? The professor's heart was not strong. Perhaps he would die of fury before he was able to receive the prize. Then she would be blamed for his death. And rightly so.

"Greta," she said. "Maybe—"

"Never!" her sister exclaimed. "We are not moving from this spot. Now we'll sit here like two old ladies who can't move. Then we'll go to bed. Ronald is coming at eight sharp."

Agnes did not reply. She peered at the garbage bags and happened to think about the gardener at Lundquist's. He had also carried black bags around. Now he was gone too, probably for good.

"Time lives a life of its own," she said.

Greta stared at her but said nothing and turned her attention to the TV.

✦

Thirty-two

The house was silent and dark. It was approaching midnight. Karsten Haller guessed that Ohler and the old housekeeper were sound asleep.

Third time's a charm, he thought as he slipped in through the cellar entrance. He felt exhilarated, not anxious at all like on the previous occasions. There was a routine to it all. He was no ordinary villain, no simple burglar, and because his motives were complex and elevated he did not doubt that for a moment. In reality he was doing justice a service by partly correcting an irregularity. He was claiming a sort of disinterested damages, if you will. Another interpretation could be that he was improving his mother's inheritance somewhat. And as a side effect he would get a few years in the landscape he appreciated most of all, the dry savanna.

But above all he wanted to create the most possible confusion in the Ohler home and inflict the most possible injury. Karsten Heller had never been a bloodthirsty or revengeful person, but the thought that the old man should have to suffer for the assaults he had committed had taken a firm hold.

The keys to the safe were in their place, no one seemed to have moved the ring since his last visit. He now moved deftly in the cellar, did not need to hesitate, made his way up the stairs, turned off the flashlight, and carefully opened the door. It was dark. Like at Melongo, that time when nature seemed to be holding its breath. He and Christian. Stock-still. Then came the scream. Both of them jumped. Christian had then shown his white teeth in a broad smile.

The house smelled different. It took awhile before he realized that they had been wallpapering and repainting. He turned on the flashlight a moment to quickly survey the hall; he did not want to stumble on a can of paint.

The door to the corridor that led to the billiard room was closed. He knew from the last time that it creaked. From his pocket he took out an oil can and sprayed the hinge. When he then pushed down the handle the door glided open soundlessly. He smiled to himself in the darkness. He was starting to get really good at the break-in game.

The floor creaked. The window at the end of the corridor was letting in a faint light that fell in across the runner. He opened the door to the billiard room, waited a moment but it was still dead silent in the house.

Karsten became unexpectedly and suddenly afraid. The previous certainty and feeling of being invincible gave way to a pulsating worry. He wanted to leave immediately but stopped to think. He was so close to the goal. With shaking hands he took out the key ring. The door of the safe glided open. A puff of closed-in air struck him.

Suddenly the room was lit up by the headlights from a passing car. Karsten checked the time: twenty minutes to one. Five minutes had passed.

The box with the money was there. He had actually not expected anything else, but still heaved a sigh of relief. Quickly he took out the bundles, stuffed them in his pockets, swept the flashlight one last time to see if he had missed anything, and locked the safe. Then he left the room, many hundred thousand kronor richer.

The tension, the weight of the money, made him giggle. He took the same way back, quickly managed the corridor and hall, carefully opened the door to the cellar. Now it can't go wrong, he thought, turned on the flashlight again, went quickly down the stairs and over to the paint can, threw back the keys, and headed for the door out to freedom. Now he wanted to get out of the house! He wanted to go home, open a beer, and count the money. He giggled again.

At the same moment the cellar was bathed in light.

In front of him was a woman with a raised gun in her hand, probably a pistol. She had been standing hidden in the darkness. The barrel was aimed at him. She stood in the middle of the cellar, partly hidden behind a pillar, with a good view in all directions. A good position, he thought.

"Who are you?"

He turned around. On the stairs stood another woman. He recognized her from the garden. In her hands she had one of the spears he had seen in the library.

"That doesn't matter," he said.

"What are you doing here?"

"Administering a little justice," he answered.

"Justice?! What do you mean?"

"My name is Karsten, and who are you?"

"Birgitta von Ohler."

"The daughter of the house?"

The woman nodded. He felt calmer at once. The hands that held the spear were shaking. He turned his head. The pistol on the other hand was not shaking a millimeter.

"Right when you opened the door to the cellar I looked out the window," said the woman with the pistol. "Bad luck for you."

He looked toward the door where he had come into the cellar.

"If you move I'll shoot you," said the woman.

"I certainly believe that," he said.

Once before he had had a gun aimed at him. That was in Johannesburg, and he had escaped. True, he lost a good deal of money and a watch, but no more than that.

"And I don't miss," said the woman. "I have three medals from the Olympics and the world championships."

"I understand," said Karsten, smiling, but was struck by the suspicion that the woman was slightly crazy.

"Liisa, he's the gardener from Lundquist's, I recognize him now."

"That's right," he said.

"And Liisa is a competitive shooter."

"Then that's clarified," he said. "But now I have to leave."

He saw a quick smile from the shooter.

"Leave?" she said. "You've broken in and then you think you can just trot off, after having been introduced?"

"Yes, you have every reason in the world to let me go."

"And that would be?" asked Birgitta.

"Your father's posthumous reputation," said Karsten Haller, turning halfway around and looking at her. "The Nobel Prize winner, the renowned professor."

"Posthumous reputation, what kind of rubbish is that?" Liisa hissed.

"What do you mean?" asked Birgitta.

"Nobel Prize or not, if I were to tell what has happened in this cellar the image of the scientist would be different."

Was there a trace of fear in the daughter's face? Did she know something about what happened in the cellar over sixty years ago?

"Now you have to explain yourself!" Liisa ordered.

"I don't want to hear," said Birgitta.

"Of course we have to hear," said Liisa.

"Calling the police equals scandal, just so you know," said Karsten calmly.

"I see your cards," said Liisa.

"This is not a poker game!" Birgitta shouted.

"Do you see that bed over there?"

"Stop! That's just filthy talk. Have you spoken with Wiik?"

"I don't know any Wiik," said Karsten. "On the other hand I do know, or knew, an Anna Haller, née Andersson."

"I see," said Liisa. "Go on!"

"We'll let him go," said Birgitta.

"Anna Haller was my mother," said Karsten.

"That's a lie! She just wanted to extort money from Daddy."

"What does she have to do with Bertram? Is that some—"

"Get out!" screamed Birgitta, waving the spear.

Karsten looked at Liisa. He saw hesitation in her eyes.

"What do you have in your pockets?" she asked.

"An inheritance," said Karsten. "Or damages, if you wish."

"Have you stolen money?" screamed Birgitta.

"Damages for what?" asked Liisa.

Karsten did not answer but instead looked at Birgitta von Ohler. When he saw her in the garden he had already felt repugnance and now that feeling was strengthened. The woman was totally out of balance. He himself felt calm and the woman with the Finnish accent seemed to be as cold as anything. He understood that he had to assure her to be able to leave the cellar. He had to give her something.

"Assault," said Karsten, ignoring the pistol and walking quickly up to the bed, taking hold of the wrought-iron headboard and shaking it so that it rattled.

He felt, in the contact with the iron and the sight of the checkered frame of flat iron bars, a violent fury.

"In this bed my mother was raped! Raped! There is no other word."

The two women stared at him.

"There is your fine Nobel Prize winner! Your father. Who is now being rewarded for his efforts."

"What evidence do you have?"

He stared at Birgitta with contempt and hate in his eyes. He could strike at her.

"Evidence! Her life was the evidence. Because she got no reward, only a life sentence."

He spit out the words. Liisa had lowered the gun.

"Are you sure? Perhaps it was mutual?" she said.

Haller shook his head vehemently.

"I know," he said in a low voice. "I know exactly how it happened."

He could tell about the pregnancy and the abortion that followed, tell about his mother's despair, about the naked and painful words in the diary, but he did not want to expose her shame. He knew what awful guilt she had felt about what happened.

It was as if her words were meant only for him. He realized now that she had saved the diary for his sake. It should not be thrown away, it should be read. She wanted him to read it. Read and understand. In order to thereby forgive her for the worry and anxiety that sometimes seized her and indirectly also affected him as a child.

"She was lured down here by Ohler," he continued. "I don't know how, perhaps with promises or that she should fetch something. She was used to his caprices. She shined his shoes and washed his underwear, so why shouldn't she obey when he told her to follow him down to the cellar?"

"Could she have been that innocent?" Liisa objected.

"Just that innocent. She did not know much about life, other than she should obey the gentry. But it really doesn't matter if she had been an experienced woman or not, a rape is always a rape. Isn't it?"

Liisa nodded.

"She came from Gräsö," said Birgitta in a toneless voice.

Karsten turned around. He had directed all his attention toward the Finnish woman.

"Yes, and from a deeply religious family besides," he said.

"You call it rape but perhaps she was in love with Bertram. And later it went further than she had imagined, and even further than what he had imagined. Perhaps they sneaked down here to cuddle a little and then they got carried away."

The Finnish woman's words made her sneer.

"You don't believe that yourself," he said. "This was 1944. She was at his mercy."

"Just like today," said Liisa.

"What do you mean?"

"That doesn't matter," she said, putting the pistol into her waistband. "It's just as well that you disappear from the house."

"Never!" screamed Birgitta.

"Calm down, Birgitta. He goes away, everything is forgotten and remains like before, that is, false and depressing. Bertram gets his prize and his glory. You can wallpaper the whole house with money if you want."

"Don't mock me! This thief and liar can create scandal just to get at Daddy. He wants to create scandal! He hates us!"

"No, I just want to disappear," said Karsten.

"He hates us," repeated Birgitta. "He hates us because we have a big, fine house, a name, because Bertram is appreciated."

"I don't want to see you anymore," said Karsten, but the words made no impression on her.

He took a few steps closer to the exit. Birgitta raised the spear.

"You hate us simply because your mother fucked my father. She wanted to! But then she was ashamed. That was it, wasn't it? She was ashamed of her sanctimonious father."

He shook his head. He didn't want to hear more, he didn't want to see her. Yes, he hated Bertram von Ohler and he hated her. He hated the whole lot!

"Go to hell," he said softly.

Liisa took a few quick steps toward them both and raised her hands in an attempt to calm the situation down.

"You and your rapist father!"

"Stop! Liisa, he's lying! He's mocking us!"

"I think you know more than you're letting on," Karsten continued. "But here secrets, dirtiness, and violence are preserved as family relics."

"Shoot him!"

"Calm down, damn it! He means nothing to you, to us. You know that. He disappears and then it will be calm. He takes the money and leaves. He isn't interested in anything else."

Karsten suddenly smiled.

"I'm going to Africa in four days," he said.

"There you are," said Liisa.

"He's bluffing," said Birgitta. "Don't you see that he wants to harm us?"

"You are the most fucked-up bitch I have ever met," said Karsten with emphasis.

"Don't talk a lot of shit now," she said, but he did not let himself be stopped.

"You don't believe in a dead woman's story, but ask her sister, she must know the whole story."

"She doesn't know a thing, she was a child in 1944," said Birgitta, now considerably calmer, as if Liisa's comment had placated her.

"Not even about the abortion?" It came out of him.

"What abortion?"

"Anna got pregnant. Down here," he said, pointing at the bed. "And down here your grandfather performed the abortion and your amazing daddy assisted. An intervention that she never would have accepted if she had known what it meant. Confused and afraid as she was she thought that the professor was only going to examine her, but she was drugged and they took the fetus from her. I know that it sounds completely improbable but that's what happened."

They stared at him.

"And Bertram was the father?" asked Liisa.

Karsten nodded.

"And after that operation she could never have children again," he said.

Birgitta laughed.

"And what about you?"

"Adopted," said Karsten. "My biological mother was killed during the last days of World War Two. I was only a few months old when father took me to Sweden on a boat called *Rönnskär*. He married Anna later. For a long time I thought she was my real mother. But that made no difference to me. I loved Anna as a mother."

"Good God," said Liisa. "What a story. What a damned mess. What if—"

Liisa and Birgitta looked at each other. Karsten sensed what was going on in their heads. If this "mess" were to come out and become generally known, that would definitely mean the end of the Ohler family's reputation. A doctor who first raped a religious young woman and then, together with his father the gynecology professor, performed an illegal abortion in a cellar, could never receive the Nobel Prize in Medicine, regardless of what he accomplished later in life in the service of research.

He saw how the insight about this was slowly growing in them. He took a step toward the door.

"Now you know," he said. "Now you know that the Nobel Prize winner rapes his employees."

"Stop!"

Birgitta's shout echoed in the cellar. At the same moment a figure appeared at the top of the stairs.

"What's going on?"

Everyone's eyes turned toward Greta, but Birgitta quickly recovered.

"It's no problem, Greta, we've surprised a thief," Birgitta called.

"Aunt," whispered Karsten, and he could not suppress a smile.

Now he felt more secure. Above all when he saw the old woman coming down the stairs.

"A thief?"

"Now I'm leaving," he said, turning around and grasping the handle to the door out to freedom.

At the same moment he got a powerful jolt in the back. He fell forward, opened the door, fumbled with his hands in the air and thudded down on the floor, just as the pain came. He twisted his body, saw Birgitta's distorted face, perceived how the spear was raised and felt as it was again driven into his body.

I have to get away, he thought. he knew what an African spear could do, and summoning all his strength he stumbled into the corridor toward the cellar entrance.

In a fruitless attempt to protect himself he put up his hand. The spear came rushing again. Now it pierced his throat. His mouth was immediately filled with blood. He made an attempt to crawl further but collapsed. Then came the fourth thrust. The spear went in just below the right shoulder blade and punctured the lung.

✦

Thirty-three

"What do we do with—"

Liisa was unsure how she should express herself. "The body," "the corpse," or simply "him"?

Birgitta had not said a word since Liisa managed to stop her violent attacks. She sat hunched over on a steamer trunk that had been plastered with stickers for various destinations.

Greta had tried to shake life into the gardener but in vain. The whole corridor to the cellar door was messy with blood.

We'll put him in the trunk, thought Liisa, but realized that did not solve the problem. He would start stinking after only a day or two.

She had decided to get rid of the body. Nothing of what had happened could come out. The police could not be involved. The professor should not know a thing. Birgitta and Greta stared at her while she laid out the strategy.

"If this becomes known, then we can forget the Nobel Prize and everything else. Besides that, Birgitta will end up in jail. For a long time. Us too, because we were accomplices."

She was not sure of that, an attorney could certainly argue that self-defense had been involved, but she poured it on to frighten Greta. Birgitta she could handle, but she did not know about Greta.

"But he broke in," the old woman also objected.

"Yes, but he died of a number of deep wounds. That's harder to explain. All in the back besides. It doesn't look good for any of us."

"But why? He's a gardener."

Liisa looked at Greta, whose eyes were still staring, scared out of her wits and not understanding.

"As if that sort can't commit a crime? He took lots of money. You saw that yourself."

Liisa pointed with the spear toward the entry where the dead man's legs were visible. Birgitta mumbled something.

"We'll bury him," she said. "We have to bury him. He is a Christian person anyway."

"We know nothing about that," said Liisa. "But we have to get rid of him."

Beneath her outward calm she was terrified. Not so much about how they would handle the situation, but more about the fury that had consumed Birgitta. The wildness of thrusting a spear into a person, again and again, frightened her terribly. She thought she knew Birgitta, they had lived together for several years, but it was clear to her that there was a side of her that had until now been concealed.

"We'll bury him," Birgitta repeated in a mechanical voice.

"Where?" said Liisa.

Greta stared at her. Liisa realized that she had to act quickly while the woman was still in shock. Soon Greta, or perhaps Birgitta, could break down.

"We'll carry him out to my car," said Liisa. "I can drive it onto the yard."

No one reacted. It was not a good suggestion, she realized that at once. It was the middle of the night and the sound of a car engine starting might waken a neighbor. Bunde might look out. Besides, she was not sure whether the gate to the garage access could be opened. As far as she could recall it was locked with a chain and a sturdy padlock. The professor wanted it that way.

"The garden," she threw out.

"It's too hard to dig there," Birgitta objected.

Liisa had a desire to run over and hug her. Birgitta's voice still sounded ghost-like, but even so Liisa could perceive something of the usual tone of voice. She was on her way back.

"At Lundquist's," said Birgitta suddenly. "The ground is soft there."

Liisa did not understand what she meant, but Birgitta continued as if it concerned something very everyday.

"He was digging for several days," she said, getting up eagerly. "I saw him digging! There's a spade in the shed by the old oil tank. We—"

"We can't do it that way," objected Greta. "We can't just—"

Liisa looked around.

"Are there any old rugs down here?"

Birgitta pointed toward a corner of the cellar.

"There are some wrapped up over there," she said. "In plastic."

Liisa hurried over to the dark corner.

"Plastic is better," she said, tearing at the bundle of rugs. "There's less friction."

She turned around and saw that at least Birgitta understood what she meant. Greta only looked confused. Liisa tore loose a large piece of plastic which she rolled up.

"Where's Agnes?" Birgitta asked suddenly.

"I'm sure she's asleep," Greta answered. "I heard strange noises and . . . I didn't want to wake her . . . she would never—"

"That's good!" said Liisa. "We'll let her sleep."

"Mustn't we call the police?"

"Greta! Wake up! Don't you understand? They'll put Birgitta in prison! *Prison!* Is that what you want?"

Liisa stared at the old woman, leaned over the dead man, and pulled out the bundles of bills that Karsten had taken. They were bloody. She threw them on the floor.

"Help me now," she said, sticking her hands into Karsten's armpits. "Take hold of the feet!"

Greta and Birgitta approached hesitantly.

"We have to get him out! Then we'll lay him on the plastic and pull him across the lawn."

Together they managed to lift the body and lug it out through the door and up the cellar steps.

It was drizzling. The branches of the fruit trees were moving slowly in the wind. Liisa sneaked up to the corner of the house and spied. The only worrying factor was the associate professor. The lights were on as usual in his tower, a faint bluish sheen that Birgitta had explained came from a plant-growing installation.

She returned to the two others.

"It looks fine," she whispered. "All the windows are dark. Did you get the spade?"

Birgitta nodded. Liisa stroked her hand across her face. The rain picked up.

She spread out the black plastic on the grass. Greta sobbed. Birgitta mumbled something. Liisa leaned over and rolled the corpse onto the plastic. She knew that she could manage pulling the body, but the hard thing would be to get it through the hedge into Bunde's lot and then across the fence to Lundquist's. The latter step was the most critical. For a short time they would not be hidden by any bushes.

"Now let's get going," she said, despite her own growing hesitation, and took hold of the plastic and pulled.

Everything went easier than she had thought. The plastic and the damp grass helped make the body seem light. Birgitta was not much help, but Greta was unexpectedly strong. Together they managed to squeeze the dead man through the hedge and over the low fence. He fell with a thud over on Lundquist's side. It sounded as if Karsten Heller sighed when the air was pressed out of the lungs.

"I'll manage the rest myself," Liisa whispered, waving aside Birgitta's protests. She jumped lithely over the fence, pulled the body into the protection of some bushes, and retrieved the spade that Birgitta tossed over. She waited a minute or two. By using the breathing technique from the shooting range she recovered her equilibrium, and her pulse rate went down. The rain intensified. The body at her feet resembled a sack. The night chill and the tension made her shiver.

The block seemed to rest. All that was heard was the incessant drumming of the rain.

After having memorized how the small plants, which she thought resembled lingonberry, were planted, she pulled them out and set them to one side. She started digging and was surprised at how porous the dirt was. It did not take long for her to shovel up a grave. Half a meter down the earth became hard and she decided that it would have to be deep enough.

After shoving the body, which now felt heavier and more uncooperative, down into the pit, she spread the plastic out like a shroud, tucked in the corners around the body, and then shoveled the dirt back in. She worked quickly and single-mindedly, and when the last shrub was replanted she allowed herself to rest a minute or two. She crouched down. The rain ran over her face. She wanted to recite a prayer, or do something that might resemble a ceremony, but found that she could only remember a few lines of the Lord's Prayer.

"Thy kingdom come, on earth as it is in heaven . . . Amen," she murmured.

✦

Thirty-four

The phone rang at six thirty in the morning. The ring was unusually muted and Ann Lindell was grateful for that; Anders needed to sleep. As far as she knew he had been up working until far into the night. She woke up when he crept into bed and glanced at the clock: 2:33. She was happy, he had started writing again. This time it probably concerned the Middle East. She fell back asleep right away.

She was sure it was Ottosson and it was not without feeling a certain excitement that she hurried out into the hall to reach the phone. The calm of the past few weeks would now be broken by something more stimulating to the imagination.

That was a morbid thought, she admitted it, but homicide was her department.

She found the phone on the couch between two cushions.

"Yes, now she's gone."

Edvard's voice sounded distant, as if he was far from the receiver.

"I thought you would want to know."

Of course she wanted to know! She collapsed on the couch. The news was expected, but still Ann felt paralyzed. She could not get out a sound.

"She died in her sleep," Edvard continued. "Calmly and peacefully."

She heard now how tired he was.

"I sensed it last night and got up. Right when I came into her room she took a deep breath, just one. I waited but there weren't any more. It was over. She was lying with her arms crossed over her chest and it looked like she was smiling."

Ann had experienced this a number of times, how the dead seemed to smile, even after a violent, unnatural death.

"She had a long life," was the first thing Ann could say.

It sounded like a platitude, she thought, but the words held much more than just the number of years Viola had lived and she sensed that Edvard understood what she meant.

Edvard hummed a little in response as if he agreed. She could picture him. He was no doubt sitting at the kitchen table staring out over the farmyard where dawn could still only be sensed. It struck Ann how alone he must feel.

"Is it very windy?" she asked.

"Yes, and it's been a steady northeaster for a couple of days," Edvard replied.

"Which she detested."

"Yes," said Edvard. "Which she detested."

She wanted to say something to the effect that she could come out, but refrained. Perhaps he would misunderstand.

"Have you spoken with anyone else?"

"No, I'm going to call Torsten, Greta, and a few others. Then the word will spread on its own. But there's no hurry."

"Are you having coffee?"

"Mmm."

"Have a sip for me too," said Ann. "Will you be in touch?"

"Yes," said Edvard.

She thought he was crying. After the call she remained sitting on the couch. She realized that a chapter in her life was about to end. Viola's illness and death had made her and Edvard reestablish contact, she had visited Gräsö, something that only a few weeks ago would have seemed inconceivable. After Viola's funeral there would be no real reason for continued contact. The story of Edvard led irrevocably to its end.

She wished she could go to the island to keep him company, console him, but that was out of the question. He would take it as a sign that she wanted them to continue seeing each other, perhaps even resume the relationship. But the feelings were not there. Or else they were so deeply pushed back that they could not make themselves known. Her reasonable self had mobilized all its forces to erase all the real or imagined feelings for the man she loved and then frittered away.

"Is she dead?"

Anders was standing in the door, looking at her. He looked as much the worse for wear as his threadbare bathrobe.

She nodded.

"Have you had breakfast?"

"No, it would be nice if you'd make some coffee."

"Sad?"

"Yes, of course. Viola was a remarkable woman. A friend."

"She lived a long time," said Anders, and Ann wondered if he had listened to her call.

"I'll put on a little java, that will perk us up."

She smiled. He was the only person she knew who called coffee "java."

"There will be one last trip to Gräsö. Do you want to come with me to the funeral?"

"Don't think so," he answered. "Funerals are not my strong suit. And I didn't know her. It's better if you go alone."

And of course that's how it was. They would both feel uncomfortable if he went along.

She heard him fill the coffeemaker and take out the mugs. Mostly she wanted to stretch out on the couch and let Anders wrap a blanket around her, but she knew that no pardon was given. She had to get up. The clock said seven. In one and a half hours she would be taking part in some kind of conference, the subject of which she didn't even know. But she was sure it would not affect her work situation for the better. A grinding meeting without meaning or purpose. She would sit there and vegetate, while the knife man Ludwig Ohrman and his ilk could stretch out on any number of couches and plan new mischief. She would have to get to work on him. He did not show up for the interview she had arranged the other day.

Ann got up with some effort, forced, but also lured by the smell of coffee.

"Now your Nobel Prize winner is taking a beating again," said Anders.

He sat hunched over the newspaper, grinning a little. He liked conflict and polemics.

"By who?"

"An Associate Professor Johansson, if you're familiar with the name."

"I am, in fact," said Ann.

She leaned over Anders' shoulder and peered at the prominently featured article. There was a photo of Ohler as well as Johansson, a twenty-year-old archive picture where the two were posing together in what apparently was a laboratory setting. Both dead serious. The associate professor looked young. She read the lead-in and the final paragraph.

"The mild-mannered old guy has sharpened his pencil properly," she observed. "Now there will be a real feud with the neighbors."

Ann briefly told about what had happened earlier. He was visibly amused and that made her happy. He was working. She was infected by his boyish delight at two neighbors attacking a third one.

"Torben Bunde has never really been in his right mind, but Johansson is all right," said Anders. "No ferocious jabs or complicated academic double-talk—instead dry and factual but still razor sharp. I can imagine how the feelings are cooling at home with Ohler. This is not some outsider grumbling but someone who's been there. That hurts."

Ann wondered whether she should tell about the connection between the housekeeper and Viola, but refrained. It was good that their conversation had left the island.

She pulled the other section of the newspaper to her, opened a page at random, and found that divine justice had arrived before the worldly kind. The first thing she saw was Ludwig Ohrman's obituary. He was forty years old, deeply mourned and missed by mother and father, and a whole throng of brothers and sisters.

She checked the date of death. *I see,* she thought, *not strange that he didn't show up for questioning.*

"I'll wake Erik," said Anders.

It had become a routine for Anders to make sure the boy got breakfast in him and left home in time. Most mornings he went with Erik to school and then took a long walk.

She knew that it was an arrangement Erik liked. Anders was something out of the ordinary where stepfathers were concerned. First he had been run over by a bus and then almost killed by knife thrusts administered by a murderer, with impressive scars as evidence.

Erik had decided to become a policeman. Ann did not bother to protest. Soon enough he would realize and start dreaming about something better.

She leaned over and kissed him on the cheek.

"Thanks," she said.

He looked up from the newspaper with surprise.

"For what?"

"For . . ."

She did not know how to continue. He smiled at her, but it was a doubtful smile and she saw a flash of worry in his eyes.

"You'll have to guess," she said at last, and left the kitchen.

✦

Thirty-five

Ronald was a taciturn young man who lugged Agnes's plastic bags and suitcases down without comment. He did not seem a bit impressed at finding himself in an aristocratic Nobel Prize winner's home. Perhaps he was eager to get going.

Agnes stayed upstairs. Even though the two rooms she had the use of were emptied of her belongings she was worried about having forgotten something. She opened wardrobes and pulled out dresser drawers, wandering around like a lost soul in the bedroom and the small drawing room. Greta had silently observed her and then went down to help pack the things in the car.

Neither the professor, Birgitta, nor Liisa Lehtonen had been seen at all.

The atmosphere in the house was unnatural. In an attempt at a joke Ronald asked if someone had died.

When everything was packed there was nothing more for Agnes to do: She had to go down one flight. Birgitta was standing in the hall, pale and without makeup, peering out through the open door, as if she wanted to check what was being carried out of the house. Birgitta said nothing when Agnes slipped through the hall and into the kitchen. It was as if Birgitta did not notice her.

Greta had made coffee and Agnes really wanted a cup, perhaps have a sandwich, before she left. She had also thought about fixing something for Ronald and Greta but she remained standing in front of the counter in the kitchen where she had worked for fifty-five years. During the first twenty years there had been a cook. After that Agnes had been the one responsible for the food.

Everything went so fast, she thought. The idea that she would pack up and move away was a foreign thought only a few weeks ago. Sure, she had thought about having passed the retirement mark several years ago, but during the past week everything had accelerated with a dizzying velocity. She could barely keep up herself. Without Greta the departure never would have been possible. Then she would have submitted to the professor's anger and Birgitta's attempts at persuasion.

Mechanically she took out bread and fixings. She made a few sandwiches, had a few mouthfuls of coffee, and quickly felt livelier. It was also as if the weather powers were in a lighter mood. The clouds were pushed aside and she could glimpse a few patches of blue sky.

Agnes did not hear Birgitta slip into the kitchen and jumped in fright when she started talking. She stood leaning against the doorpost. Her expression was that of the injured party, it was the sullen Birgitta Agnes knew so well. She had nothing new to say but instead repeated her arguments that Agnes was putting them in a difficult position.

Agnes decided not to defend herself. She realized that it was pointless.

"So you don't even notice me anymore?" Birgitta complained.

"I just didn't hear you come in," said Agnes. "Would you like some coffee?"

Birgitta shook her head. Bitterness made her ugly. She took a couple of steps toward Agnes and was preparing to go on renewed attack when Greta came into the kitchen. She ignored Birgitta. Agnes sensed that they had had a dispute.

"Everything is stowed away. Ronald is waiting in the car."

"Doesn't he want a sandwich?"

"No, he wants to get going."

Agnes sensed that her sister was at least equally eager to leave the house. She had seemed strangely absent the whole morning, blamed it on sleeping poorly.

"Well, then we'll say good-bye," said Agnes, extending her hand.

Birgitta sobbed. Agnes felt sorry for her in a way, understood that in the future she was the one who would have to take the blows when the professor got worked up and shouted about things large and small. On the other hand her way of reacting with anger was insolent. If she had only been sad Agnes could have given her a hug and consoled her like in the past.

At the same moment the professor entered the kitchen. Behind him Liisa could be seen.

"See to it that you leave now!" he hissed.

Even Birgitta looked dumbfounded. Greta shook her head.

"Goodbye," said Agnes, extending her hand.

The professor pretended not to see it. Instead he turned toward Birgitta.

"Now that the servants have abandoned the house you'll have to see to—"

"We can talk about that later," Birgitta cut him off.

The professor stared. Agnes knew that he loathed being interrupted. She saw besides that he was dizzy.

"Thanks, then!" said Greta, making an effort to continue, but Agnes stopped her by placing a hand on her sister's arm.

Agnes did not want any trouble. She just wanted to disappear from the house.

"Hags," the professor snorted.

"I am no hag to you!"

Greta held up an index finger in front of his face as if she were scolding a child.

"Is this the thanks I get?" the professor shouted. "Here we have fed you all these years. You've had it good here. Agnes! Don't say otherwise, don't try to lie!"

Agnes had not expected an affectionate farewell, but not this anger either, this aggressiveness, this injustice.

"Silence!" Greta thundered with Aron's voice. "You should be grateful that we have been so loyal for all these years."

She also assumed some of her father's features: the face which despite its wrinkles stood out as sculpted, the prominent jaw and flaming eyes. The preacher who did not stand aside.

"Loyal," the professor said with a sneer.

He twisted his lips but the effect was missing when he was forced to support himself with both hands on the back of the chair in front of him so as not to fall down. He was breathing with great exertion.

"Daddy!" Birgitta pleaded.

Despite Agnes's renewed attempts to silence her Greta did not let herself be stopped. She placed herself close to the professor and forced him to meet her eyes. Agnes could glimpse fear in his eyes for the first time since she had been in the house. Was it due to Greta's fury or was he worried about having a heart attack? It would be embarrassing for him to ask for a pill, it would be an illustration of his dependence and weakness.

"We know about everything that has happened here in the house," said Greta. "Everything! And there are so many skeletons in the closet that it's enough for a whole cemetery. Last night I rescued you from disgrace, but now I don't know if I did the right thing. You have bullied Agnes all these years and it is a miracle that she put up with it. But now it's over. We have done our part. And we don't deserve to be scolded."

The words positively rushed out of Greta's mouth. She talked about the long shifts and the lack of freedom, the constant attending. Agnes stared at her sister. She recognized all this, but what was the disgrace Greta mentioned?

"Daddy," Birgitta pleaded again, "we don't care about that! Come!"

By pulling him on the arm she tried to get her father to leave the kitchen, lead him away from the verbal barrage. But such a retreat was inconceivable, Agnes understood that. That went against everything the professor stood for. He was not the one who stepped aside. On the contrary, he shook himself free and appeared to be recovering from the attack of dizziness. Then came the counterattack.

"Not free? If there is anyone who hasn't been free it's me, who has taken responsibility for everything and everyone. Have you ever had to make a single decision about anything? Get out, you ungrateful cows!"

Greta's reply came like a whiplash. "So you said that to Anna too?"

The professor stiffened. Liisa who had so far kept in the background took a couple of steps into the kitchen.

"Anna disappeared without saying anything," said the professor.

"She was struck dumb," said Greta. "Silenced. I don't know what happened, but I can guess. And then the old professor went out to Father and talked nonsense about Anna."

"You know nothing about that," the professor snarled.

With his superior manner the professor had retaken command. It was as if nothing really had any effect on him. Greta did not have the same experience either in the art of being disrespectful and shameless. She closed her eyes for a few seconds and when she opened her eyes again she looked completely powerless. It was as if she had shot off all of her ammunition and more than anything wanted to disappear from the house and Uppsala.

"Ronald is waiting," said Agnes, in an attempt to make contact with her sister.

Greta raised her eyes and took her hand. Together they left the kitchen, went through the hall, opened the door, and stepped out onto the stairs. When Agnes caught sight of Ronald, who was leaning against the car—unexpectedly enough with a broad smile on his face—she squeezed her sister's hand. She was happy about Greta, about the smiling Ronald from Gräsö, and about being free. She had made it through.

✦

Thirty-six

There was something strange about the flower bed. He saw it immediately, even if it took awhile before it became completely obvious. It meant he had to take out the binoculars. He had done that before, sneaked it out between the plants in the tower, to check the surroundings. He was ashamed, but not enough to keep him from doing it.

The perennials were sitting wrong. Haller would never be guilty of such amateurish planting. Maybe he had been in a hurry, been sloppy, been eager to get away? No, he had not gained any time by planting that way. It was simply poorly executed.

However, in the long run it did not matter much, the wintergreen would quickly spread over the whole surface and hide the mistake.

"Strange," murmured the associate professor.

Then he caught sight of the bicycle that was leaned against Lundquist's wall, which made him even more perplexed. Haller had said that he had finished the work but perhaps there was some task he had forgotten on the front side of the lot?

He looked at the clock. They had decided that Haller would come by for mid-morning coffee. Gregor was curious about the gardening books Haller was bringing. "Duplicates," he had said, but the associate professor suspected that partly it was an excuse for a visit. There was something vague and introverted about Haller. It was obvious that there was something on his mind, perhaps it would come out today? He smiled to himself, satisfied over the sprouting friendship with the gardener.

Why did it feel as if the end was approaching? Not his own death, he did not want to imagine that, but something ominous—he smiled at the ridiculous word—rested over the house and the whole block. An endpoint was approaching. Perhaps it was something that Torben Bunde, quite certainly unconsciously, expressed in his article about Ohler and the Nobel Prize? The associate professor could not put his finger on what it was other than that it was about existence in the nature reserve that constituted the Kåbo district.

Perhaps it was only his customary dissatisfaction making itself known? He had become a recluse, somewhat of a misanthrope. It was not something he was proud of. But the lifelong feeling, since he left his parental home in Rasbo, of not feeling really at ease with his colleagues, his position, had developed over the years into a slightly contemptuous attitude toward his surroundings. He was no longer indulgent, but instead condescending, sometimes spiteful, when he thought back on his experiences. There was no reconciliation of old age.

With the publication of the article in *Upsala Nya Tidning*—only a month ago a completely unimaginable action—he had joined an academic quarrel, but also, through his conclusions about the inbred isolation and camaraderie of the research world, placed himself outside, distanced himself. It was as if he recounted his own private quarrel that had followed him his whole life. Nice to finally speak out, he might think now, if a trifle unpleasant to make himself known.

Now he was tagged, out of the game. Even if perhaps he won some people's sympathy he had defined himself out, pooped in his own nest, as his uncle would have put it.

For that reason he looked forward to the gardener's visit. Haller stood for something else.

What had originally caught his attention was not Lundquist's flower bed but instead the big car that was parked on the street outside the professor's house.

The associate professor could not figure it out. He did not recognize the young man who was lugging out sacks and suitcases from the house. At first he thought hired help had been brought in to do a big cleaning but when the housekeeper's sister showed up on the sidewalk he realized that something else was up.

And now his suspicions were confirmed. The sister and Agnes came out together. They got into the car without ceremony. They drove off. It could be explained in many ways, but the associate professor was suddenly convinced that Agnes had resigned her long service with Ohler and now definitively taken off.

It pleased him. He liked the thought that the professor would live alone in that gigantic house.

✦

Thirty-seven

During the first few days on Gräsö Agnes grappled with a sense of unreality. Her childhood and youth were there. The terrain, physical as well as emotional, was carved for all time into her awareness. Every stone in the hills around the house and every breeze that swept around the corners, the slightly raw aroma of the sea and the slightly musty smell in the corners of the house, everything was familiar, yet so foreign.

She had walked down to the sea. There was a westerly wind and it felt warm in the sunshine down by the pier. There was no boat there anymore, hadn't been for many years, but the shore was still a natural destination for a stroll. Submerged in the tangled grass was the last rowboat the family owned.

She walked around and breathed, and every breath was like a slow, successive airing of the old life.

Agnes had not wanted to discuss or even comment on the strange, mournful parting from Ohler. Greta seemed to be of the same opinion. She seemed in a strange way unwilling to talk with her at all, beyond what was required so that they could function under the same roof. The change was tangible. In Uppsala she had been talkative, almost tenderhearted, and un-expectedly physical. Now she seemed pensive, hesitant in her movements and lost in her own house. But above all silent. Agnes had caught her cry-ing but her sister would not say why, other than that she was tired and felt out of sorts, perhaps it was a cold coming on. Agnes did not believe that for a moment. It had been years since Greta had a cold. No, it was some-thing else, that was clearly written on Greta's tormented face.

There was so much Agnes wanted to ask about, not least what Greta meant when she said that she rescued the Ohler family from "disgrace," but she decided to wait. Agnes understood that something had happened the night before while she was asleep, not least due to the frightened ex-pression on Birgitta's face and Liisa's unexpectedly passive demeanor the next morning.

Even though she was the one who had been in Ohler's household for so many years, Greta stood out as the most well informed. That especially ap-plied to what concerned Anna. That the old professor would have gone out to Gräsö and "talked nonsense" to Aron about Anna was news to Agnes. She could not remember the visit. That was not really so strange; in 1944 she was only a child. But she suspected that Anna's disappearance had to do with that visit, even if she did not really understand how. She really wanted to know, but there was no need to rush. Soon enough she would bring it up with Greta.

Why had Anna quit so suddenly? Greta had spit out something about her guessing what had happened. What could it be? Agnes could guess too. Perhaps Bertram had assaulted her sister? Just as he had done with her, thirty years later.

Just as every time she remembered that June evening in 1973 she felt em-barrassed. Not so much for his fumbling hands and sweaty excitement, but rather because she actually liked it. She could not lie to herself. After the first awkward, slightly rough treatment Bertram had been tender, ca-ressed her across her back, whispered about how long he had wanted her and in that way managed to excite her.

She knew that all the things he was saying were lies but they were neatly packaged and she let herself be deceived, grasped at his assurances as if they were famine food, starved for love as she was. The memory of what played out that June evening always made her face beet red. So too this time.

Afterward both of them acted as if nothing had happened. Without saying so she was grateful to him in a way. She had experienced the closeness of a man, and to start with she waited—with mixed emotions and feeling very guilty—for it to be repeated. But Bertram took no further initiatives.

Had he been after Greta too? It was not impossible. Was that perhaps the origin of her sister's anger? But who would really want to talk about it so long afterward? Definitely not her and surely not Greta either.

The Andersson family had always functioned that way: What was unpleasant was repressed, possibly to be resolved later. But the right time usually never appeared. Either it was too close, the wounds too fresh and sensitive, or else it was too long ago to start rooting around in.

Greta had spoken about skeletons in the closet in the Ohler household, that there were so many they could fill a whole cemetery, and that was surely correct. On the other hand there were plenty of skeletons in the Andersson family's closets too. The two families had been intertwined for so many years that there were probably quite a few skeletons in common.

But why pull them out of the corners? Was it necessary, or even desirable? Agnes did not think so. She was happy to have gotten away from Uppsala and Bertram. Now she wanted to enjoy life. She probably did not have that many years left and did not want to let old unresolved grudges poison that time. She had had enough during her years in Kåbo. Now she wanted to live.

She approached the rowboat and its leaky belly. She carefully set her foot against the planking, pressed a little, and the wood gave way. It was the boat Aron used to row out in to catch a little herring in the spring, or perhaps put out a few nets. Mostly out of old habit. Soon the boat would disappear completely, become one with the grass.

There was something very desolate about the old dock. Autumn had taken hold. Everything collapsed, turned gray. Agnes longed for ice and snow, the winter resting period.

She walked carefully out on the pier, though it rocked and creaked alarmingly, and remained standing a good while surrounded by water. It splashed below her feet. Far off in the distance the islets Jankobben and Änglaskäret could be glimpsed. She repeated silently to herself one of the prayers from her childhood.

"Amen!" she concluded, raising her head and looking toward the sky.

A great calm came over her, now she was quite convinced that it was right to move home to the island. *Best that I go up*, she thought, *before Greta gets worried*.

There was a car in the farmyard. She recognized it immediately. The calm she had achieved was immediately changed to worry that in turn quickly turned to anger. She felt that she had abandoned Greta—a ridiculous thought, as her sister could very well take care of herself, but ever since the showdown at Ohler's Agnes felt more strongly than ever that she and Greta were connected. They had no one else they could rely on completely.

She hurried inside. In the kitchen Birgitta and Liisa were sitting on either side of the table. Greta was standing by the counter. They gave each other a quick look. Agnes wanted to laugh. Greta was in a fighting mood. No one could get the better of her.

"They think we're short of money," said Greta.

Liisa sighed. Agnes listened to Birgitta's protests, a stream of words. She was very nervous, Agnes understood that immediately, she was talking constantly and had a hunted expression on her face. She made a gesture with her hand toward the table.

Only then did Agnes see the money that was piled in front of Birgitta. It was a thick bundle of five-hundred-kronor notes held together by a rubber band. She realized that it must be tens of thousands of kronor. Something burst. She went over to the table and leaned over the woman she had seen grow up, took hold of her ears and pulled. Birgitta was forced to get up. She shrieked.

"Shame on you! How dare you come here with money!"

It took a second or two for Liisa to react, but once she did it all happened very quickly. She threw her arms around Agnes and basically lifted her up completely off the floor. Agnes was forced to let go of Birgitta's ears.

Greta started laughing loudly and uncontrollably. Everyone stared at her. Suddenly she fell silent and covered her face with her hands.

"I only meant well," said Birgitta.

Liisa reached over, took the bundle of money, and tossed it down into her bag that was on the floor.

"You didn't at all," said Agnes, who was still furious. "You want to create dependence, gratitude, and guilt. That's your tune."

Liisa put her arm around her partner. Otherwise she had been strangely quiet and not said a word. That surprised Agnes, because otherwise the Finnish woman would be in control, inciting Birgitta with acid comments.

"Whores!" Greta screamed suddenly. "Get out! I know what you go in for."

"Greta, calm down. They'll go now."

But Agnes was speaking to deaf ears, because her sister went on.

"I've heard enough! You're going to protect Bertram for . . . and now you're going to buy silence but—"

"I think you should keep quiet about whoredom," Liisa interrupted in her iciest voice. "And silence is good for all of us. Isn't it?"

Agnes did not understand a thing, other than there was something ugly and dreadful here. There was a wild animal lying in wait here. Here was Greta's worry.

"Go now," she said.

They left. The sound of their car faded away. Greta left the kitchen. The clock in the parlor struck four. Agnes sank down on a chair. She heard her sister's desperate weeping but was not able to get up, could not manage any more stress. It felt as if everything was her fault.

✦

Thirty-eight

Ann Lindell was standing in front of an open grave, a pit down into the darkness, where the lid of the casket had just disappeared. It was raining, which is as it should be. There was a cold wind from Öresunds-grepen.

The cemetery was very close to the ferry landing and there was scraping and creaking as the clumsy ferry docked. She heard the heavy thud as the steel plate clattered against the abutment on land and how the cars drove off. Somehow she thought it was wrong. Shouldn't the island have stopped for a while when its oldest inhabitant was being buried?

Ann could not feel any sorrow that paralyzed her inside. Viola had lived almost a century. On the other hand she felt very melancholy. She was taking leave of a person she had liked very much, almost revered, for her great wisdom and warmth.

———

Edvard Risberg took a step back and placed himself beside her. He had been one of the pallbearers. It was strange to see him in a dark suit. He looked official in a way that was unlike him. He was aware of that. He seemed ill at ease. His face was closed.

It felt as if she was also burying her old life. After this she would never return to the island. He surely sensed that, which explained the weight in his face. He wanted her back, she knew that. His wordless, austere attitude, which in the beginning of their acquaintance she was attracted by, now stood out as only gloomy and oppressive.

The last lines in the story about Ann and Edvard were written in lower-case letters. There was no showdown, no harsh words were exchanged. Before, she would have feared his anger and been lost in shame. She had overcome that. Not completely, and definitely not when she was on the island, but enough to be able to reason with herself and not wallow in destructive self-contempt.

She sneaked a glance at him. He had aged, the wrinkles in his face had deepened, but he still had an energy that radiated. Even in a black suit in a cemetery. She did not understand why he wasn't living with a woman. Perhaps there would be a change now when Viola had departed this life.

The ceremony at the grave was blessedly brief. Ann was so cold she was shaking. The group of funeral attendees, perhaps a hundred, slowly broke up. Ann nodded at Agnes and Greta Andersson. They had exchanged a few words earlier. Ann felt how they were keeping an eye on her and Edvard, certainly curious whether they could spot a somewhat more intimate contact between them.

"I wish she had been my mother," Ann said suddenly.

Edvard did not say anything, perhaps due to the fact that his two sons were approaching. Ann placed herself in front of Edvard, pushed her arms around his body, and gave him a hug. He responded by putting his arms around her and squeezing. They stood like that a couple of seconds. Ann closed her eyes.

When she released her hold tears were running down her cheeks. *God how I loved that man,* she thought, and felt an impulse to strike at him, throw herself forward and pound on his chest.

She turned around and headed for the parking area. Never again Gräsö. She would make it to the ferry that was waiting.

✦

Thirty-nine

Ten days passed before worrying made him call. There was some-thing wrong. Not only in the flower bed and the fact that the bicycle still stood leaning against Lundquist's wall. A planting can be unsuccessful or sloppily done and a bicycle can be left behind, but that Haller should wait so long to be in touch was not likely.

It was not just the books that the gardener promised to stop by with but more the hope the associate professor had seen in Haller's eyes.

Haller had radiated loneliness, expressed in a kind of resigned noncha-lance and evasive insinuations. He himself had taken his share, but hit back. But the associate professor had also glimpsed something else entirely, a kind of eagerness to be friendly and accommodating, which surely stemmed from the joy of having found someone like-minded.

They were two lonely men with a common interest. Chance had brought them together. Both had seen the possibilities of a friendship. Would Haller frustrate that now by staying away, break his promise about "the duplicates"?

The associate professor did not think so. That was why he called the police.

The woman who took his report was very polite, asked questions, and little by little as he explained what had happened she acquired a sympathetic tone in her voice. It sounded as if she shared his worry. The associate professor, who to start with expressed himself cautiously, careful not to stand out as a senile and curious old man, became more forthcoming.

He told how he perceived Haller as an extremely lonely person. Sympathetic and social, but lonely. He put great weight on the flower bed, that a professional would never plant that way. To the question of why the plants were planted so amateurishly the associate professor could not give an answer, other than that Haller must have been very confused.

They talked for perhaps twenty minutes. Then he went up to his tower, satisfied with himself, happy about the conversation. The police had encouraged him to contact the neighbor to find out if he had had any contact with the gardener. But the associate professor was doubtful. Perhaps that was too obviously sticking his nose into other people's business.

The bicycle was still there. He had only caught a glimpse of Lundquist once since then. He probably did not care that the wintergreen had been planted wrong. But the bicycle, didn't he wonder about that? That made him decide to contact Lundquist.

Just as he took out the phone book it struck him that he had not thought about calling Haller himself. The policewoman had not said anything about that either, perhaps she assumed that he had tried to reach him by phone but failed. He looked up his name. There were not many Hallers. Karsten lived not far away, on Artillerigatan. Within walking distance, thought the associate professor.

After a moment's hesitation he dialed the number. It rang ten times before he hung up. He looked up the neighbor's number. Lundquist answered after two rings. The associate professor told him how it was, that he was worried. There was no reason to beat around the bush. Lundquist did not seem to be the type who appreciated small talk.

No, he had not seen Haller. Not heard from him either, no bill had come, but he was not particularly worried about that. He had determined that all the work ordered was done and was satisfied with it. He had not noticed Haller's bicycle.

The associate professor apologized for the trouble—certainly unnecessary—thanked him and hung up. But he was not relieved in any way; on the contrary, his worry increased. Something had happened to Haller, he was sure of it. Could he call the police again without seeming completely nuts? He stared at the direct number the woman had given him. He resorted to magic to decide. If the sum of the figures in the telephone number was an odd number he would call. He quickly added the six digits and the result was twenty-seven. He immediately picked up the phone before he had time to change his mind.

✦

Forty

"Reported missing" was an ominous term, he had always thought that. It had to do with an experience in his childhood, he understood that very well. When he was thirteen years old his grandfather had disappeared. No one could explain how or why, neither then nor later. He was and remained missing, Fred Emanuel Nilsson. Suicide, it was said, but that was an explanation Sammy Nilsson never bought. The grownups put the lid on, never wanted to talk about what had happened, and were disturbed and at last angry at his constant speculations.

Was that perhaps why he became a policeman? Fred had been Sammy's favorite relative. A person like that would never kill himself, was his teenage thought. He was still convinced, more than thirty years later, that Fred had not disappeared voluntarily.

Random harvest, he thought. He stared at the hastily jotted-down information and remembered the conversation he had had with the gardener.

There can't be that many Hallers. According to directory assistance there were two in Uppsala. One of them was Karsten. Sammy got no answer.

He called the person who made the report, Gregor Johansson, and got a little more meat on the bones.

He went to Lindell's office. The door was open. She was studying the map hanging on the wall. Sammy studied her figure, noted that she had put on a few kilos.

"I have someone who's been swallowed up by the earth," he said.

Lindell turned around.

"You and your missing persons," said Lindell.

She smiled at him. He knew that his fixation with missing persons was well-known in the building. Everyone in homicide knew that he regularly checked all reports that came in. It had become a habit. It had never had any significance for investigative work, but that did not matter. There were those who joked about it, but Lindell knew better than to tease him. She was also the only one who knew the background. He had talked with her about the Fred Nilsson mystery.

"Yes," he said, "you know how it is. But this is a person we've met recently."

He told about the associate professor's report.

"Strange," said Lindell. "But it's probably a coincidence."

Sammy looked at the notes again and nodded. They looked at each other. They both knew that he would check up on it. She grinned.

"Good luck," she said.

Sammy Nilsson immediately went to Artillerigatan. The building had three entries and Karsten Heller lived in the middle one on the third floor. Lind and Svensson were the names of his nearest neighbors. Sammy pressed on the doorbell and waited. After half a minute he crouched down and opened the mail slot. On the floor in the hall not unexpectedly was a drift of newspapers and mail.

The air that streamed out through the mail slot was fresh, he could not detect any odor of the sort that bodies exude when they have been lying dead for several days in a warm apartment.

He straightened up and remained standing indecisively in front of the door. There were several alternatives. One was to contact the management of the co-op apartment association and perhaps get someone to open the door. That could entail complications. If there were ordinary reasons that Haller was not at home, he might have opinions later about the police going into his apartment.

Sammy decided to wait but in a final attempt to get clarity he rang the nearest neighbor's door. A woman in her seventies opened almost immediately. Perhaps she had been watching him through the peephole in the door?

He introduced himself and explained his business. The woman reacted immediately and unexpectedly strongly.

"I knew that something had happened," she said, and Sammy saw that she was on the verge of tears. "He would never go somewhere without telling me because I take care of his flowers when he's away. I'm sure you saw how it looks?"

"How does what look?"

"In Karsten's window. They're drooping. Above all that fine flower from Africa. You should see the kind of plants he has."

"Yes, he does work with gardening," said Sammy.

"Exactly! He's a good man. Never any problems. He helps me sometimes. I actually thought about going into his apartment today. Maybe he's gone away for a few days and simply forgot to tell me."

"You have a key?"

"Yes, how else would I go in and water?"

"Do you think that Karsten Haller would take it amiss if I borrowed the key and went into the apartment?"

"Perhaps he's sick? Perhaps he's lying in bed and can't communicate?"

"That might be."

The woman took down a ring with two keys that was hanging on a bulletin board right inside the door.

"Go on in," she encouraged him.

He stepped over the mail and newspapers that formed a neat little pile inside the door, at the same time as he formed a picture of how the apartment was arranged: the kitchen to the left, living room straight ahead, bedroom to the right, and then the toilet.

In the living room a drooping plant was seen on the windowsill, just as the neighbor pointed out. He called out a "hello." It could actually be the case that Haller was in bed, severely ill.

It only took a momentary glance to determine that the room was empty but to be on the safe side he crouched down and peeked under the bed. Dust and a shoe box.

He opened the two closets, where there were strikingly few clothes. Sammy counted half a dozen shirts and a couple of jackets in one. In the other were piles of garbage bags.

The living room gave a strange impression. Besides the many potted plants there was an armchair, an old teak table, and a TV on a bench. Against the one short wall stood a sparsely filled bookshelf but there were lots of notebooks of a kind that Sammy recognized well. They were of Chinese manufacture, with red spines and hard covers. He pulled out one of them and randomly opened to a page. Columns filled with figures: a workbook. Here was information about gravel, topsoil, and rented machinery. All neatly noted. He put the book back on the shelf.

A bachelor apartment, Sammy noted a little jealously. Sparse furnishing was something he had always wanted, but then he would be forced to get a divorce, and that was the most unimaginable scenario he could think of.

He went out into the kitchen. On the table was a passport and travel documents placed in a plastic sleeve. At the top a ticket issued to Karsten Haller. He was supposed to travel to Johannesburg a week earlier.

He remembered the man in the garden. He had stood out as frank and open, made an almost garrulous impression. What had they talked about?

Sammy did not remember, everyday things surely, after Haller assured them that he had not seen anything peculiar in the neighborhood. After that the change had come, when he commented on Professor von Ohler. Haller's facial expression darkened, the good-natured look disappeared.

South Africa. Sammy rooted in the brochures that were in the plastic sleeve. There was nothing about any hotel or other special activities such as a safari or the like. He took out his cell phone, called the travel agency that was listed as seller of the ticket, and was met by the message that many were calling right now but that his call would be answered as soon as possible.

Lindell on the other hand answered immediately and he asked her to assign some trainee to check out the hospitals. Perhaps Haller had been in an accident?

They ended the call. He checked around the apartment one more time, trying to see something that deviated from the dreary, unimaginatively furnished apartment. On the table in the living room were several notebooks. He opened one of the books but realized that it was also a kind of diary but of a different type than Haller's workbooks. Here were no lines with the number of hours worked, no list of various materials.

On the cover page the year 1942 was given. The style was old-fashioned and shaky but completely legible. It was about cleaning. He browsed ahead: preparations for a dinner in May. All the courses were noted.

He picked up the next book, January 1, 1943, was at the top of the first page. After a few pages about the weather the entry described the aftermath of a New Year's celebration. Here was a more personal text. The woman, because he assumed that it was a woman's diary, commented on the guests who had been at the New Year's dinner the day before. A certain building contractor D had evidently "declaimed," ended up in a quarrel with P about the "awful war," and left the company in anger.

Sammy Nilsson closed the notebook. Almost-seventy-year-old diaries could not give any explanation for why Karsten Haller was missing.

He remained standing in the room. Should he continue? It was definitely not his area to ferret out missing persons, but it was a situation that bordered on the unsolved mystery of his own grandfather.

On his way to the car Lindell called. No Haller had been admitted to a hospital. Sammy told about the ticket to South Africa. He heard from her voice that she was becoming more interested. She's bored and needs a mystery too, he thought, smiling to himself.

"Shall I pick you up?"

Lindell laughed. He took that as a yes.

They had been in his tower before. That time the associate professor had been enthusiastic; now he looked worried, almost tormented.

"You see," he said, pointing.

"What?" asked Sammy.

"You see those small green plants, those are wintergreen. They don't sit in formation, zigzag if I may say so. It's so amateurish that I don't think Haller would have planted that way. Unless he was in a really big hurry . . . but no . . . an experienced landscaper will still plant zigzag. You do it automatically. Do you understand what I mean?"

Sammy nodded. Lindell looked the most thoughtful.

"It's not the homeowner who—"

"I asked," the associate professor interrupted, shaking his head, "but he hasn't touched the flower beds. He didn't even understand the question."

"And Haller's bicycle is still there," Sammy noted.

They stood quietly, pondering the fact that the landscaper seemed to have disappeared into thin air.

"So if it's not Haller or the homeowner—"

"Then it's someone else!" the associate professor exclaimed.

Sammy saw how irritated Lindell was at having been interrupted a second time.

"Did he say anything about Africa to you, that he was going to travel?"

The associate professor looked completely uncomprehending and shook his head.

"So many strange things are happening here now," he said.

"I saw the article you wrote," said Sammy. "That was brave. Criticizing an old colleague and neighbor can't be easy."

"Of course," was the associate professor's curt reply.

"What other strange things have happened?" asked Lindell.

"Well, the housekeeper at the professor's has quit. That alone. She has worked there for however many years. And quitting now when he'll get the Nobel Prize . . . I mean . . . and then this thing with Haller. He seemed so unbalanced . . . you understand, he was the one who threw that stone at Ohler's house. I shouldn't reveal that, but this feels so strange."

Sammy and Lindell gave each other a look. Lindell nodded. *What was that I said?* she seemed to want to say.

"Did he talk about why?"

"No, not really," said the associate professor.

"Was he the one who put the skull by Ohler's gate too?"

The associate professor's face suddenly turned bright red.

"It was you, wasn't it?" said Lindell.

The associate professor nodded.

"A silly prank, I admit that, but it's an old doctor's joke. I was subjected to it myself in the fifties. Now in retrospect I admit that perhaps it wasn't so well-advised."

"So Ohler understood that it was someone in his field, so to speak?"

"I would presume so," said the associate professor.

Sammy Nilsson grinned.

"Did he know it was you?"

"No, he doesn't think I have the courage. I did it more for my own amusement. To prove something, not sure what. I am an old man but not without . . ."

He hesitated but shook his head when Lindell suggested the word "passion."

"That's too strong a word," he said with a cautious smile, which more expressed sorrow than anything else. "Am I going to be charged?"

"No," Sammy Nilsson decided. "Do you know whether Ohler is at home?"

The associate professor nodded.

"And his daughter too, and her . . . girlfriend. They seem to be living there now."

The two police officers left the associate professor. If it weren't for the gloomy background and Haller's disappearance, Sammy would have made fun of the whole situation. But now there was something heavy and ominous about it all. They recognized it: discomfort. They felt it as a scent. Without commenting on the visit with the associate professor they walked toward Professor von Ohler's house.

A middle-aged woman answered the door. Sammy Nilsson immediately saw the resemblance. It must be the daughter, he thought, and introduced himself. Lindell stood passively by his side. That was the division they always used. One active and the other waiting, observing.

"We're investigating a disappearance," he continued. "There is a landscaper who has worked in the area and who now has disappeared without a trace."

The woman stared at him. Her face expressed nothing. Passive, waiting for a continuation.

"Karsten Haller. Is the name familiar?"

She shook her head.

"You are Ohler's daughter, I understand," Sammy continued indefatigably.

"Why do you understand that?"

"You remind me of your father. Haller? Doesn't ring any bells? He worked on the neighbor's yard. I thought possibly that—"

"No, as I said, that's not anyone I know. Was there anything else?"

"Perhaps your father knows Haller. Perhaps he's done work here?"

"I would have known about that," said the woman.

She was shaking.

"Perhaps we can continue to speak inside?" Sammy suggested.

"I don't think so. I'm a little busy and as I said, we don't know who this Haller is. No one in this house knows anything of interest."

"We have reason to believe that he knows someone in the house."

"My father is a public person."

Sammy remembered when he and Haller met. Haller's undisguised anger when he brought up Professor von Ohler. An anger that he did nothing to conceal.

"We believe that Haller has reason to feel a certain animosity toward your father. A feeling that does not seem to originate from any type of general indignation but rather seems to have a personal connection."

The woman snorted.

"Well, we don't seem to be getting any further," said Sammy without showing anything he was feeling. On the contrary he extended his hand and looked sincerely friendly.

"Thank you, and I apologize for disturbing you."

The Ohler daughter closed the door.

"Animosity," said Lindell, sneering.

Sammy Nilsson shook his head.

"The bitch is lying," he said.

"Yes, it's obvious," said Lindell.

They went out onto the street. When Sammy closed the gate behind him he turned around and looked up toward the house.

"If it had been a drunk woman we could have forced our way in," he said. "Now we're standing like two beggars on the stairs."

"We had nothing."

"Doesn't matter. We could have forced our way in anyway. Or rather, a drunk woman would have taken for granted that we would run right in."

They knew that they would drop the whole thing. A disappearance, which besides might very well have a natural explanation, was not their responsibility. Even if there were no formal obstacles to snooping further there were practical limitations. Ottosson would not give his approval. Even though at the present time it was calm at the squad, there were many old cases to sink their teeth into.

✦

Epilogue

It nauseated him, this false pomp. He cursed himself for having turned on the TV. He already knew. He knew what it looked like. "There is no justice," Ohler had said, and that was right. There are injustices here, illustrated by this sea of refined and decked-out persons, the elevated of society within academe, culture, and business, all weighed down by their own importance.

Why should he stare at the spectacle? The last thing he saw before the TV screen went black was the close-up of a face he recognized very well. It was an old colleague from the university in Lund whom the associate professor knew was very critical of Ohler. Now the professor was sitting there, taking part in the celebration, laughing along.

Gregor Johansson got up with great effort. The autumn had been difficult. It would get even worse. He was surrounded by darkness.

Besides, his body was starting to protest. Perhaps next year he wouldn't be able to care for his garden properly? *Then I might as well die,* was a thought that constantly returned.

With even greater effort than before he made his way up into the tower. The garden was just as desolate and depressing as a closed-down amusement park during the winter. The snow that had fallen around the first Sunday in Advent had disappeared in an unfortunate thaw. He loathed these abrupt leaps between bitter cold and warmth, between deep snow and bare ground. Black frost was a word that meant the death of plants.

Suddenly he perceived a movement at Lundquist's and had a déjà-vu experience from the fall. It was not the landscaper this time but instead Winblad's setter that was sniffing around. It was an uncommon sight. Willie, which was the dog's name, was very disciplined and never left the yard, even though it always went around loose. The associate professor had also on some occasions praised Winblad for his good hand with the dog.

Now the setter was standing by Haller's planting on the back side of Lundquist's lot. The associate professor could see with the binoculars how Willie was wagging his tail and nosing at the magnolia. Don't you dare lift your leg, the associate professor thought.

The dog went sniffing a turn around the flower bed, as if he was a critical inspector. Then he started digging in the dirt.

So that's how it happened! It was Willie who had also rooted up the plants before. Winblad had discovered it and tried to put them back. The associate professor laughed. The mystery was solved.

The dog continued to dig, more and more eagerly.